Ylc

Once Tom too[...]
she learned of [...]
from what had [...] her husband's
exuberant, inexperienced caresses.
Tom went slowly; he savored each bit of
her, his caresses lasting and treasuring,
his sensitive fingertips learning each
changing texture.

Just as Curry had seen Tom's hands, tan
and strong, linger on newly sanded
wood, loving the velvety smoothness, so
now he stroked her from shoulder to
thigh, again and again, until Curry was
lost in sensation....

After All These Years

KATHLEEN GILLES SEIDEL

Harlequin Books

TORONTO • NEW YORK • LONDON
AMSTERDAM • PARIS • SYDNEY • HAMBURG
STOCKHOLM • ATHENS • TOKYO • MILAN

For my parents,
because this one is special.

Published July 1984

ISBN 0-373-65002-7

Chapter One

Tom Winchester didn't mind being thirty-six. Not in the least. Sure, there were things wrong with his life. He had a wife who was happier when he wasn't living with her than when he was, and his left leg had never been the same since its little encounter with some Southeast Asian shrapnel. But these problems did not have a thing to do with age.

He would not have done time in his twenties again for anything. At twenty-one, he'd been in Vietnam; at twenty-two, he'd been in an Army hospital in Tokyo; at twenty-six, he'd been running a machine in a lumbermill. These were not exactly places he wanted to visit again.

But in his thirties, he had found work that kept him on the road, work that kept him from having to be in a place long enough to hate it. To a log cabin in Wisconsin, a Quaker meeting hall in Pennsylvania, a plantation outside Charleston, a Spanish mission north of San Diego, wherever there were old buildings and the money to restore them, Tom went.

He called himself a carpenter although he was not. But he couldn't stand being called an historic preservationist; that made it sound like he wrote grant applications, took developers to court, fought zoning laws, and he did none of that. He was a craftsman; he did the actual work, returning the keepsakes of America's past to their original condition.

Skilled and knowledgeable, with standards of perfection that had exasperated his wife, Tom was good at this work. Very good. A man down in New Orleans had been waiting for a year and a half for Tom to come solace his nineteenth-century termite-tunneled staircase, and a family society in eastern Massachusetts kept telling Tom that they wanted no one else to restore the paneling in their ancestral cottage.

Tom was now in South Dakota, his footsteps echoing hollowly through the empty rooms of a weathered farmhouse ten miles outside Gleeson, a little town about halfway between the James River and the Old Sioux.

But he wasn't here to restore this house, to turn it into a little tribute to the harsh life of Dakota farming. Although Tom had woodworking skills that had stirred a staid preservationist magazine to its first italics, although he could tell at a glance whether a piece of wood had been milled with an eighteenth-century whipsaw or a nineteenth-century sash saw, he was here on this June afternoon for the most routine sort of remodeling. He would patch plaster, put in a new dishwasher and garbage disposal, and carve the smallest bedroom into two bathrooms.

This was Tom's childhood home, where he had grown up, where he had only spent the briefest time since his return from Southeast Asia, and he was readying it to be sold. His father had retired to Florida last winter, and the house hadn't sold and wouldn't, Tom thought, not without a new kitchen and more bathrooms.

Tom moved through the familiar rooms, his mind half-occupied with plans, with thoughts of plumbing lines and electrical circuits, and half-occupied with memories. He paused at the window of his old bedroom, his boot resting on the sill, his arm across his knee, staring out across the sweeping fields. The spring wheat was green, and wild flowers, black-eyed Susans and Queen Anne's lace, littered the ditches alongside the blacktop road. He couldn't see town—in this part of the country the prairie rolled in gentle swells and after the Dust Bowl, farmers had planted lines of trees between fields to break the fierce wind's force—but he could see the radio tower, a thin silver line against the blue sky. As a boy, he had lain in bed, staring at the tower's red lights, wondering what happened to the sound, where it went.

Well, now he knew where the sound went. He'd been there, and it hadn't been worth the trip.

Suddenly Tom minded being thirty-six.

How simple things had been in childhood, back when he was a boy. Pleasures were so acute, so pure; nothing in adult life had come close to the glorious rush of freedom when school was finally out for the summer. Life had such intensity, such immediacy: the sharp smell of wild onions, the chill of a creek during spring thaw, the unfamiliar shape of a girl's body inside a soft sweat shirt.

There had been three of them who had shared those times—two boys and a girl, the boys born within a week of one another, and the girl only two months later.

Memories—Huck swinging so high that his bare feet thrust into the green mass of the cottonwood trees on the far bank, when the old rope frayed through, sending him and the tire crashing, splashing, into the creek below, with the sound of Curry's clear laughter ringing through the summer air.

One of Curry's long braids getting caught on a fence and her impatient jerk that left strands of corn-yellow hair snared on the twists of the barbed wire, the sun bleaching them to glistening hominy.

The smell of damp hay during a summer thunderstorm, the three of them in the hayloft, leaning toward one another, as a pocketknife was passed around—three quick slices and bloodied fingertip smeared against bloodied fingertip as if shared blood could have made them closer than they already were.

The gasping and choking when, crowded together on the seat of a pickup, they had passed around a small pint bottle, their first one; their high spirits becoming giggles and Tom noticing the feel of Curry's leg against his own.

And at last Curry, looking nothing at all like herself with her mass of curly hair, hair the color of sunshine, piled on her head and the tan of her

arms and neck hidden under the lace of her grandmother's Edwardian wedding dress; Curry es-
corted by Tom's own father down the aisle of the
church to where he and Huck stood, awkward in
their rented tuxedos.

But of course it had been Huck who had
stepped forward, Huck who had taken Curry's
hand.

Tom shrugged and turned from the window.
That had been a long time ago. It had been the
best, the sweetest time in his life, the time before
growing up, before marrying, before that jungle
war, but what was the point of remembering? Better check the attic joists. Attic joists made sense;
memories didn't.

But as he moved to the low-ceilinged closet to
hoist himself through the attic's trapdoor, he
heard a noise. A door opening, then a voice.

"Hello. Anyone here?"

Someone must have seen his out-of-state plates
and had stopped in to check. That would be just
what people did around here.

He walked down the hall to stairs, stopping at
the landing, glancing across the banister.

And there in the hall below him, the sunlight
from the open door throwing a bright rectangle
across the dusty floor, stood a boy, tall but not
quite full-grown, with hair light brown, almost
sandy, and a few freckles across his nose, and a
grin that—

It was Huck. Dear God, it was Huck. Tom
vaulted down the remaining steps. "Huck!" he
cried. *It's you; it's really you. At last, it's—*

"Sir?"

Sir? Why was Huck calling—

Tom stopped, sick. It wasn't Huck. It couldn't be. Huck was dead, wasted in the central highlands of that country neither one of them had heard of until they had to go fight for it.

If it weren't Huck, it had to be... Slowly Tom walked across the room and extended his hand. "You must be Huck James's boy."

The boy blinked, surprised. "Yeah, I guess I am."

Tom cursed his own clumsiness. Of course the boy was surprised. He wouldn't remember the man he was named for; he wouldn't think of himself as Huck James's *boy,* but as Huck James himself. And Tom knew him to be sixteen. Sixteen-year-olds don't like to be called "boys."

"I'm Tom Winchester."

What would he say if the name meant nothing? *I knew your parents once.* No, that was wrong. *I'm Tom. I'm the reason you're called Huck. That's what they called us—"Huck and Tom, Tom and Huck."*

The boy's face was politely blank. "Pleased to meet—" But then sweet recognition. "Oh, you're Mom's friend!"

Mom! He was talking about Curry. Someone calling Curry "Mom"—how odd that sounded.

"Yes, I am, and I was hoping to see her," Tom said. "I wanted to ask her about this business of selling the house and barns without the farmland, if she thought it made sense." He had worked out what he'd say, what reason he'd give for knocking on her door when he had kept away for so many years.

"She's home now," the boy—her son—answered. "Why don't you come with me? I can show you the back way...if you don't mind climbing a fence, that is."

"I don't mind." *And I know the way. Through the field, over the fence, across the creek on three stepping stones, and through the orchard. I know that path. Slogging through the mud and bamboo, through the mottled, watery light of the strange jungle, I was on that path with its smell of sweet Dakota prairie.*

Silently Tom followed young Huck outside. The path was much fainter now than it had been when he had run down it two, three, four times a day.

"You go to the high school?" he asked. *We went there, the three of us, driving together every morning, tossing our books in the backseat every night, not taking them out until the next morning.*

"I'll be a junior next year."

"Do you like it?" *We hated it, sitting in those classrooms, with the town kids, learning things we didn't want to know, being inside when we wanted to be outdoors.*

"Well enough. I play basketball, that helps."

"On the school team?" *We didn't do that; we were country kids, and we had chores in the afternoons, chickens and hogs to feed, water to pump, peas to weed.* "What position?"

"Well"—the boy's face went a little red—"our center graduated last year, so I'm hoping...although I'll only be a junior."

How Huck, the other Huck, had sneered at the high school team, jeering that they were slow, awkward. Had it been a pose, had he longed, desperately longed, to be on the team, unable to admit it even to himself?

No, don't think that way. Don't let the memories change on you. That's what happened when you were here last; just two hours and all the memories changed. Don't let that happen again.

Just as there had been three of them, there had been three houses too; they lay in a triangle. The smallest house, a little four-room renter's place, now torn down, sat at the crossroad of a blacktop and a dirt lane. Down the road a piece, perhaps a hundred yards or so, a drive jutted east from the blacktop, leading up to a white frame farmhouse and its little fort of outbuildings, a hay barn, a cow barn, another for the calves, a brick dairy, a white chicken coop. And around the corner, off the dirt lane, was a second white farmhouse. It sat to the south of the lane so that the Winchester property backed up to the side of the Trent place.

It was to these three houses that three couples had come after their war, the Second World War. Cal and Connie Winchester took over his uncle's place; Curt and Beth Trent moved in with her mother; Hal and Myra James rented.

How strange the pictures of them now look, the snapshots Beth Trent's mother had carefully arranged in a green-bound volume.

They looked determined to have everything. Raised in the Depression, separated by the war, they now seemed ready for their lives to start: they had places to live and ways to support themselves; the women were pregnant; and the babies, born so close together, were healthy and lively.

The photographs showed it all. Younger than their children were now, they were captured forever in black and white, standing in front of the hulking shape of a new Ford or on a picnic with the three babies, the men in loose pants and laced shoes, the women in flowered skirts, their hair flat against their heads, blossoming into pin-curled poofs at their ears. The pictures made them look happy.

But an icy highway ended it all—a car swerving off the road, killing its four passengers, Curt and Beth Trent, Howard James, and Connie Winchester, when the children were just barely two.

So the little girl, Curry Trent was her name, was raised by her grandmother; young Thomas James Winchester was with his father; and Howard Jr., already called Huck, had his mother; but most of all, the three children had each other, and they were always together.

They were adventuresome, inventive, and independent, but although no one fully realized it, they weren't alike. The two boys were misnamed. This Huck was the imaginative one, always thinking up new adventures, new games to play, new places to explore. And if it was Huck who got them into trouble, it was Tom who could get them out of it. He was the one who could figure out how to get them across a rain-swollen creek; he was the one who found a way for Curry to climb down from her bedroom window; if they were five miles from home at ten forty, out of gas, with their learners' permits allowing them only to drive in daylight, and with Curry's curfew in twenty minutes, it was Tom who managed to get her home.

And the girl was their diplomat, the liaison between them and the adult world. On the rare moments when they admitted that they needed permission to do something, Curry was the one who asked for it, even if she was asking Huck's mother or Tom's father. When they were in town, she did the talking for the three of them, donning the excruciatingly polite manners her grandmother had, upon occasion, starved into her.

The three had thought that nothing could split them, and they had taken a blood oath on it one stormy summer afternoon. "Stick together and answer straight," they had promised, pledging loyalty and honesty. To parents, grandparents, and teachers, they would willingly, even automatically, lie, but they swore to tell each other the truth. And they swore they would never abandon each other. If a chicken coop had to be cleaned, they'd do it together; if a broken window had to be explained, they'd do it together.

Of course, they had made those promises at a moment when broken windows and stolen apples were all they knew of sin. Being a girl, Curry entered the adult world first. And for a time she was taller than the two boys, taller and alert to things they didn't understand yet. Tom followed her there next, and as he grew taller than she, he looked at her more carefully. And one afternoon, the sun golden in the August sky, he had found her coming up from her grandmother's garden, balancing a line of scarlet tomatoes along a forearm held close to her body. He had taken some of the tomatoes from her, newly careful that his hand not touch her. He who had as a baby been bathed with her, who had as a boy hauled her into the hayloft by grabbing the seat of her jeans, who had lain flat next to her watching rabbits, now felt as if her flesh would burn him. Curry's well-known face atop this strangely soft body was an irresistible mingling of the familiar and the unknown. And when Tom asked her if she wanted to come out for a drive, neither of them had mentioned their friend Huck.

But teenage love rarely lasts, and after a year, a hot summer night ended it, this little romance that few but Huck had even been aware of.

Huck too was tall by then. He could tell wonderful stories and his temper was as sunny as Curry's hair. And he had learned from Tom's mistakes.

Through the last two years of high school they were an odd combination of three and two. They all drove to and from school together, sometimes Tom driving, sometimes Huck. They would leave afterward, the chores of rural life keeping them from joining others for Cokes at the drugstore or afternoon record parties in someone's basement. They kept out of most town things, sports, clubs, but when they did go into Gleeson at night for pinball or a movie, Curry went alone with Huck.

And suddenly they were all doing grown-up things, marrying, having babies, fighting a war.

It never occurred to either of the boys not to go to this war. Although they were husbands and, by the time they left, fathers, although they understood nothing of the issues at stake, although they could have taken farm deferments, they both went.

Huck joined the Marines. His father before him had been a Marine, and Huck had been raised on stories of his father's heroism and courage. Tom waited for the Army to draft him.

"I'm going," he had said, "but they'll have to come get me."

It was the first important thing they had not done together, and Huck's not coming home was the second.

Life hadn't been easy for Tom after Vietnam. He had been wounded, and as his leg was healing, he had gone to Bemidji, his wife's hometown in northern Minnesota, and soon after found work in a lumbermill.

He loved wood, the smell of it, the clean, living feel of it, but his job at the mill had been running a machine, and his M-16 Army rifle had already taught him how cold and dead a piece of machinery can feel.

It was a union shop, and other vets envied him. The union kept telling how secure his job was, and what kind of pension he could look forward to—all as if he and his machine were serving a life sentence together.

It was hard times for Tom. Awkward with the

wife he felt he hardly knew, confused by the daughter who was nothing like the baby he remembered, he felt locked-in, trapped in a job he hated, uncertain of how all this had happened or why he was doing it, only knowing that twenty-five was too young for a man to feel this way.

If there had been more money, Tom would have left. But the only thing he knew about being a husband and a father was that husbands and fathers paid the bills, and so he stayed with his wife, Trish, and their four-year-old, Diana, supporting them financially and in no other way.

He might have turned to male friends as did so many others, to hunting partners and drinking buddies, but Tom had had a friend once and he couldn't imagine ever having one like that again, so he went home after the whistle blew and tried to bury the aching blankness by working on his house.

It was a rickety frame house set well back from the road, nothing much when they moved in and a little jewel of comfort and convenience when Tom was done. Someone offered him four times what he had put into it, and forgetting to discuss it with Trish, he had taken the money.

When he sold the second house out from under her, she suggested that half of this money should get a split-level in some new subdivision for Diana and her, and if Tom wanted to invest the rest in some other broken, crippled house, then it was pretty much up to him, but she was done camping out in plaster dust, thank you.

It was during this third house that Tom started

learning about preservation. It was an old house and he wanted to make it as it had originally been. His efforts to find authentic copies of hardware—the wood moldings and balustrades he could duplicate himself—linked him with the preservation community, and for these people a craftsman of Tom's skill and high standards was as treasured as a government grant.

So for the last six years or so Tom had done only preservation work, earning enough to keep his daughter, now fifteen, in designer jeans or whatever it was that she and her mother believed life's necessities to be. He visited the two of them between projects, but he often felt much closer to the long-dead builders whose work he was trying to reproduce than he did to either his wife or his daughter.

He'd not seen Curry since before he'd left for the war, but she and Trish dutifully exchanged Christmas cards, and he'd kept track of the news. Her life hadn't been easy either. After Huck had been killed, she had had to work. Her grandmother had gone senile and when the old lady finally died, Myra James, Curry's mother-in-law, had taken her place, a long, hard fight with cancer turning her into another old lady who was again taking her time about dying.

But Curry had stuck it out, still living in the same house she'd grown up in; she hadn't hit the road as he had done. If her troubles made her restless, if dreams had haunted her, no one knew about it. Curry had what it takes; Tom wasn't so sure that he did.

Chapter Two

Whatever sterling character traits Curry James possessed, they were not, at the moment, helping her. She was taking apart her dishwasher. Not that she knew one thing about dishwashers—she didn't. She had no idea at all whether taking it apart was going to make the rinse cycle start rinsing, but she was certainly going to try. There had been any number of times in Curry's own life when all she had needed was to have her screws tightened and her washers put back on straight. If it had worked for her, it ought to work on a dishwasher. And she was certainly going to give it her best shot before calling a repairman.

It wasn't that Curry couldn't afford a repairman. She had plenty of money, but she had made every dime of it herself, doing something she hadn't particularly liked, and she had no intention of wasting it on a repairman who would promise to come between eight and ten and would show up long about three thirty.

Curry was being watched by her friend Bonnie Crown. Bonnie remained at the kitchen table, wanting no part of this mechanical disemboweling. Bonnie believed in repairmen.

In fact, Bonnie frequently believed that other people knew more about things than she did, and at the moment, she was paging through a book that was trying to tell her how to understand her natural beauty.

"Listen, Curry, this is great. If we can just figure out what season we are, this book tells us everything."

Curry looked over her shoulder. "What are you talking about?"

"This book. It says women are one of four color types, one for each season, and once you know which type you are, it tells you exactly what colors to wear—makeup, scarves, shoes, everything."

Since, at the moment, Curry wasn't wearing makeup, a scarf, or shoes, and, with the exception of shoes, did not really expect to be wearing any in the near future, she didn't particularly care.

Bonnie figured as much, but as always, she was enthusiastic enough for the both of them. "Listen, the wrong color 'may make your complexion look pale, sallow, or "muddy"'; will accentuate lines or shadows around the mouth and nose, dark circles under the eyes; will accentuate blotches, if any; may age your face—'"

"That sounds okay to me," Curry interrupted. "It's probably better than I look now."

"That's not true."

And it wasn't. Curry James was not one bit beautiful, she didn't care enough to go to the bother involved in being beautiful, but she was, in the words of one local farmer, "one hell of a fine-looking woman."

Her features were unextraordinary, but very expressive, and when Curry smiled, whether with her sparkling laughter or just a quick grin, it always seemed as if someone had just washed the world's windows.

Her hair was as bright as her smile, its blond a genuine yellow-gold without a trace of pale silver. It was thick and she wore it long, cascading past her shoulders to the middle of her back. Had it been any shorter, it would have been distinctly frizzy, but its weight tamed the frizz into natural waves. That this casual style was, at the moment, rather fashionable was accidental. She had been wearing her hair like this since her grandmother told her she was too old for braids. Gran had urged for a shorter, smoother look, which had sounded fine to a twelve-year-old Curry until the beautician presiding over this undertaking had been misguided enough to mention that Curry would then have to start sleeping in curlers. That had been the end of that.

Bonnie was not deterred by what Gran had once described as Curry's "simply appalling lack of vanity." "First," Bonnie announced, "we need to do our color history. What outfit have people complimented you the most on?"

Curry thought. "My wedding dress."

"Oh, come on. That doesn't count. Everybody always tells brides that they look great."

Curry stared at a small elbow-shaped piece of

metal, turning it around, wondering what it was. "Then I am in trouble," she said, looking up, "because that was the only time both Huck's father and our best friend ever told me I looked nice. 'Like a regular female' was how Tom put it."

"All right, we'll skip that step. Let's look at our coloring."

"My hair is yellow."

"But it's skin tone that counts, and we are to look at the undertones and not be led astray by sallowness or ruddiness."

Curry sat back on her ankles. "I have no idea what you are talking about."

Bonnie sighed. "I don't either. We're no good at this, Curry."

"You should have known that I wouldn't be."

"I know, and this book keeps telling you to rely on the reactions of your friends."

"But the lady who wrote that book is bound to have a better class of friends than we do. What are we supposed to do? Ask the Dungeons and Dragons crowd?"

Another one of Bonnie's self-improvement projects had gone considerably better than this one seemed to be. When Curry sold the paint store that Bonnie had worked in, Bonnie had suggested that they both take a class at the local community college. Curry, with no particular plans except that she wasn't selling paint anymore, agreed, and both women became full-time students. As a result, they spent most of their days with eighteen-year-olds and were nearly friends with a group of very young men who, in their free time, played Dungeons and Dragons, an elaborate fantasy-adventure game that neither Curry nor Bonnie had quite figured out yet.

The Dungeons and Dragons clan cared a great deal about wizard's robes and elfin capes and even less about other clothes than Curry did.

But Curry sometimes felt a little defective because she was so uninterested in typical female concerns. "Which one of these seasons lets you wear your kid's jeans?"

Bonnie flipped through some charts. "Summer. Summer lets you wear denim."

"Good, then I'll be summer. I always liked summers."

"'The summer woman,'" Bonnie read, "'is most often a poised, gracious, even-tempered person, ideal in classic clothes and soft prints. She's the elegant, but feminine, type.'"

"Now doesn't that describe me just perfectly?"

"No. Anyway, you don't get to pick your season. It's determined by your skin—the undertone business that we can't figure out."

"Why are you all of a sudden so worried about this?" Curry asked. "It wouldn't have anything to do with your birthday, would it?" Bonnie had just turned thirty-five the week before.

"Oh, probably," the birthday girl sighed in reply. "Didn't turning thirty-five bother you?" Curry was now thirty-six.

"No, not in the—no, wait, I take that back. The week I turned thirty-five was one of the worst in recent memory."

Bonnie looked surprised.

"Don't you remember?" Curry prompted. "That was when Huck was grounded."

Last year Curry's then fifteen-year-old son had gotten into the sort of trouble that most American males get into at his age. It had been a fairly routine little adventure into the wonders of mixing beer with one's learner's permit driving skills, and Curry had to go pick him up at the police station. Like the other parents, she grounded Huck for two weeks, a punishment that hardly bothered some of the other boys because their parents enforced it so leniently.

But when Curry James did something, she didn't fool around. She had taken the keys to Huck's car and she drove him to school every morning and picked him up after basketball practice each night. Because they lived in the country, there was nowhere Huck could walk to; he had nothing to do but be sullen and make his mother's life miserable, something he did with quite notable success.

So Huck's punishment was much harder on Curry than it was on him, but unlike some of the other parents whose sons' campaigns to drive them crazy succeeded, Curry stuck with it, bearing up with the long, inconvenient drives and Huck's resentment, having decided she could take anything he could dish out, except for his death.

But in general, Curry and Huck got along just fine. She hardly ever ordered him around, but when she did, she meant it and he knew it. If she ever stuck out her hand for his car keys again, he might waver for a moment, but he would hand them over.

Although he didn't know it, Huck was proud of his mother. He had always liked it that before she sold her paint store, she could be depended on to sponsor floats and Little League uniforms. And although for a year or so in junior high he was embarrassed because in a crowd of mothers, his would be the only one in jeans (not realizing, of course, that in the crowd of mothers, only his had a shape that looked good in jeans), he now liked it when his friends would say, "Gee, Huck, she's just not like other mothers."

Curry was much more than just proud of Huck; sometimes she couldn't believe that this young man—already five feet eleven inches and still growing—had anything to do with the six-year-old who had gone off to first grade only yesterday.

Because Curry had had to work, Huck had learned to be self-reliant very early and that had given him more self-confidence and poise than many sixteen-year-old boys. He played on the high school basketball team, made respectable grades, and looked almost exactly like his father had at his age.

Good looks, athletic abilities, and a car are an unbeatable combination in a small-town high school, and when she was in town, Curry was often stopped by some pair of girls, their mouths shining with braces, blushing and whispering, "How's Huck, Mrs. James?"

"He's just fine," she'd answer without pointing out that if the girls had classes with Huck, there'd be days when they saw him more than his mother did.

Bonnie, who was much more interested in people's children than her own natural beauty, which was fortunate, since people had more children than Bonnie did natural beauty, pushed her book aside. "How's Huck doing this summer? Is he surviving Tracy's absence?"

Huck had been dating Tracy Morgan for nearly six months, and when Tracy's reports of her dates with him started to leave considerable blocks of time unaccounted for, her parents, determined to raise a "nice" girl, had shipped her off to a summer-long art camp.

Curry was certain that the two had not made love. Huck had come home from too many dates bright-eyed and restless, and being his mother did not keep her from knowing exactly what was wrong with him. But she could understand why Tracy's parents had sent her away. Small-town summers are long; in Gleeson, the movie changed on Wednesday, and everyone had seen it by Thursday. No matter how many jobs, lessons, or chores parents loaded their teenagers with, they still had too much time to kill. The nice kids hung out at the A&W, the other group lounged in front of the drugstore, and then they'd get in their cars and drive.

And if this random, aimless driving worried parents, the driving was certainly preferable to the parking. More girls got pregnant in the summer than during the other three quarters of the year.

Although Huck complained abut Tracy not being around, he had plenty of other friends, and, his mother suspected, not having Tracy around at all was easier on him and his rapidly maturing body than whatever it was the pair did do together during those blocks of unaccounted-for time.

But still the summer worried Curry. Huck was at an age when boys got into trouble, and she said so now to Bonnie.

"The books might say," Bonnie advised with her usual caution, "that maybe he needs a male role model."

"I don't know about that, but I do know that he needs to be busy, and it looks like his job at the hardware store is about to fall through; they keep giving him shorter and shorter hours, and it's only June."

"What will he do if he gets laid off? Would he do my math for me?"

"Probably not. He wouldn't work a single algebra equation for me all year. 'I'll *help* you with your homework,'" Curry mimicked Huck mimicking her, "'but I won't *do* it for you.' You try your best to raise your kids right and then they turn into juvenile delinquents who won't do your algebra for you." Curry frowned at her screwdriver. "But seriously, I don't know what he'll do if he's laid off. Shoot baskets all day, I suppose. Drive me crazy." She stuck her head back into the dishwasher. "Maybe I should throw him out. Think of what I would save on groceries."

"Oh, don't," Bonnie pleaded. "My girls would want him to move in with us"—Bonnie's two prepubescent daughters thought Huck James was the finest creature to grace the earth—"and my icebox isn't large enough."

Huck did eat a lot. Curry had been raised on stories of what a horde of grasshoppers can do to a wheat crop, but stripping a field bare in two hours seemed paltry compared to what Huck and his friends could do to a refrigerator.

"Speaking of Huck"—Curry lifted her head out of the dishwasher, listening to the screen door open and then slam—"that must be his wings fluttering."

Bonnie pointedly moved her chair out of the path to the refrigerator. "I don't want to get trampled."

Curry's kitchen was as large as farmhouse kitchens usually are. The first floor of her house was hall-less; the rarely used front door opened directly into the dining room, and to the right of that was the "front" room, which was where one took the minister to sit when he came calling.

Although these two rooms were large and quite comfortably furnished, Curry and Huck almost never used them. Even in South Dakota, ministers don't come calling anymore—a social change that was a profound relief to Curry. She felt that any attempt to confide her problems to her minister ought to begin with the fact that it had been she, twenty-five years ago, who had launched the softball that happened to pass through the church's one stained glass window. But as it was, she had no occasion either to make this confession or use her front room; she often said that she wasn't entirely sure that she remembered where it was.

Nor did she and Huck eat in the dining room. They walked through it on the way to the stairs. A gate-leg walnut table was folded against one wall, but it was used only as a place for Huck to pile the quantities of clutter that his life generated—worn-out basketball shoes, cans of motor oil, and homework assignments. Curry often thought it would make sense to substitute this table with a packing crate that every month or so she could parcel up and ship off to the Salvation Army—although someone would have to have let his life degenerate to truly grievous straits before he could possibly benefit from the things that Huck had abandoned.

Instead they lived in the kitchen. That room extended along the entire back of the house, big enough for a rocking chair and an oak table that, with both its leaves in, could seat eight on Curry's grandmother's patterned-back chairs. Oak cabinets, studded with white porcelain knobs, extended to the ceiling and a few braided rag rugs lay on the wood floor. The kitchen looked rather like a magazine illustration for the currently fashionable "country kitchen," except Curry's kitchen did not have copper pots hanging from the ceiling—Curry was incapable of keeping the bottoms of her pots shiny enough for display—and it did not have the regulation fireplace that its modern imitators did. Curry's house had been built back in the days when people were proud not to have fireplaces. A house without a fireplace meant that you could afford a furnace.

The kitchen opened out onto a screened porch,

and it was the porch door that Curry had heard bang a moment before. She distinguished just one other set of footsteps besides Huck's. That was surprising. Unless he was with Tracy, Huck tended to travel in a pack.

She glanced up at the mass of shadows that appeared in the door. Following Huck was a man, taller than he, with broad shoulders and rather shaggy brown hair and eyes of a surprising blue—

Curry's hand flew to her throat. It was Tom. After all these years, suddenly, out of nowhere, Tom.

"Hello, Curry." His voice was deep, with a low tremor charged by memories.

Oh, Tom.

But years of training, of growing up along with two boys who had detested "mush" with every fiber of their beings, checked Curry's impulse to hurl herself into his arms. She stood up slowly. "Well, I'll be crumbed and deep-fried. Is that really you?"

"No, but it's close enough."

"What are you doing here?"

"Fixing up Dad's house."

"It sure needs it."

He looked wonderful, tall with a good solid build to him. And so familiar. Different, of course, older, but still . . . just wonderful.

Curry should have followed that impulse; she should have run to him, letting him swing her off her feet, nearly cracking her ribs as he hugged her, his shoulders solid beneath her hands, and then he would have set her down so she could turn her face up for his kiss. She should have let him know how it was to see him again, how for an instant the world had stopped and it was early spring again with the wild strawberries and purple milkweed blooming by the side of the road and the meadowlarks singing in the cottonwoods.

But it was too late now, the moment for such rapture was gone, and she introduced Bonnie to him. "And this is Tom Winchester," she finished. "We ate sand out of the same sandbox."

With a warm smile, Tom shook Bonnie's hand. "More than that, Curry," he said over his shoulder. "I told you where babies come from."

"You did? I don't remember."

"That's good. I had it wrong."

"Have you figured it out yet?" Bonnie laughed.

"Just barely. My daughter's fifteen, and believe me, sometimes I haven't the faintest idea where she came from."

"You have a fifteen-year-old girl?" Huck looked interested. Very interested. In fact, fifteen-year-old girls were the third most interesting thing in Huck's life, eclipsed only by basketball and sixteen-year-old girls.

"You knew about Diana," his mother said.

Huck shrugged and hoisted himself up onto the kitchen counter. "I forgot."

Tom was looking around the kitchen. "Curry, what have you done with the decals? The place doesn't look the same without them."

"That was pretty much the point."

Up until her grandmother died, the kitchen in this house had looked like farmhouse kitchens generally look, which is, of course, nothing at all like the magazine illustrations. The walls, the cupboards, the ceiling, the oak chairs and table, had all been painted a shade of gray-green that was particularly reminiscent of a stagnant pond. Adorning the cupboards and the chair backs were decals of orange-red roses that were perhaps intended to match the maroon linoleum floor.

Although Curry had, at the time, made her living selling paint, she also sold paint remover, several cases of which had been required in the excavation of this room.

Tom was examining the floor. "Was this under that red stuff?" He knelt down to admire it. "This is wide-plank white pine; you can't get that anymore." Then he looked up, shaking his head. "But, Curry, why'd you polyurethane it? It feels like a bowling alley; with a floor like this you ought to be able to feel the life in the wood."

Curry shrugged. "If I had to wax a wood floor and in a kitchen, no less, all you'd feel is waxed-up crud. You'd have to bring in an iron lung before you'd feel any life in the wood."

Tom laughed and stood up.

How bizarre, she thought. *Here we are talking about waxy, yellow build up, as if we saw each other every day, as if we were still fifteen.*

And for a moment, it seemed unreal that Tom was actually here.

Bonnie was speaking. "So you are Huck's father's friend, the Tom of Huck-and-Tom."

Tom's face seemed to go tight, and Curry spoke

quickly. "I bet it's been a long time since anyone called you that."

"Yes, it has," he acknowledged and then turned to Bonnie. "We were very close as kids . . . all three of us were."

"Hey, Mom," Huck put in, "with a Tom and a Huck, why didn't people call you 'Becky'?"

"As I recall," Curry said, not looking at Tom, "it was tried once or twice, but it was not repeated."

"Why not?" Huck wondered.

"You tell him, Tom." And now she looked at him, never doubting that he would remember.

Tom grinned. "If you want the truth, kid, it was because she was bigger than we were."

"She was?" Huck stared at Tom, who was several inches over six feet.

"It was awhile back," Tom admitted. "But a couple of years ago, weren't all the girls taller than you?"

Huck groaned. "I hated that."

"I know," Tom commiserated, "and then by the time we got big enough to beat her up again, we stopped wanting to."

"Yeah," Huck agreed cheerfully, "I know that feeling too. In fact—"

"I think," Tom interrupted, "that this is a conversation that maybe you and I should continue at a later date . . . away from these ladies."

Huck said nothing, just drumming his heel against the lower cabinet, but Curry knew from the brick flush coloring his face that he was about to expire with delight. Tom was talking to him like a grown-up, and if Huck couldn't play center on the varsity team, if he couldn't do some very natural and ordinary things to Tracy Morgan's body, he would probably settle for being talked to like a grown-up.

Bonnie seemed as pleased with Tom as Huck was. "You said you were here working on your father's house. Do you do that professionally?"

"I have," he answered.

"Bonnie, you remember," Curry put in, "that article I showed you about him."

The local librarian had called Curry when the preservationist magazine had had the article on Tom. It had been a highly flattering piece, praising his skill, his perfectionism, his commitment to preservation despite the absence of the academic background typical of most preservationists.

The article had embarrassed Tom; he probably would have been more comfortable if it had been a smear. And now he groaned, "Oh, Curry, did you show that to people? You're as bad as Trish."

"Trish?" Bonnie was interested.

"My wife," he replied.

"Oh."

Curry took pity on her. "His ex-wife."

Tom frowned. "No. At least not as far as I know. Last I heard we were married. Do you know something I don't?" He seemed to think that this was a genuine possibility.

"Why, no," Curry said hastily. "I just assumed ... I mean, the two of you aren't exactly on the best of terms."

"I don't know about that. We're certainly on better terms than when we were living together full-time."

"That's what my husband thinks too," Bonnie said, "only he *is* my ex-husband."

Tom smiled at her with the sort of immediate intimacy that Curry sometimes felt for other widows. "Lousy marriages are great fun, aren't they?"

"Oh, for sure," Bonnie agreed. "But if you don't live with her, why aren't you divorced? Don't you believe in it?"

Tom shrugged. "I guess what it comes down to is that I don't hate her as much as I hate lawyers."

"You do spend a lot of time with lawyers if you are trying to get divorced."

"They're just everywhere," Tom concurred. "It's gotten so that in my line of work, you can't even start measuring until the lawyers all say it's okay."

Curry had no such prejudice against lawyers. She figured that they were a lot like hired guns, extremely useful until they forgot that you were paying their meal ticket; that was when they got dangerous.

This conversation was starting to bore Huck and he slid off the counter to draw a bead on the defenseless refrigerator.

Young Huck James was capable of great body control and even a measure of physical grace; his moves on the basketball court left a number of teenage girls feeling a faintness that, to their parents' great relief, they did not fully understand. But as with most adolescents, grace wasn't yet automatic for Huck; he had to be trying. When he wasn't concentrating, he could be as clumsy as he had been at twelve. So as he slid off the counter one of his rather generously sized feet landed on top of Curry's array of dishwasher screws and sent little metal bits skating across the kitchen floor.

"Oh, Huck," Curry sighed. "Those were in order. Now I'm never going to get them back in."

"Sorry, Mom," he apologized. "I'll help."

"You don't know anything more about dish-washers than I do."

"Do you want me to take a look at it?" Tom offered.

"No, don't worry about it. I'll call a repair-man."

"Don't do that. Repairmen never do a good enough job. They're in too much of a hurry."

When Curry was paying someone by the hour—or by the minute, as always seemed to be the case with repairmen—she wanted them to be in a hurry. A big hurry.

But before she could protest, Tom was on the floor in front of the dishwasher, and Huck, having decided to let the refrigerator live for another hour or so, had dropped down next to him and seemed ready to hand him tools. Clearly it was out of Curry's hands.

Well, why not? she thought. Wasn't it silly to protest politely that no, she really *wanted* to call a repairman, that she *loved* calling repairmen, when, of course, like any sensible human being, she'd a lot rather that Tom fix it now if he could? She didn't have to go all polite and insincere.

After all, as hard as it was to believe, this was Tom.

"Well, this does look like fun," Bonnie said, collecting her purse and natural beauty book, "but I have to go fix supper."

Curry walked her out to her car and then started her own supper preparations. As she was pulling out the iron skillet and the shortening, Huck happened to glance up.

"You're actually going to fry the chicken?"

Some years ago Curry had decided that life was simply too short to spend it watching drumsticks swim around in hot grease. So she had taken to rolling chicken in crushed cornflakes, sticking it in the oven with a pat of butter, and calling it fried chicken. Huck complained at length, but since it had taken him a good year to notice, Curry didn't pay any attention.

"Well," she defended this unusual effort, "I was assuming that Tom would stay for supper."

Huck turned back to Tom. "She sure must like you better than she likes me."

"She's just known me longer, that's all."

Curry started to unwrap the chicken that was defrosting on the counter. "You will stay, won't you? I'm sorry we have to eat so early, but I have a class tonight."

"Class?"

"Didn't you know? I sold the store, you knew that, and I am at school full-time now."

Tom sat back on his haunches. "School? As in college?" Curry nodded. "With majors and term papers and things like that?"

"I'm a history major."

"History? You mean memorizing dates and all?"

Curry set down the Crisco can. That seemed like an odd remark for a man who was manning the barricades in the nation's fight to preserve its heritage.

"It's just that she has a crush on her history professor," Huck announced.

"Huck!" Curry glared at him for a moment, but her gaze softened as she understood. Huck was trying to impress Tom, and it never occurred to him that perhaps he should not do it at his mother's expense.

"Actually"—Curry silently dared Tom not to laugh—"I'm going to be a high school history teacher when I grow up."

Tom dropped the screwdriver. "A hi— But, Curry, you *hated* school; we all did."

"I know I did. That's why I think I will be a good teacher. I adore school now, but I remember what it's like to hate being there."

Tom picked up the screwdriver again. "That might just make some sense."

"Thank you."

"I said might. We can't know for sure, now, can we?"

Curry got home from class a little after ten. This was earlier than usual; normally she went out drinking after class. There was a group that went— a couple of kids from the Dungeons and Dragons crowd, Curry, sometimes another housewife-student, and the professor, Dr. Wheeler.

Huck hadn't been entirely right when he said Curry had a crush on Dr. Wheeler. She didn't write his name over and over again in her notebook and she didn't fantasize about him sweeping her off her feet—he was, after all, younger than she. Nonetheless, she did feel a certain tension in his presence that could only be half attributed to the fact that he was her best teacher.

But in class tonight, she had had trouble even paying attention to what he was saying about South Dakota history, the subject of this shortened summer school class. She was thinking about Tom, about how extraordinary it was to have him back.

But supper hadn't felt extraordinary at all, that was what was so strange. It felt perfectly normal to have him sitting right there, eating fried chicken, talking to Huck about sports, to her about the crops and the farmer who rented both her land and his father's. It was almost as if all the years hadn't made a bit of difference, as if he hadn't left Gleeson and married and—

Tom's marriage. He had said nearly nothing about Trish, nothing beyond the rather startling fact that he was still married to her.

He had met Trish while Curry and Huck's father were honeymooning out in the Badlands of western South Dakota. Trish had come to Gleeson to visit a sick aunt and Tom, whose world must have felt rather empty without his two friends, had taken up with her. After she left, he went up to see her in Minnesota a couple of times and then came home, announcing that he was going to marry her.

"You'll stand up with me, won't you?" Tom had said.

"Sure." Huck had grinned. "I like wearing rented clothes."

"Actually, I was asking Curry." It turned out that Tom had unconsciously described the adventures of Curry-Tom-and-Huck in such a masculine fashion that Trish's mother had reminded him that he needed to choose between Curry and Huck for his best man.

"I'm not sure I like that." Curry frowned.

"Sure you do," her husband told her. "But, Tom, didn't you ever let it slip that these two fine fellows had married each other? That might have tipped her off."

"Or made her think that we were all a little on the strange side," Curry put in. "A little on the strange side," was South Dakota's useful phrase for those rare moments when one had to discuss homosexuals, psychopaths, or other communists.

"I don't know," Tom replied. "I guess it didn't come up."

The first impression that Curry made on the good people of Bemidji was not a particularly feminine one either. Rather than drive with Tom's father, she and Huck had borrowed a motorcycle and had ridden it up from Gleeson. When they parked in front of Trish's home and swung off the bike, they were probably indistinguishable: dusty jeans hugged their long legs, loose leather jackets hid the difference in their builds, and their heads and hair were masked by their helmets.

But Tom knew who they were and came bounding down the porch, pulling a pastel-clad Trish by the hand.

Curry jerked off her helmet, and the glowing mass of golden hair tumbled forth. Carelessly she flipped it back over the shoulders of her leather jacket and started to speak to Trish.

"Good God, Curry," Tom interrupted her, "you look wonderful."

Surprised, Curry drew back, frowning at him, not quite sure if he were sincere.

Huck came up. "Hell, Tom, you'd look this good too if you had the honor of carrying my child."

Curry was newly pregnant, a fact that the young couple regarded with exactly the same mindless enthusiasm that they had once had for the coming of Santa Claus.

Now it was Tom's turn to stare. "You're going to have a baby? You?"

Curry shrugged. "It seems like it. So if I look great, it's because it's afternoon. In the mornings I look like a green sponge."

Curry and Huck had both been very eager to meet Trish, never occurring to either of them that she wouldn't instantly fit in, that she wouldn't be a part of their little team just as surely as if she had been in the barn that stormy afternoon when their blood had sealed an oath.

But two hours later when Trish's mother, considerably startled by this high-spirited pair, had shown them to their room, they looked at each other amazed. "Tom?" they wondered together.

For Trish had, at least on first glance, been everything the three had sneered at: sheltered, fastidious, delicate.

"She must be pregnant," Curry concluded. "Did you have a chance to ask him? That would be fun, us all having babies together."

"He says not," Huck answered. It didn't cross either of their minds that this was not exactly a question that one was supposed to ask a bride-groom.

"Well, why, then?" Curry demanded.

"He said something about she's the kind of girl a person is supposed to marry."

"What does that mean?"

"Beats me. But if he's right"—Huck swatted Curry across the seat of her jeans—"I made a ter-rible mistake."

"You sure did," she acknowledged calmly.

Curry understood it better now. Tom, she sus-pected, had married an idea. Although none of the three had had ideal "Dick-Jane-and-Sally" homes, Tom had had it the roughest. In general, his father ignored him, occasionally issuing stern and vague orders.

Curry now found it curious that Huck's mother, Myra James, had not done more for Tom, had not been more of a substitute mother to the boy. If Curry had been in her situation, the sole surviving woman out of six friends, she certainly would have mothered whatever children still lived.

But Mrs. James had not, and Tom had grown up with rather hazy notions of what it was that wives and mothers did. So when it looked like time to get married, he had chosen the first girl who seemed to fit his story-book images. That wives and mothers came in great variety and that it was more important to find a woman suited to him than to these domestic roles was not something that had apparently occurred to him.

And Trish's reasons for marrying Tom, Curry further suspected now, were no better. Undoubtedly he had coaxed and bullied her into going to bed with him, and she had enjoyed it more than she had expected.

Well, Tom was quite an attractive man. Curry hadn't really thought about it before; the bonds that had tied the three of them had been so deep that physical appearance had never mattered. But this afternoon, seeing him for the first time in years, noticing the way Bonnie's eyes followed him, she had paid attention.

As a boy, Tom had been on the skinny side, and he still had hints of that wiriness in the lithe way he moved, but he had filled out with a man's solid muscle. He wasn't classically handsome, and he looked exactly like what he was, a man who made his living with his hands, a man who'd hang himself before spending the day in an office. He'd been wearing a blue work shirt and well-worn jeans, rubbed to a light blue at his knees and at one patch on his right hip where his tool pouch must normally hang. Thrust into his back pocket had been a pair of worn leather gloves, a splash of beige in the blue of his clothes, just as his eyes were a sparkle of blue in the tan of his face beneath the dark brown of his curl-rumpled hair.

His smile had a warmth to it, a warmth that was undercut with a slight edge, reminding you that this man was an adult, someone who had fought a war and screwed up a marriage.

What's he like in bed? The thought came unbidden.

As a merchant in a small town, Curry had acted as if her heart, her mind, and other bits and pieces of her anatomy were still kneeling in prayer at her dead husband's shrine. But, of course, that wasn't so. Her thoughts, sometimes even her pulse and breath, were a great deal less respectable than her behavior. She did not feel the least bit guilty about this. In fact, she rather enjoyed her wayward thoughts.

But she wasn't sure she liked this one. In high school she and Tom had never "gone all the way," as they used to say, but they had spent their share of time on her grandmother's back porch or in Tom's car, parked along the Jenny Wren road.

He had always been pushing, first trying to touch her breasts, and then when she finally let him do that, he immediately started tugging at her sweat shirt. They had been like adversaries, he assaulting, she defending, locked in the panting competition of so many teenage romances.

Of course, it had been entirely natural. Tom had been just barely fifteen; desire had been new, more urgent than it would ever be again, and it never occurred to most boys that age to try to please a girl.

But Tom was hardly fifteen anymore. His hair was longer, his body stronger, his leg wounded. The years must have changed much about him. Surely this had changed too; surely he wasn't still just interested in his own pleasure.

But he might be. Curry suspected that lots of men were interested only in themselves. That's what she'd tell herself when sometimes she'd glance at the TV screen while Huck was watching a football game, when her breath would quicken at the sight of those splendidly built men gathered in a huddle—"Oh, well," she'd sigh, "they're probably no good anyway."

Such suspicions had kept her out of several casual affairs when she went to paint conventions—she wasn't going to bed with some joker just so that he could have a good time.

What was Tom like? Maybe she should ask him. "Hey, Tom, are you any good in bed?" They'd made that pact; he'd have to answer straight. Except that he'd be laughing too hard to talk.

Well, it didn't matter. Even though asking probably made more sense than wondering about it, she wasn't going to. There were questions that she'd promised herself she'd never ask him, and if she wasn't going to ask him those, she certainly wasn't going to ask him to rate his own performance in bed.

She could just ask to see his scar. That might be fun.

Curry was not entirely surprised when she pulled open the door from the screen porch to see that Tom was still there. He and Huck were at the kitchen table, making their way through a half-gallon of ice cream. They hadn't bothered with bowls; the square carton sat between them. Melting ice cream had started to ooze through its seams and form little puddles on the table.

Huck started talking as soon as Curry came in. They had been over to the old Winchester place, and Huck had to tell her in great detail exactly what Tom planned to do. "... run the plumbing lines so just in case they ever allow gray water systems..."

Curry did her level best to listen.

"And, Mom, you should see Tom's camper, it's so cool. He ripped out everything, and it's like a little workshop. His tools are so organized; I mean, the hammers are all lined up according to size, and..."

A place for everything, and everything in its place. Curry thought that a complete waste of time.

At last Huck ran dry, and Tom stood up to leave.

"I'll walk as far as the creek with you," Curry offered.

Reminding Huck to put the ice cream away, she led the way out of the kitchen and was at the screen door when she noticed that Tom had stopped on the porch.

"Is this the same glider that was always here?" Then he answered himself. "Of course it is. They don't make wrought iron half this sturdy anymore." Tom gave the green-cushioned glider an affectionate push. "I certainly do have memories of you," he told it.

It creaked a fond reply.

Curry smiled. "Do you remember it as the place you learned about sex?"

"Not at all. I learned about frustration on this glider. I learned about sex in the backseat of my car with Betty Lou Spencer."

Curry was halfway down the steps. She glanced over her shoulder. "Betty Lou Spencer? You're joking."

He shook his head.

"Well, you'd better keep quiet about it. She's Betty Lou Toggin now. She bought Webster's fabric store and is a regular community pillar. In fact, she and I were the first women to join the Downtown Merchants' Association."

"You and Betty Lou? In the Downtown Merchants' Association?"

"Yes. Just because you remember us as wearing padded bras and saddle shoes doesn't mean that we still do."

"You didn't wear a padded bra."

"I did too," Curry defended her right to be counted as a member of her generation. "Gran bought it for me. Two, in fact, and they were different, so sometimes I looked real pointy if I wore the one that had stitching around—" Curry stopped. She'd been about to demonstrate how the apparatus had been constructed when she noticed that Tom was watching with a fair amount of interest.

"Well, never mind," she said. "The point is that even if Gleeson is still going by the same old script, the next generation of players has taken over."

Obviously Tom hadn't been thinking. If he had realized that Betty Lou hadn't been permanently embalmed in her sewn-down pleats and penny loafers, if he had thought about her as a woman with a husband, a family, and a business, he would have never said what he just had about her.

"Of course," he apologized, "it's just hard to think of you two as grown women, liberating the Downtown Merchants' Association."

"That's okay. When we did it, the newspaper called us 'girls.'"

Tom laughed. "I love this place."

It was a warm night. The barn was a mass of shadows, and in the orchard, the few surviving crab apple and plum trees were low, shadowy shapes in the starlight. The night was quiet and still, the only sound the fading of Tom's laughter and the tinkle of a set of wind chimes.

Tom glanced up. "Huck's wind chimes. He made those in metalshop, didn't he?"

Curry nodded.

"Did you bring them over? Or did his mother?"

"His mother? Tom, I *am* his—" She stopped. They were talking about different Hucks. "My son made those wind chimes," she said gently. "I don't know what happened to the ones his father made."

"Oh." Tom thrust his hands in his pockets and started walking.

Curry caught up with him. "You've been away a long time."

"Yes. Too long, I guess."

"Then, why—"

Again she stopped. This was what she had sworn to herself that she would never ask him, that she would never expect him to explain, that she would never hold against him.

But there was a time when she had felt that he had betrayed her, that he had dishonored the pledge they had all made that thundery summer afternoon.

After the two men in the dark green Chevy brought the news from Vietnam, the news about Huck's father, it had been dark and crazy days for Curry, and only the routine needs of her small child got her out of bed in the morning. She desperately needed someone to talk to, someone to remember Huck with, and there just wasn't anyone.

Gran got too confused—she didn't always remember that Huck was dead or she'd think it was the baby Curry was talking about. Huck's mother did want to talk about him all the time, but her talk was more than Curry could stand. It seemed like Mrs. James had it all wrong; it wasn't Huck she was talking about, but some fantasy son, some cleaned-up, homogenized fantasy that didn't have a thing to do with the Huck whom Curry had loved.

When Tom gets here, she kept telling herself, *I'll be able to talk to him. Tom will remember, he won't have forgotten what it was like.*

Tom was still over in Vietnam, but Curry had

been sure that as soon as he was back, he'd come to her. Even before he went to Trish, he would come to her.

But Tom had been wounded, and Trish and her parents had told the Army to fly him to Bemidji. She had written Curry, saying that he was still in a lot of pain, but he'd come to South Dakota as soon as he was better.

Curry started to pack to go to Bemidji. If Tom couldn't come to her, she'd go to him. That was part of the pact, "stick together." Myra and Gran could take care of the baby. He was almost two; he'd be okay without her for a couple of days. But Gran was having one of her clear spells, and she had come to the bedroom door, watching Curry pack.

"You can't go without an invite, girl."

"Gran, this is *Tom*. I don't need an invitation to go see him."

"Maybe not. But he's with his in-laws, and you can't turn up there unless his wife or her mother asks you."

"But, Gran—"

"You aren't kids anymore, young lady. He's got a wife, and you've got yourself that baby. It's time you started acting like adults and that means you wait to be invited."

So she had sunk down next to her suitcase, miserable and lonely, but resolved to wait until he came back home on his own.

And then one cold January day she'd been in town and heard that he had come and gone. Come and gone without stopping, without seeing her.

It had stormed the day before, the year's first hard blizzard, but the sun had been out in the morning, and the snow was covered with a brittle crust of ice. As she drove home the fields were glittering, so bright they almost blinded, and she had to squint to see.

Curry pulled off her left glove, pressing the tip of her forefinger against the cold steering wheel, as if she wanted to freeze off the thin scar left by a pocketknife one summer afternoon. Tom had the same white line across his finger. How could he have forgotten what it meant? How could he have left without seeing her?

Both Tom and Huck had gone off to war, promising to come back. Both had broken their promise.

Curry was desolate. The blank, aching misery of Huck's death now seemed absolute; she'd lost Huck, and now she'd lost Tom too. Just as surely as if he had also died, Tom was gone.

She had to face this on her own. No one was going to make it easier for her. No one was going to step in and take over her grieving. This was it; it was hers. She'd have to do it by herself.

And she did.

Curry shivered, chilled by these memories. The cold of that white day so many years ago seemed, for a moment, more real than this summer night. But that January had been a long time ago. It no longer mattered why Tom hadn't come to her. At least not much.

But he knew what she had been about to ask. "Why didn't I come back?" he finished for her.

"Although I suppose you heard that I was back once."

She shook her head. "No, Tom. I mean, yes, of course I heard, but no, you don't have to explain. Those were black times; nothing I did made sense; I don't know why what you did had to make sense either."

"I wish I could explain, but I..." His voice trailed off.

There was no point in him feeling bad about what had happened so long ago. She had survived, and she was very glad to see him now. Surely the time they would have together would be brief, just as long as it took him to finish his father's house. She did not want to waste it accusing him and blaming him for something that was over and done with.

"Well, even if you could explain," she said lightly, "I don't have time to listen. I've got an appointment with the bank first thing in the morning."

"The bank?" Tom's voice immediately filled with a Midwesterner's basic distrust of banks.

"Oh, it's nothing." Curry flicked her hand. "Just routine."

And then just as if nothing had changed, just as if they were still living in those bright, confident days when they believed tomorrow would always be there, they went their separate ways, neither one bothering to say good-bye.

Chapter Three

The next morning found Curry, her legs making a rare appearance beneath the hemline of a skirt—although it was only wheat-colored denim—trying hard not to frown at her banker.

"... we've all got to tighten our belts," he was saying. "No one would expect it of you if you didn't have enough for your boy, but ..."

Of course, Curry knew that the new owners of her store couldn't pay her this quarter. She had eyes, didn't she? There wasn't a building in town that didn't look just a little dingier than it did last fall. People weren't painting, not with what crops had done the last two years. The whole town felt it, not just the farmers.

If the Ransom brothers were mismanaging the store, Curry would have been at the counter at 7:30 A.M. on July 1, demanding cash, but they were doing a fine job. It wasn't their fault it hadn't rained last year. There just wasn't a blessed thing anyone could do about a long, dry spell. But right now the crops looked better than they had in years.

Anyway, what was her alternative? She could foreclose on them, but that would mean she'd have the store back, and if she had wanted it back, she wouldn't have sold it in the first place. The banker knew that just as well as she did; he was wasting everyone's time trying to smooth-talk her into doing what she didn't have much choice about.

So after Curry figured he had said enough to make himself feel important, she agreed to rewrite the note—or rather sign the rewritten note.

"That's real neighborly of you, Curry," he said, standing up.

Curry smiled dryly. "Well, I'm sure you're being just as neighborly on the notes you hold." This bank had foreclosed on less than a handful of farms since the Depression, but there was nothing people in these parts had longer memories for than a family farm up on an auction block.

The banker mumbled something about "as much as we can" and "we do have repsonsibilities to our stockholders, though." He then walked with her not just out of his office, but past the wooden railing that separated the new accounts desk from the tellers' counter, and all the way to the front door, holding it open for her.

This was first-class, best-client treatment—Gleeson's equivalent of free Super Bowl tickets—and Curry didn't much like it. Just because she'd been able to raise her boy herself and so all the money from the Veterans' Administration was sitting in C.D.'s waiting for Huck to go to college didn't mean she was one whit better than the town's other

Vietnam widows, just luckier. Being a widow with a young child was a lot easier when you didn't have to pay rent and when you had both a great-grandmother and a grandmother around to baby-sit. And having a head for business hadn't hurt either.

Outside the bank, Curry glanced down the block, wondering if she ought to stop in the paint store. No. Bad news she'd have delivered herself; if she had had to have the money, she would have marched right in there. But as long as the bank was interfering, let it finish. If she told the Ransoms, they'd feel obliged to thank her and it would get all embarrassing.

Trying to remember if she had any errands to run as long as she was in town, she saw a figure, more familiar than it had any right to be, coming out of the plumbing and electric supply store across the street.

"Hey," she called out. "Now, wait, don't tell me—" She snapped her fingers. "I've got it. You're that Winchester boy."

As she was speaking Tom had crossed the street with an easy gait that gave no hint of his once-bad leg wound. "How did you know?" Clearly he had been hearing that all morning.

"I know this town. I didn't stop being the 'little Trent girl' until I'd been a widow for four years."

"What happened then?"

"Oh, I decided there wasn't much reason for the hardware store to be carrying paint as long as I had a better stock of it."

"What did you do? Go ask him nicely?"

"Hell, no. I just undersold him by ten percent all season long, fifteen if he were having a sale. Even sold at a loss for a couple of days, but he finally told the Sherwin-Williams people to come pick up their display."

"'This town ain't big enough for the both of us'?" Tom laughed.

"Well, it wasn't," Curry defended herself. "Now he's got space for a line of auto parts that are cheaper than what the gas stations have; that's what people needed. And he's making more off those than he was off paint. He can't be too unhappy about it, or he wouldn't have given Huck a job this summer."

"I stopped in and saw him."

"Huck?" Curry was pleased. She was glad that Tom liked her son. "Listen, you got time for coffee?"

"Sure. At the bakery?"

"Ain't nowhere else."

Downtown Gleeson looked the same as hundreds of other small-town Main Streets. It was only four or five blocks long with an I.G.A. at one end and the Woolworth's and the picture show at the other. To city people the street looked wide; there was angle parking on both sides, and the buildings were so low—not a one was over two stories—that it threw the proportions off. And there wasn't much traffic, even though it was Friday morning. Three stores were boarded up, but if the weather and the wheat prices held, things would look better next year.

The bakery, a block down from the bank, specialized in white bread, donuts, cupcakes, and peanut brittle. On Tuesday they made pumpernickel bread and on Fridays Swedish rye. They also had a lunch counter and a couple of tables where the local merchants gathered for coffee.

Nodding at someone she knew, Curry reached out to open the bakery door, but as she did her hand landed not on the handle's cool metal, but on something warm.

Surprised, she looked down. Her hand was resting on Tom's. He had reached around her to open the door. Almost embarrassed, she pulled her hand away.

He noticed and smiled mockingly. "I've got problems, but doors I can handle."

Well, was it such a surprise, she thought almost defensively, that she had reached for the door herself? After all, she must have gone through doors at least a thousand times with Tom. He'd never opened them before. In fact, almost no one held doors for her. Her son did not, neither did the Dungeons and Dragons crowd at school. Back when she'd had her store, if a man was carrying a couple of gallons of paint out to his car, she had certainly held the door for him. In general, Curry was a woman quite capable of opening the doors in her life. She'd just never been the sort of person for whom men quickened their steps in order to reach a door first.

But so far this morning, Tom and the banker had held doors open for her. That was certainly a strange set of bedfellows—Tom and a banker. Tom would probably faint if he knew that he was in such company, even if what they had in common was as little as this.

When they finally made it through this particular door, all heads at the counter swiveled, checking out the newcomers.

"Hey, Curry, we don't see you around much anymore," a voice called out.

"No, Pete," she answered. "Can't say that you do. How are the kids?"

She and Tom went to a table.

"Coffee, Curry?" Janelle, the white-uniformed waitress, called from behind the counter.

"Two," she answered, never occurring to her to let Tom do the talking.

Janelle came to their table carrying two white mugs and a glass coffeepot. Curry introduced her to Tom. "You remember, Janelle was two years behind us."

Tom smiled at the waitress. "How old do we have to get before people stop introducing us by what class we were in high school?"

"It keeps a person honest." Janelle laughed as she poured the coffee. "Last time I tried to tell someone I was twenty-nine, he started to pull out the yearbooks." She sat the pot down, then leaned over and straightened the napkins, the sugar, the salt and pepper. Curry thought it rather unnecessary fidgeting until she saw Tom glance at Janelle's left hand. He was checking for a ring, and Janelle was making it easy for him to see that there wasn't one.

Well, aren't we all being big-city swingers here?

No, it made sense. Janelle was a widow, too;

her husband had been killed in Vietnam a couple of months after Huck. While some of the other men in the bakery were good-looking in a clean Midwestern way, they were all numbingly familiar, universally married with kids and dental bills. But Tom, sitting back from the table, one elbow hooked over the chair back, one foot propped up, smiling a warm and lazy smile . . . well, no wonder Janelle was interested.

"Hey, Janelle," someone called out, "what about a refill over here."

"Sure thing." She picked up her coffeepot and smiled at Tom. "Hope we'll be seeing more of you."

Tom smiled back, his blue eyes twinkling, and after Janelle left, he must have noticed Curry's expression, for he started to laugh. "Now, is it my fault that there are more women on the loose than there are men?"

"Are you used to come-ons like that?"

"Come-ons? Oh, Curry, that was nothing."

"I could tell her that you're married."

"Be my guest. It's not something I hide."

Curry made a face at him, but before she could speak, Burt Morris, the editor of the town's weekly paper, came to the table.

"Hi, Curry. Long time no see. Do you miss us?"

"You and the rest of the fellows, sure, but I can't say that I miss paint. I never did like the stuff much."

Morris laughed. "Well, you sure got out when the getting was good."

"Blind luck." Then Curry introduced Tom, mentioning that he had been a friend of Huck's father's.

After Morris left, Tom asked, "What was that all about?"

"All what? About you being a friend of Huck's father's? I thought you were." Then more seriously—"Or did you mean about me liking paint? It's the truth; it's—"

"No," Tom interrupted. "About you getting out at the right time. I thought—" He stopped.

"You thought I lost the store?" Curry frowned. "Look, I said I sold it, and I did. If I'd gone bankrupt, I'd have said so."

Everyone in town had thought Curry crazy to sell her store just after its best year ever, and if she'd been a man, they probably would have carted her off to the state mental institution. But she had sold so much paint and wallpaper that year that she just didn't think she could look at another gallon of the one or roll of the other. She had had it with people who bought seven gallons of specially mixed paint and then didn't like the color. She was sick of women who spent two months looking at wallpaper before they picked out something for their bathroom. Hell, wallpaper never looked the same up on the wall, so why go blind looking through the books?

All that had never bothered her in the store's early years. She had needed the money, and earning it had been enough of a challenge that she really cared whether people found the right wallpaper, and she would experiment endlessly with a customer until he liked his paint color. She'd felt good at the end of the day if these efforts had made a lot of money. When she didn't feel that way anymore, she sold the store.

She explained this to Tom. "Does that seem harebrained to you?"

"To me? Curry, you're looking at a man who turned in a union card."

"With no regrets?"

"Not a one."

He was pulling something out of his pocket. He set it on the table. It was a pocket tape measure, a good one with a locking mechanism and all. Printed across the side in red letters were the words "Gleeson Paint Supply, Curry James, Proprietor."

"Who'd you shoplift that off of?" she asked.

"Watson at the plumbing supply place. I traded mine for it."

"Is this a grown-up version of marbles and baseball cards?"

"And at the hardware store, there was a folding carpenter's rule. Said the same thing."

"I gave away good stuff," Curry acknowledged. "Everyone else passed out these dippy little calendars at Christmas, but I figured if I wanted good will, I ought to give out things people would use. Those tape measures were the best, though."

"Was that the year you put the hardware store out of business?"

"Out of the *paint* business, Tom, just out of the *paint* business. And it was the Christmas before, actually. It was phase one."

He shook his head. "This is hard to get used to."

"This?"

He tried to explain. "This you." He pointed at the measure. "'Curry James, Proprietor.' The cutthroat killer businesswoman. The lady Downtown Merchant. Someone who gets called 'Mom.'"

Curry laughed. "What does your kid call you?"

"Not 'Mom,' that's for sure."

But before he spoke, he had looked startled as if his having a daughter was something he hadn't thought to compare to her having a son. And in a way, of course, it wasn't comparable. He just visited Diana; he wasn't really carrying the full load of being a parent.

But Curry didn't think she should say anything about his relations with his family. It was odd enough just thinking of Tom having a family of his own.

She guessed she was making the same mistake he was. He'd come back expecting that Gleeson wouldn't have changed and she, in turn, was surprised when things happened to remind her that he wasn't sixteen and skinny anymore—when he opened a door for her, when he spoke to strangers with an adult's ease, when women watched him, when he checked their left hands.

Just as he had to get used to her being a businesswoman, student, and mother, so she had to get used to him being grown-up and male.

Curry thought she'd probably pick it up a lot faster than he would.

"You like him, don't you?"

"Like who?"

Curry stared at her son. "Tom. That person you were just with."

"Oh, sure, I like him fine."

That was high praise from Huck, but Curry was not surprised. It had been two weeks since Tom had arrived and he had seen more of Huck than the boy's mother had. From the beginning, Huck was fascinated by what Tom was doing to the house and haunted him during every free moment. Tom was clearly willing to explain what he was doing and to show Huck how to do things, even letting him try them for himself, although, as he later told Curry, "I don't know what's come over me. I don't usually let anyone else use my tools, not even to bang a nail."

Curry was ready to start making cracks about how Tom Sawyer got the fence whitewashed when this Tom asked Huck to start working for him when he wasn't at the hardware store.

"There's plenty you can do, and I can pay you minimum wage, just like they do at the store."

"Oh, Mom, can I?" Huck pleaded. "The store only has me working Saturday afternoon and Thursday night this week and next."

"Why, Huck," she said, "it's entirely up to you." This was rather a new phrase in their household, and it tended to mean that Curry approved of either alternative. "It's your summer; if you want to hold down two jobs, it's your business."

Huck certainly did want to, and his comment

after their first day was "He sure does like things done right, doesn't he?" Since Curry herself rarely did anything completely right—perfectionism was another thing, along with frying chicken, that life was too short for—she figured this was good training for Huck. If he could work for Tom, he could work for anyone.

But it seemed to be going very well; the only complaint was Curry's silent one that in her role as concerned, interested, responsive parent, she was learning a great deal more about remodeling techniques than she wanted to know.

But other things about Tom interested Huck besides what he knew about buildings. "He's been so many places. Did you know he's seen both the Atlantic and the Pacific?"

Neither Huck nor Curry had ever seen a body of water so big that you couldn't see the other side.

"And he's been to New Mexico and Maine," Huck went on, the places obviously sounding very exotic to him. "It's neat hearing him talk about them. Man, I'd like to travel like that some day."

Listening to him, Curry felt guilty. She and Huck had hardly been anywhere. He'd been to Boy Scout camp and such, but as for your regular, two-weeks-in-August, family vacation...well, when you had your own store, it was hard to get away.

Perhaps they should have.

"I'm glad you like him," was all she said to Huck.

"Yeah, I do." Huck opened the refrigerator and took out the milk carton. "It doesn't seem like he's your friend. It's hard to remember that he grew up with you and my dad." Huck took a long swill of milk.

She had long since quit trying to stop Huck from drinking straight out of the milk carton. He didn't have a drug problem; for that Curry was willing to forgive him any number of mildly unsanitary practices.

"Have you ever asked Tom about your father?" When he was six or seven, Huck had suddenly become very interested in his father, wanting to hear stories about him, have his picture in his room, but that interest had faded long ago.

"No," Huck replied. He put the milk back in the refrigerator and started rummaging for something to eat. From behind the door, Curry heard his voice. "I did ask him about the military, though."

"The military?" Curry had no idea, simply no idea, that Huck was at all interested in the military, and quite frankly, she wasn't sure that she wanted him to be.

Huck must have sensed the surprise in her voice, for when he emerged from the refrigerator, banana in hand, he was a little defensive. "Well, guys at school do talk about it, you know."

"Of course." Curry made her voice very calm; the least variation in tone sometimes made Huck feel as if the entire adult world were besieging him, and if Huck thought he was being attacked, he clammed up beyond all prayers, his entire vocabulary dwindling to "It's okay" and "Forget it."

"What did Tom say?" she asked in as bored a tone as she could muster.

"He was real straight about it. Talked about how hard basic was for him, not the physical stuff, but the way they turn you into a soldier first and a person second. He said that's probably necessary to get guys to do what they do in combat, but it was kind of tough for him."

Curry knew Tom; to relinquish control, to give up authority over himself, to take orders, would have been terribly, terribly difficult.

Huck continued. "But he did say that the Army was okay for some people and that there were some pretty good reasons to join up, but some bad ones too."

"Like what?" Was Huck considering enlisting after he graduated? Curry wanted him to go to college.

"He said that you shouldn't join up just because you don't know what to do with yourself."

"Have you been thinking that you should?"

"Well, Mom, I mean, isn't it pretty pointless to go to college when you don't know what you want to major in and all?"

Huck's interests weren't very clearly defined. His math skills were excellent, but Curry suspected that he liked being good at math more than he liked math itself. He hated Spanish, he loved basketball, but beyond that, his likes and dislikes depended on his mood. Curry hadn't realized that this bothered him. "What did Tom say about college?"

"That college was probably a pretty good place to figure out what you wanted to do."

Oh, bless you, Tom, Curry thought. *I could have said this; his teachers could have said this, but he listened to you.*

"He said," Huck went on, "that he'd bet you didn't start off college knowing you wanted to major in history."

"It never crossed my mind." In fact, Curry had dreaded her first history course. "Huck, listen, you have time; it may not seem like it, but you'll find something that interests you. You don't need to feel like you have to enlist."

"That's what Tom says. But, let me tell you, I'm sure going to be ticked off if going to college makes me want to be a high school history teacher like it did you."

"I don't think you need to worry about that."

She knew enough not to push Huck any further. This was how talking to him was; if she ever sat down to talk about something serious, they got absolutely nowhere, but if she waited, he generally got around to telling her what was on his mind. "By the way, did Tom say if he was coming to supper?"

"I don't know. Was I supposed to ask?"

"It wouldn't have hurt; but I can ask him."

She found Tom sitting on the front porch of his father's house, doing something with some fine steel wool and a short piece of wood. She dropped down on the steps and took a swig out of the beer can that was sitting next to him.

"What are you doing?"

"Making a leg."

"Who for? Yourself? Isn't it a little short?"

"There was a time when I didn't find jokes like that particularly funny."

"I'd be surprised if it bothered you now."

He smiled. "Of course it doesn't. Especially from you." He held up the wood, and Curry saw that it was intricately carved. "It's a leg for a walnut server, some French piece. I'm doing it for an antique dealer down in St. Louis."

"Is there a lot of work like that?"

"I could probably do it full-time if I wanted ... although I need a workshop and all."

Curry was, as always, practical. "Is there money in it?"

Tom shrugged. "Maybe if I wanted there to be. I've never really talked price much. I just do it for fun; I usually carry something around with me, to work on for a break."

Of course he only did it for fun. If he did it fulltime, if he set up a workshop somewhere, he would have to stay in one place. Maybe she and Huck hadn't traveled enough, but Tom traveled too much. Hell, you couldn't even call it traveling; he was running, running away.

"Do you have much money, Tom?" She would never dream of asking anyone else such a question, but of course it was different with him.

He nodded. "It's out of character, but I do ... or rather Trish and I do."

"How did you make it?"

"Houses. I didn't mean to; it just sort of happened. We own a couple of houses in Bemidji; I fixed them up and her uncle rents them out for us. And then . . . do you remember back before interest rates went up and real estate prices were going up by the month?"

"Sure."

"Well, I was in Chicago, not really knowing what to do with myself, and I found a couple of houses on the North Side that were nearly condemned, so I bought them and did some work on them, and . . . well, it was criminal, I should have been arrested. People shouldn't make that much money . . . but I sold them all to lawyers, so I didn't feel bad."

Curry laughed. She was glad Tom had money. It was pleasant having money. Of course, she spent almost nothing, but it was good not to have to worry about it. "Do you spend much?" she asked him.

"Just on my tools. I do spend a lot on them, almost as much as my daughter spends on clothes."

"Boys are nice that way." And then Curry remembered what she had come to say, the not-so-nice-part about having male offspring; that some of them went off to war and didn't make it home. "Huck says that he asked you about the Army."

"Oh?"

"Yes, and I really appreci—" Curry broke off and looked at him suspiciously. "What do you mean 'Oh'?"

"Nothing."

"Come on, Tom. Did he ask you about something else?"

"Not really. But we've been working together for more than a week." Tom leaned down and took his beer back from her. "Things have come up."

"Like what?" At his polite smile, she grimaced. "Like sex, I suppose."

"Is that so surprising?"

"Yes." When Huck had been born, Curry had had a working knowledge of both reproduction and sexual pleasure that had been entirely adequate for her own purposes. Her theoretical knowledge was nonexistent. When she realized that she was going to be raising a son on her own, she went to the library, checked out the books that the librarian normally kept in the back room, and made sure that Huck knew all about fallopian tubes and testosterone. When he had taken Human Development and Family Life, which was his school's polite name for sex education, he complained that it was all "junk" he already knew.

"What on earth did he want to know?" Curry asked Tom now.

"Well, it wasn't exactly the most direct of all converations I've ever been in, but I think the bottom line was how you can be sure that a girl is having a good time."

"Oh."

"I was impressed," Tom unknowingly echoed half of Curry's thoughts, the feminist half, not the mother half. "I certainly never worried about that at his age."

"I know."

Tom's laugh was quick, surprised. "I suppose you do."

"Well, what did you tell him?"

He shook his head. "Those are trade secrets, my dear." And when she frowned, he continued, "Don't start yammering about answering straight. He wouldn't want you to know that he had asked me."

Curry sighed. She tried hard to respect Huck's privacy; it wasn't easy sometimes. She stood up. "Oh, well, I came over here to see if you are ready for supper."

Now he frowned. "Curry, I've eaten with you almost every night since I've been here. I just can't go on imposing."

"Tom, you aren't imposing; I've got to feed Huck, and anyway, since when did you start acting like a grown-up?"

"Like a grown-up? What do you mean?"

"All this Curry-I-can't-impose-on-you business. That's polite grown-up talk."

Tom shrugged as if he agreed with her, but he did not stand up, taking a swallow from his beer instead.

He was in jeans and a T-shirt, and the narrow ribbed cuff cut across his biceps. A leather tool pouch on a broad belt was strapped low across his hips like a gunfighter's holster. It was a perfectly ordinary way for a working man to dress, but Tom looked . . . well, anything but ordinary.

"Do you raise such a fuss about having dinner at a woman's house if you're sleeping with her?"

He choked and set down the can. "I beg your pardon?"

"You heard me. If you're sleeping with someone, don't you let her cook for you?"

He was trying not to laugh. "Curry Trent, what kind of question is that?"

"Listen, buster, my name is Mrs. James, and I need to know if I'm going to have to sleep with you just to get you to come to supper."

"Oh, absolutely, and you'd better be good too." But he stood up and unbuckled his tool belt, getting ready to go with her.

Nonetheless, Tom's concern was genuine. He usually never minded the solitariness of working and living alone, but it had been so easy to take up with Curry and her son, so pleasant to clean up after the day's work and go sit in that polyurethaned kitchen and be with the two of them.

Both of them were entirely willing to absorb him into their routine, and with typical self-deprecation, Tom told himself that it was because it was summertime. Curry was taking only one class; Huck, of course, wasn't in school at all and seemed, rather surprisingly, not to be dating anyone. If he had come in the winter, surely they would have been too busy with their own lives to waste so much time with him.

On Thursday evenings, though, they all went their separate ways: Curry had her history class; Huck had to work at the hardware store, and so Tom went back to his remodeling chores, shaking his head over these new work habits of his. On every other project he had worked obsessively, stopping only to eat and sleep, but now he was just putting in an honest day's work and then quitting, spending the evenings with Curry and Huck. It was a good thing, he thought as he picked up a screwdriver to take down some shelving, that Huck was helping him. Otherwise he might never get done here.

He frowned. These shelves didn't have cross braces that were screwed into the studs as they should have. Instead they were awkwardly fastened into the wall with nails driven at a slant through the uprights. He turned to get a crowbar, then stopped, staring at the shelves, at how much was wrong with them.

He should have showed me how.

Tom had built these shelves. It was one of his first carpentry projects, done during a rainy summer week when Curry and Huck were still in bed with a late case of the measles that he had recovered from more quickly than they.

The shelves were miserably built. Knowing nothing, he had simply held each shelf at a right angle to the upright and pounded some nails in. He had used tenpenny common nails, and they had split the wood, their points sometimes protruding underneath the shelves. He hadn't cut dadoes into the uprights; he hadn't put cross braces across the back. It was an effort marked by utter ignorance.

And it would have taken his father ten minutes to explain how to do it right.

That was so typical. It had not occurred to Tom

to ask his father for help; it had not occurred to his father to offer.

What a waste. A man and a boy ought to work together. It seemed right somehow. He probably would have loved it if his father had spent more time with him, showing him how to do things, sharing the pleasures of work done well. Curry's son certainly seemed to like the time the two of them were spending together.

In fact, it surprised Tom that Huck liked working with him. He had always assumed that he was nearly an impossible person to work with because he was so methodical, so insistent that everything be right; that's why he generally worked alone. But although young Huck had his mother's practicality, her willingness to cut corners, he was also willing to do things Tom's way.

And it was more than the work. Curry's comment made him realize how much they did talk about. Of course, most of their conversations were about carpentry, cars, and sports, but occasionally other things came up—the military, sex, ambition, drinking. Huck had questions, questions he couldn't ask his mother, and Tom, remembering a pledge he had once made, answered straight.

His own father had issued him advice on such matters just once. "You keep out of trouble, you hear? Especially with that little Trent girl."

What he and Huck, *his* Huck, not this one, would have given to have a man they could talk to. They hadn't known that that was what they needed, but it had been. They too had so many questions; there was so much they didn't understand, and there was no one they could go to.

Would it have been different if that car hadn't crashed? Would Cal Winchester have been less aloof if there'd been a woman in the house? Or could he and Huck have talked to Howard James or to Curt Trent, Curry's father?

How many little families had been blasted apart. He had lost his mother; Curry had lost her mother and her father; and, the saddest irony, both Hucks, both this generation and that one, had lost their fathers.

Tom suddenly cursed. There was one person in all this who had two living parents; having a father might not be doing her a bit of good, but she had one.

Quickly he unstrapped his tool belt, locked the house, and took his truck into town, stopping at the first gas station with a phone booth. He pulled out his wallet for his telephone credit card—his single concession to the cashless economy—and dialed.

"Diana? It's—"

"Dad!"

He didn't know how she did it, but Diana always recognized his voice, sounding thrilled to hear from him. He didn't deserve it, but that joyful "Dad!" still stirred him more than almost anything else in his solitary life.

Like most fifteen-year-old girls, Diana adored talking on the phone, and that his call was long distance gave it an extra fillip of excitement that made her even more chattery. So it was an hour later that Tom hung up the phone with a smile. He straightened and then immediately grimaced as his leg protested against the hard time it had just served.

Coming out of the phone booth, he saw some men he'd known as boys and what with talking to them, he didn't get back into his truck until after ten.

As he was driving out of town across the railroad tracks, past the grain elevator, he noticed that a familiar bar had apparently changed hands. The sign was different. He slowed. He was curious about it, but he didn't plan to stop. He rarely went into bars by himself; if he was drinking alone, which had, on occasion, been known to happen, he wanted to be alone when he did it.

But glancing around the parking lot, he noticed a very familiar car, Curry's car, and unthinkingly he pulled in.

The bar was different than it had been. It was now clean and clearly trying harder than the other rundown joints that littered the outskirts of town. Tom glanced around and instantly saw Curry's corn-colored hair.

Eagerly he moved toward her. What a first-class drinking buddy she would be. Women generally weren't. They didn't know how to drink. They either got weepingly drunk or they'd primly sip one glass of white wine all evening long. But not Curry. She'd know how to get started and she'd know when to stop. She'd be—

Tom stopped. Someone had already beaten him to it. Curry was there with a man. Her hands were curled around her beer mug and she was leaning forward, talking to this guy he didn't know.

Why was he surprised? Just a couple of hours ago he'd been telling himself that she had a life of her own, and very likely this fellow was it. It seemed odd, though. In high school he and Huck would have thought it unnatural if she had dated anyone but the two of them, and now too he had trouble imagining her involved with someone who was a dead stranger to him.

But she'd been a widow for fifteen years, hadn't she? Surely she had the right to have a beer with a man every decade or so.

As he turned to leave Curry glanced up and caught sight of him. Her familiar smile brightened the bar. "Tom, get your sweet ass over here."

There was no way out. "I saw your car," he said as a greeting, "and came in, hoping to see you get arrested for public drunkenness."

She laughed and gestured to the man across from her. "Dr. Wheeler, this is a friend of mine, Tom Winchester—"

So this was one of Curry's teachers. Funny, none of *his* teachers had ever looked at him the way Wheeler was looking at Curry.

"—and, Tom, this is my history professor."

Good job, Curry. Tom extended his hand. *A fine, etiquette-book introduction that would do your grandmother proud, except I don't know the man's name.*

Dr. Wheeler was only in his late-twenties. Tom was not going to call him "Dr. Wheeler."

The professor hastily stood up and took Tom's hand. Clearly he hadn't planned on it at first.

"Nice to meet you, Wheeler," he said as he slid into the booth next to Curry. He noticed that there were a few other mugs on the table, as if other people had been there too.

"Are you a student at the college, Tom?" Wheeler asked pleasantly.

"Me? God, no."

Curry pinched his leg, quite unintentionally nipping some sensitive flesh around his scar tissue. "No, s—" Tom bit off the nearly automatic "sir." "My work takes me on the road a lot."

"What do you do?"

Wheeler was clearly on automatic pilot; showing polite interest in a student's friend was probably a familiar routine. Tom felt patronized. "Odds and ends, mostly carpentry and woodworking," he answered.

"Oh, Tom don't lie." Curry turned to Wheeler. "He's a—what do you call it? He restores old buildings."

Wheeler looked slightly more interested. "What sort of buildings?"

"Just old houses," Tom said with a shrug.

Curry was glaring at him. She clearly wanted him to make a monkey of himself. Oh, what the hell, there wasn't much he wouldn't do for her, why not this?

Obediently he mentioned some of the houses he had worked on.

"The Armstrong Mansion in Rhode Island?" Wheeler was surprised.

"Was that ever a sweetheart of a house," Tom

remembered her fondly. "Even the millwork on her—"

"So you must have worked for the guy who won the National Trust's award," Wheeler interrupted.

Tom blinked. "No, I didn't work for him," he answered carefully. He was him.

"You didn't? That's strange, but I thought he ran the whole job."

Tom shrugged again, and Curry demanded an explanation. Wheeler told her how the National Trust, a nonprofit organization chartered by Congress, gave annual awards for work in historic preservation. One of the awards a few years ago had been given for the work on the Armstrong Mansion.

"Did you win that award yourself, Tom?" Curry demanded.

She did know him, didn't she? He nodded.

Wheeler was clearly impressed. "So you really are big time," he said flatly.

Tom denied it. "I'll never do another project like the Armstrong place again. I felt like I was just a general contractor, supervising other people's work and having to worry about them not doing it right. I hate that, and preservation has become this 'field' now. People go to college and major in it. The best projects anymore, the really big ones, involve so much administrative crap, the red-tape, the zoning laws, the government grants, I hate all that."

"But wouldn't it be worth it?" Curry asked.

"Not to me," he answered. "I can't stand filling out forms."

"Why? What's wrong with forms?" Wheeler was surprised. Filling out forms was probably a very routine part of his life.

"I don't know." Tom flicked his hand. "Those little boxes. They ask questions that have really complicated answers and then give you a little five-space box to do it all in. Like 'previous job.' I haven't had a surefire honest-to-God, time-clock job in years. But if I put that down, I'll sound like a vagrant." He took the last swallow of Curry's beer. "Of course, I usually don't make it that far on a form. I get stalled up when they ask today's date or whether or not I'm married."

"Whether or not you're married?" Wheeler asked in surprise. "I can understand not knowing the date, but whether you're married, isn't that pretty clear-cut?"

"Not in the least."

Curry laughed. "You're taking it too seriously, Tom. Just tell the closest approximate five-space lie and be done with it. So what if someone thinks you're a vagrant?"

But before Tom could list the reasons why he didn't want people to think he was a vagrant—the primary one being his own suspicion that he *was* one—they were interrupted by the return of the two kids who were clearly in Wheeler's class along with Curry.

After Curry trotted out her grandmother's good manners and had introduced them all, Wheeler spoke to Tom again. "What do you do if you don't do full-scale restorations anymore?"

"The woodworking parts of somebody else's projects or I help people get started. In a couple of days I can usually date the various sections of a house and help them decide if they need to call in three thousand architects."

"You do your own dating?"

"Show me a nail, and I'll tell you when it was made."

"Listen, Winchester"—Tom noticed that he was no longer the schoolboy Tom—"would you be willing to come talk to one of my classes?"

"Me? What about?"

"What you do. My students still think of history as textbook stuff, and they don't know that historians do do something besides teach."

"No way, man, I'm not a historian."

How he hated labels like that, any kind of label. They flattened you, made you sound like something you weren't. Like "historian" or worse, "preservationist"—they made you sound like you sat behind some Civil Service desk with a diploma on the wall. That was the splendid thing about Curry; she hadn't been able to remember the phrase "historic preservationist," and had to resort to "what-do-you-call-it?" He liked that one; he should start listing it as his occupation, a professional "what-do-you-call-it?" Except you probably needed a college degree for that too.

Curry was watching him and then suddenly she glanced at her watch and shoved at him, once again managing to push hard on his thigh. "Let me out, Tom, I've got to get home."

Stiffly he slid out and stood up.

One of the kids noticed his stiffness. "Were you lamed by a wizard or a troll, good sir? By magic or the sword?"

Magic, wizards? He stared blankly at the kid. What on earth was he talking about?

"That's Dungeons and Dragons talk," Wheeler interpreted. "They want full details of all old war wounds."

"It's from some shrapnel that I picked up about a year after the Tet."

The boys were instantly silent, and for a moment Wheeler said nothing either. He fidgeted with his mug, turning it around and around on the small white napkin.

They hadn't expected him to answer, Tom realized. They hadn't expected it to actually be an old war wound.

"You were in Vietnam?" Wheeler asked slowly.

"Sure." Tom looked at the professor. He was younger and would have turned eighteen just about the time American combat troops were leaving Nam. He wouldn't know any vets, just what he read about in the papers or saw in the movies.

What he saw in the movies. Oh, great.

Of all the labels, this was the one Tom hated the most, and indeed Wheeler was looking at him like he was a laboratory specimen.

"Come on, Curry," he said abruptly. "I'll walk you to your car."

The bar had been air-conditioned, and the night felt warm.

"Are you all right?" Her voice was low.

He decided to pretend she was asking about the leg. "While I am delighted to have you poke at absolutely any part of my body that interests you, I do wish that you'd start with something other than my left leg."

Curry wasn't the type to go soft with sympathy. "Sorry, I forgot," she said, "but that's not what's bothering you, is it? It was that Vietnam talk."

"It's nothing that hasn't happened before." And then to his surprise, he heard himself going on. "Damn it, Curry, I can't stand everyone assuming that I am some haunted dope fiend just because I was there. Lord, if enough people go on expecting me to do something weird, that'll probably make me do it." He slung his arm around her throat, pulling her back against him, holding his finger to her forehead as if it were a gun. "Aren't you worried that I will wig out and take you hostage?"

She loosened his arm but didn't move away. "You aren't exactly the most well-adjusted person on the face of the earth, Tom Winchester."

"No," he acknowledged. She was right there. He let his arm rest on her shoulders as they started to walk again. "But while I am perfectly willing to blame the government for everything that is wrong with this country, it does seem to be pushing it to say my being a lousy father and worse husband is the fault of the United States foreign policy."

"But—"

"I'm not generalizing," he said as they reached her car. "I don't know about other guys, only myself. Some of them did pick up terrible drug habits; thank God, I didn't. Others did feel like they had done something worthwhile and deserved a regular hero's welcome; I sure didn't feel like that, and so I won't blame the war for the way I am."

She started to speak.

He interrupted. "I know, I know. You don't have to say it. What am I complaining about? At least I came home."

"I wasn't going to say that."

He hardly heard her. "There's a label for that one too. They call it 'Survivor's Syndrome'—guilt because you are still alive, and they . . . and he—"

Curry's light eyes were soft, the color of the earliest morning sky. He couldn't stand to look at them.

Oh, Huck, why you? One in ten. Why you?

"My God, Curry, how do you stand it? With that kid looking so much like him?"

"It's not a problem." She spoke calmly. "When I look at Huck, at my son, that's who I see—him, not his father."

Tom cursed. "His father—that drives me crazy, to hear people talk about him that way, as 'Huck's father,' all the time 'Huck's father.' You've all just turned him into a word. He *is* Huck."

"No, Tom." She shook her head slowly. "He *was* Huck. He's dead. And what really matters about him now is that before he died, he had a child. That's what's left of him, that's what he is now—'Huck's father.'"

Tom grabbed her left hand, turning it up to the light, knowing what he'd find there, the thin white scar across her forefinger, almost identical to the one on his. Huck had had one too.

She pulled her hand away. "He's dead, Tom. It isn't disloyal to say that. It's the truth. And being Huck's father is more than most of those boys have."

She stood on her toes to kiss his cheek. The brush of her lips was soft, and suddenly Tom felt himself moving forward, pushing her back against her car with his body, his head bending as his mouth searched for hers.

She was alive. These long years he couldn't bear to think about Huck so he hadn't been able to think about her either. He had pretended her dead too. It was easier that way, not to have to think of her alone, of her without Huck.

But she was alive, and more than alive. She was a woman, the shapes of her body soft against him. And the forces in him that were still alive, urges that had died with so many of those boys, hungered for her, for the touch of her hand, for the feel of her body beneath him, for the warmth that was woman.

But she wasn't any woman; she was Curry, and he'd shoot himself before using her when anyone would do.

Quickly he stepped back. "Sorry, Curry," he said as soon as he could. "That's what growing up in the Midwest does to you; kissing people in parking lots is second nature."

Chapter Four

Tom was lying, Curry knew that. It might have been a while since she had felt a man against her, but she hadn't forgotten. That kiss wasn't second nature. It was first, plain and simple. He had wanted her.

And she was flattered.

But she was also deeply concerned. Not by the kiss—such kisses were probably very routine in Tom's life even if they weren't in hers. No, she was worried by the things that he had said before. Beneath his easygoing Midwestern manner, Tom was a man in knots. It was clear that he had never fully acknowledged the death of Huck's father. Was that one reason that he'd stayed away from South Dakota? Had his one very brief visit been just too painful?

Well, Curry couldn't blame him. It hadn't been fun.

But she'd done it; she'd stayed put and done her mourning like a sensible woman, not running from her grief as he had. And she was a lot happier and healthier now than he was.

What could she do? How could she help him? He'd have to do it alone just as she had done. Unless he took off again. He always had that way out.

She might have worried about him more, but as had happened so often in Curry's life, she had something more immediate, more pressing, although perhaps not more important, to worry about. She had a final to study for.

That Thursday evening had been the last class of this two-credit minicourse—even South Dakota herself considered her own history only worth two credits—and the final was on Tuesday. Curry needed to study. So to the great amusement of both Huck and Tom, she went around for four days clutching a set of exam study notes and mumbling to herself.

As she always did with tests, Curry studied way too much—it was the only thing she did in excess—and she found the test easy when everyone else thought it hard. When she picked up hers in Dr. Wheeler's office two days later, she found she had done very well indeed.

They chatted briefly about the class.

"Do you know what you're teaching next fall?" she asked.

"The European history sequence; I hope you'll sign up for it."

"I wouldn't miss it."

He laughed. "Don't get your hopes up. American history was my specialty; I've got a lot of work to do when it comes to the Europeans."

"Well, get to it. I want my money's worth." Tuition at the community college was dirt cheap as colleges go—a class cost less than a couple gallons of top-quality paint retail. Curry felt that the money she had spent for Colin Wheeler's courses was one of the best values she had ever had, and she hoped that he knew it. She thought about trying to tell him, but she knew she'd just end up making some sort of joke.

She stood up. "I guess I'll see you in the fall."

"Right." He too stood up and seemed about to open his office door when he suddenly stopped. "Actually, Curry, why wait that long? Would you like to have dinner with me this weekend?"

"Dinner? With—" She broke off, took a breath, and tried again. "That would be very nice, I'm sure."

I'm sounding like my grandmother here.

"Would Friday, tomorrow, be okay? About seven?"

She nodded.

"Then tell me how to get to your house."

Why? And then she realized. This wasn't a meet-your-professor-and-talk-about-class appointment. This was, as Tom would say, a surefire, honest-to-God, time-clock date.

She was thirty-six, for heaven's sake; she had a kid in high school; she had a blast-from-the-past kissing her in parking lots. Why on earth was she going out on a *date*?

Curry didn't feel a bit less strange about it on Friday, and at quarter to seven she was rummaging through her already disorganized kitchen drawers, looking for her mascara—mascara being both the beginning and the end of her most elaborate makeup routine. "I know I have some. I'm sure I used it for the Morrises' Christmas party."

Huck was sitting at the kitchen table. "It's July, Mom. Christmas was seven months ago. We can't ever keep track of things for that long."

He was enjoying her ill-ease a great deal more than any truly sympathetic son would—if there were such a thing as a truly sympathetic son. "And anyway, it's just a date, isn't it? I go out on dates all the time. It's no big deal."

Curry remembered the first time he had taken a girl out. It had been a very big deal indeed.

"They're all the same around here," he continued. "You go to a movie and then you go park," he added with an innocence that didn't fool Curry for one instant.

She jerked open another drawer. "I hardly think we will do either of those."

Or will we?

"You sound like you're sure planning on having a great time."

"Keep this up, Huck, and I'll turn you over my knee and spank you."

He grinned. "Just try," he dared.

The screen door slammed, and Curry groaned. Huck was bad enough; she didn't need Tom too.

"Mom's going on a date," Huck announced as soon as Tom stepped into the kitchen.

"A date?" Tom swiveled a chair and straddled it.

Curry glared at him. "Is that so weird?"

"Did I say one word?"

"You said two."

"Then let me have two more—with whom?"

"She's going out with her history teacher," Huck told him. "Man, I'd never go out with my history teacher."

"Well, Huck," Tom said pleasantly, "that just might be because your history teacher is twenty years older than you...not twenty years younger."

"Dr. Wheeler is twenty-eight," Curry said tightly, "and although I may look it, I am not yet forty-eight."

Tom tilted his head, clearly curious about the edge in her voice. "That's a pretty shirt."

Curry regarded him with suspicion, her eyes narrowing, but he returned her gaze innocently. "Well, don't blame me," she said, abandoning her search for the mascara. "Huck's girlfriend forced it on me."

Tracy Morgan's father owned a clothing store, and if Tracy was there, Curry entrusted herself to the girl's care, invariably emerging from her clutches with something utterly unlike what she had intended to buy. Her last visit had resulted in this cotton shirt, which, although of a soft orchid color, was cut for all the world like men's long underwear with a front placket and ribbed cuffs. Tracy had said it would look very chic bloused over a silver belt. Curry had pointed out that she didn't want to look very chic, she just didn't want to get arrested, but she had bought it anyway and was wearing it now—although she had to pass on the silver belt, since the closest Curry could have come to a silver belt would have been to cover a leather one with aluminum foil.

"Hey, Huck." Tom changed the subject. "I didn't know you had a girlfriend. How come she hasn't been around?"

"Her parents shipped her off to art camp all summer so that I wouldn't sleep with her."

Curry glanced at him in surprise. Of course, Huck had to know perfectly well why Tracy had been spirited away, but he had never said so in front of his mother.

"Parents, what a pain they can be," Tom commiserated, having apparently forgotten that he was, at least on this one, a member of the enemy camp. "Do you miss her?"

Huck grinned. "Parts of her."

Curry suspected that this was an exceedingly crude remark, but she decided to let it pass. "Well, I miss her. She'd know what I ought to wear."

Curry was fast deciding that this rather expensive new shirt looked like she had robbed an old man of his winter undergarment and then had tried to hide her crime with a package of Rit dye.

"Good Lord, Curry," Tom remarked, "if we had known how much going out on a date bothers you, Huck and I would never have put you through it."

"Oh, shut up."

But he had a point. Why was she so nervous? Colin Wheeler was hardly a stranger. She had seen him at least three times a week all last year, often more. They hadn't exactly been friends, but she felt like she knew him fairly well. She could tell when he was struggling to stay patient with a very slow student. She sensed his disappointment when people weren't as enthusiastic about history as he was. She could see how he fought against showing the anger he felt at the indifference and contempt the other history professor had for the students.

He was an excellent teacher and a very nice man. So what was to be nervous about?

"I am perfectly calm," she told Tom. "And now you get out of here."

He looked blank for a moment, but then understood and got up.

Huck protested. "Why does he have to leave?" He thought of Tom as his friend and not as a factor in his mother's usually tepid social life.

"Because," Curry replied, "I don't think I should have to explain why some disreputable man posing as a childhood sweetheart is hanging around my kitchen."

Tom laughed. "You think you'd have trouble explaining me? What about *him*?" He jerked his thumb at Huck. "Does your date know that you have a son older than he is?"

"Out," Curry ordered.

"I'm going. I'm going. Come on, Huck, I'll buy you a—"

"Tom." Curry's voice was cautioning.

"—a glass of milk."

"He only drinks out of the carton." And then she added automatically, "Be home by midnight, Huck."

"You too, Mom, you too."

Colin Wheeler arrived soon after the other two left and disconcerted Curry further by knocking on the front door. But to her relief and surprise, it did open.

"I hope I'm not late," he said. "I didn't realize you lived so far out."

Curry glanced at his watch—she didn't wear one in the summer—he was a minute or so early.

Was he a little on edge too? Did he feel as odd about going out with her as she did with him?

The thought made her feel better.

"I thought," he was saying, "that we'd drive over to DeSmet for dinner, if that's okay with you. There's supposed to be a good rib place."

Curry had been there. "I don't know how good it is, but it's a lot better than anything in Gleeson."

As they walked out to his car she found herself noticing him in a rather different way. He wasn't as tall as Tom, nor as broad-shouldered or strong. Well, that made sense. Tom rebuilt houses. Colin taught, read, and wrote. That's what Curry had liked about his classes—how much he knew history.

But we aren't in class anymore.

In the car she asked him about his own history, where he was from, what his background was. She'd been curious about him for a long time.

He was from suburban Kansas City; his father was a doctor, and his family had been very Johnson County. He'd gone straight from college to graduate school to teaching. He hadn't planned on being in a community college, but, as he said, "it's nearly impossible to get a job in history and even harder if you are a white male."

He did like the community college. "Much more than I thought I would."

"Do you like Gleeson?"

"Again—better than I thought I would, except that everyone's married."

Curry laughed. "That's not fair. We're a big-time city; we have a divorce almost every year."

He smiled. "Do *you* like Gleeson?"

"Sure, but I've never lived anywhere else, so I don't really have anything to compare it to."

"You grew up here?"

"Same house my whole life."

"The same house? You're joking."

"No. First with my parents, then my grandmother, then my husband, and now with my son. Other people keep moving in and out. Me, I stay."

He looked at her oddly, clearly having trouble imagining that someone would stay in one house for her whole life. "Do you think that it's good for people to be that . . . well, that fixed?"

It's better than running away.

"Maybe not," Curry said instead. "My son's starting to get itchy feet, I think. Maybe he and I should have traveled more."

"What are you going to do after you get your associate's degree?" Colin was asking.

The community college just gave a two-year degree, which wasn't enough to teach school on. "Once my son graduates from high school, I'll finish up at university in Brookings. It's not a fun drive, a little over an hour, but I can probably get a three-day-a-week schedule."

"Will you try to teach here or do you plan on moving?"

Curry James? Leave home? He had to be kidding.

"I'll stay here. One of the history teachers at the high school will be retiring just as I finish. The School Board knows that I'll want the job."

"You're that sure of getting it?"

"No, but they're sure that if I don't, I'll run for School Board myself and make their lives miserable."

Colin laughed. "You'd run for School Board? You're amazing."

And as they talked through dinner it became clear that he did think her amazing—at least that was the polite term for it. Curry realized that he found it hard to understand her life. Not just that she had never moved, but all the other differences between being a country kid and an upper-middle-class suburban doctor's son. He couldn't understand why someone as bright as she hadn't gone to college right out of high school, and she didn't quite know how to explain that it had never occurred to her, and if it had...well, she had wanted to get married.

"Maybe if Huck's father—my husband—had come back, he might have gone with his VA benefits, but who knows?"

Colin spoke a little gingerly. "Your husband was killed in Vietnam?"

Curry nodded. She knew what he wanted to ask, and the questions didn't bother her anymore. "I don't understand that war, and I don't think he did either. But he chose to go."

"Does it seem like a waste?"

"Well, sure, but if he had died defending Sioux Falls from a Russian invasion or something clear-cut like that, I wouldn't have missed him any less than I did."

That wasn't a straight answer. It did matter that Huck had died in Vietnam. Once her personal grief had softened, Curry sometimes felt a larger emptiness. Huck had been special, blessed with inexplicable, unfailing enthusiasm, a willingness to try anything new, a cheerful confidence that all things would always turn out well, and when Curry read in her history books about Manifest Destiny, about the type of people who settled the frontier, who were splendidly foolish enough to set out West in a covered wagon, she thought about her husband: he seemed like those people, terribly American.

But he was gone—"wasted" had been the military slang for such deaths—and his son was more like she, also American, but of another type: practical, hardworking, but without that bright spark, without his father's dreams. And it seemed as if something were missing, not just from her own family, but from American life as well.

But these weren't the sort of things Curry ever said aloud. How would this man understand anyway? He hadn't known Huck; he probably thought that only the nation's riffraff had gone to Vietnam, the thick-skulled, the leather-brained.

But, Tom, you'd understand, wouldn't you?

Colin clearly didn't know how to respond to her simple statement of personal loss. "I guess I haven't had a lot of experience with death." He sounded apologetic, as if he felt young, naive.

Curry shrugged. "I just seem to travel in the wrong circles, that's all."

She didn't much like it when people clucked admiringly about how hard her life had been. Everybody had their troubles, and everybody did what they had to. Even the people who lost their marbles; maybe going bonkers was the way for them to survive.

This conversation was going nowhere, Curry decided. What should they talk about? He probably didn't much care about the wonders of living with a teenager, or how a better crop would help out paint sales. What did she talk about when she was with people?

Colin picked up the check, starting to sort through his pocket for the tip. "Are you ready?"

"Sure."

He glanced at his watch. "I have been living around here for ten months, and I don't seem to have found the night life yet. Have I been looking in the wrong places?"

"I doubt it. There's the movie, a couple of bars if you are over eighteen, and the bowling alley and video games if you aren't."

"And Dungeons and Dragons, of course."

When Curry laughed, his expression suddenly changed. "You know, you have the most wonderful laugh. I love listening to it."

And to her horror Curry felt her face grow warm. Good heavens, she was blushing. Curry James—blushing? Curry James sold paint and took apart her dishwasher; she couldn't keep track of mascara and she didn't have doors opened for her. Women like that didn't blush. What on earth was wrong with her?

Colin stood up. "The movie's no good this week, and the bars are noisy. Shall we just go back to my place?"

"That sounds fine," Curry said...and then wondered what she had just agreed to.

You're a big girl now, Curry. You don't have to hand over your heart and soul along with your body.

On the way home, once again she had trouble thinking of something to talk about so she started asking him about his European history course next fall, and they talked about that, what texts he would order, which other students might enroll, the sort of things they would have talked about if they had been student and teacher, having a beer after class.

But when he pulled into the drive of what must be his house and Curry reached for the door handle, he stopped her. "Wait a minute."

He stretched his arm along the back of the seat and then in a minute brought it in around her shoulders. It was the first time he had ever touched her.

With the other hand, he lifted her chin and bent his head and kissed her.

It was a soft kiss, a nice kiss, Curry supposed, but what she was most aware of was simply how different this kiss was from Tom's.

When it was over, he leaned his forehead against hers. "I've wanted to do that for a lot longer than I should have."

Curry had thought she knew his expressions, but this was one she hadn't seen before.

He let his fingers slip down her throat to rest on the ribbing at the neck of her shirt. "About the class next fall..."

"What about it?"

He cleared his throat. "Look, Curry, I really want you to come inside with me—surely you know that—but if you do, you've got to promise that you won't take another class from me ever again."

Not take another class from him? "Why not?"

"Because professors shouldn't get involved with their students, and I don't want to be in the position of having to grade your work if you're more than my student. It's not fair to me, you, or the other students. Do you understand that?"

"But I'm a history major."

"There's another history professor."

But there wasn't, not really. Dr. Mathers was a dreadful teacher, and although Colin would never say so, Curry knew that he knew it.

"What about it?" he asked again. His fingers slipped under the collar of her shirt, brushing against her skin. "Will you come in?"

It felt good to have a man touch her ... but this wasn't just a man; he was her professor.

Curry shook her head. "I'm sorry. You're too good a teacher."

He sighed and reached for the ignition to start the car again. "I suppose I ought to be flattered."

"You don't exactly sound like it."

"Part of me certainly isn't." Glancing over his shoulder, he started to pull out of the drive. "But you probably made the right decision. I'm afraid I don't do anything as well as I teach."

The house was dark when Colin left Curry off; Tom and Huck weren't home yet. She sat down on the back steps. The moon was full and the night was only the softest gray. The first evening primroses gave the breeze a faint lemony smell, and Huck's wind chimes tinkled softly.

Are you disappointed?

All year long she had thought that Colin Wheeler was the most interesting person she had ever met, but now she realized what he knew about history was interesting—the man himself wasn't nearly as intriguing.

No, she wasn't disappointed. She was relieved. She wanted to go on being his student. She didn't want to get to know him better; she didn't want to go to bed with him.

The age difference mattered. Not to him, at least as far as Curry could tell, but it mattered to her; Colin hadn't done anything except go to school and now teach. His life had been comfortable and sheltered; the worst thing that had ever happened to him was that he was teaching in a community college, not a four-year school.

Curry had lost both parents, then a husband, raised a son, run a business—Colin had done nothing like that. He wouldn't know what it was like to live through a long dry spell when it just kept not raining, when you had to start wondering if it would ever rain again.

Dry spells of the heart changed a person. Troubles made you different; it took another survivor to understand just how. Surely that was part of why she and Tom still felt as close as ever.

Tom—how often she had thought about him this evening. Oh, well, it must just be the contrast. Although at the beginning of the evening, Curry had been telling herself that she knew Colin, it had only been his professional self that she had known. Otherwise he was a stranger, someone who was hard to get to know, someone who made her nervous, who made her blush while Tom was . . . well, Tom was Tom.

And if you're so eager to go to bed with someone, why not Tom?

Curry wasn't sure what the answer to that one was.

As she was standing up to go inside she heard a car, and in a moment knew that it was Huck's. She sat back down, waiting until the car drove up and then the doors slammed.

"Hi, Mom," Huck called as he came up the walk. "Did you have a good time?"

"Yes."

"Did he try to kiss you?"

Curry looked up at him. "Do I ask you questions like that?"

"No, but you sure want to."

Huck went inside to pillage the kitchen, and Tom sat down on the step next to her. "You're home early for someone who had a good time."

She shrugged.

Tom stretched out his feet and linked his hands behind his head. "As I recall, there's not a lot to do in this town. What did we always say—go to a movie, then go park? Have things changed?"

"No, and the movie this week was a dog."

"And I suppose you think you're too old for the Jenny Wren road." Tom rolled his head to look at her. "Doesn't he have a place of his own?"

"You're prying, Tom."

"So I am," he agreed. "Why didn't you go home with him?"

"Maybe he didn't ask me."

"But he did. He may be young, but he's normal."

"There was a condition attached, and I couldn't accept it."

"A condition? Did he want you to wear a mask? Put on a rubber suit?"

Curry smiled. "Hardly. He just wanted me to promise not to take any more of his classes. He doesn't want to have to grade someone he's involved with."

"So he made you choose between him as a man and him as a teacher, and you chose the teacher."

"A good teacher is hard to find."

Tom shook his head. "If I ever made a woman choose between me as a man and me as a carpenter, I sure as hell hope that she doesn't choose the carpenter."

Curry remembered Colin's remark. "Which are you better at, being a man or being a carpenter?"

Tom laughed. "That depends entirely on how you define 'being a man.'"

"But you're a very good carpenter."

"Yes."

Curry looked over at him. He was leaning back on his elbows now, and his thumbs were hooked in the pockets of his jeans. She had seen him planing a board the other day. The board was between two sawhorses and Tom had straddled it and, plane in hand, had paused every few passes to test the feel of it, his hand smoothing across the board, lingering longer than need be, because he loved the way the wood felt. What were those hands like when they were on a woman? Did they linger on her, loving the way she felt?

"It's hard to get to know new people," she said suddenly.

Tom didn't seem the least surprised by her remark. "That it is. I have a lot of trouble getting cranked up to make the effort anymore."

"Is that why you haven't started seeing anyone while you've been here?" As far as Curry knew, he hadn't visited anyone except male friends and their wives, no single women, of which the town did have a few.

"That's why I didn't call what's-her-name from the bakery. Janice, was it?"

"Janelle. And why not Bonnie? She was interested, you know."

"I know, but I rather imagine Bonnie wants a bit more from a man than I can give."

"You're probably right."

They were both silent for a moment. Then he spoke again. "But what about you? From the way Huck was talking, it didn't sound like you've been seeing many men."

"Ask Huck. He'll tell you anything you want to know about me."

"I know that. But it didn't seem fair, and I figured if I asked, you'd tell me."

How right that was. They might not always be blurting out their hearts and souls to each other, but if one asked a question, the other would, of course, answer. "There's never been anyone important since Huck's father died. This town is not exactly crawling with available men."

"Really? That's a shame."

Was he feeling sorry for her? He'd better not be. "Good Lord," she said abruptly, "you know this town. First of all, hardly anyone ever moves here, so it's always the same old faces, and second—"

"Do I count as one of the same old faces?"

"You don't exactly add much to the town's pool of eligible men, Tom Winchester."

"Well, I am married," he acknowledged.

"That does tend to disqualify you. To say nothing of the fact that you don't have a steady income, that you can't stay in one place for more than two months, that you believe you are hopelessly screwed up, that—"

"Don't forget my leg," he added helpfully. "The minute I get tired, I start to lurch around like a broken Veg-O-Matic."

Curry grimaced. "You don't exactly add up as the answer to every young girl's dream."

"I don't have herpes," Tom defended himself. "That's something."

"In this day and age, it certainly is. In some circles, that qualifies me as extremely eligible."

"Not in South Dakota, friend. Eligible around here means husband material, and that you ain't."

"So have an affair with me."

"What?"

Curry had expected him to ask; she knew that someday it had to come up between the two of them; she'd just been thinking about it herself. After all, they weren't kids, they cared deeply for each other...but something was wrong here. This wasn't the way it was supposed to go.

"Are you serious?" That was all she could think to say.

"Can you give me a good reason why I shouldn't be?" He sat up and reached for her.

"Hey, Mom, isn't there anything to eat around here?" Huck's familiar lament drifted through the open window.

"How's that for a good reason?" Curry asked as she stood up.

Tom cleared his throat. "Not bad."

Are you serious? Curry had asked.

Well, Winchester, were you? Tom asked himself an hour or so later.

His body's answer was easy. He may have aged more than twenty years since he first felt her against him; he'd been through basic under the hot Carolina sun, picked off leeches during the monsoons, watched his leg get shot open, crashed through a rotting roof, and popped a rib hoisting a beam, but his body still wanted hers.

That was the real reason why he hadn't called those other women. Janelle would have been fun, and Bonnie sweet, but how could he possibly be interested in anyone when Curry was around? Who else had her smile, her laugh, her grit? There was no other woman like her; there never would be.

But still, when he had reached for her, it had been all wrong. He'd been with women who had children, and he never touched them when their children were near. It wasn't fair. Huck had still been rattling around the house; there was no way Curry would have submitted to any but the most casual embrace, and subconsciously he had known that.

So why make a pass at her that must inevitably fail? Had he wanted it to? Was he just repeating patterns that had started twenty years ago?

Twenty years ago . . . it had been natural, of course, that Curry, the girl, would mature faster. Suddenly she was bigger than Huck and he, and her grandmother made her shave her legs and wear a bra. As soon as she was in the orchard, out of the sight of the house, she would pull her arms inside her sweat shirt, wriggle out of the hated bra, and cram it into her jeans pocket.

Funny, she stopped doing that just about the time he started to like it. For he started noticing girls before Huck did, and once he had started, it didn't take him much longer to figure out that Curry was a girl too.

How ideal it must have been, he thought now, for a boy to have a girl like that. She was, most of all, his friend. The three of them still drove to school each day, copying homework, sneaking in a few pinball games, trying cigarettes, swapping chores, doing everything healthy young country kids do together. In the daytime it was still the three, sticking together, answering straight, sworn together by a blood oath.

But as the afternoon light faded from the cottonwood grove down by the swimming hole, in the evening on her grandmother's glider or parked out on the Jenny Wren road, he was alone with Curry, and she made him feel things he had never felt before.

They learned together. When they were children, they had explored the creek, now they explored this. Their kisses lengthened until they became soft and open. Her hand that had lingered at his neck began to move, gliding over his shoulders and his back. The careful upright positions eased, she leaning back as he kissed the curve of her throat, leaning more and more until at last they lay next to one another, pressing against each other. The hand that he had kept at her shoulder slipped downward, finding, with a jolt that felt like the shock from an electric fence, a softness, and he heard her sigh when he touched her there.

And then she started coming out without her

bra, and he'd feel the thin cotton of her shirt tight against her, his hand moving, the shirt moving, and inside it, her breast moving, and what he felt beneath his fingertips taught him that at moments like this, her body changed too, a stiffening that mirrored what was happening to him, the aching swell that was sometimes almost a physical pain.

But like nearly everything else in his life, he had ruined it. He had pushed her too far.

There were times when it seemed like she was being mean, when she would push him away as he tried to pull her shirt free of her jeans, when she would jerk back if his hand started to wander below her waist. She had to know how he felt; why did she make him stop?

He didn't expect her to let him go all the way, but he knew from talk around school that there were girls who would touch a guy, sometimes even letting him unzip his jeans. Curry wasn't like those girls, with their short black skirts and teased hair, but she was a good sport. Surely if she understood what it would mean to him, she'd do it.

So one night Tom had taken her hand and pulled it down to the front of his jeans.

Curry gasped and tried to pull it free. And if he had let her go, this would have been no different than the other times when he had tried things she wouldn't do.

But the touch of her hand was like nothing Tom had felt before, her struggling only making it better. He was stronger than she, and he held her hand tightly.

Suddenly she went still. "Nobody, Tom Winchester," she said clearly, "nobody makes me do stuff."

His grip loosened; she pulled herself free, opened the car door, and started to walk.

She would not get back in.

"I'm not afraid of you," Curry replied to Tom's entreaties. "I just don't want to be with you."

It was night, and they were four miles from home, but Curry was emphatic. She'd rather walk than be with someone who tried to push her around.

Helpless, he drove home, stopping at Huck's. He knocked at the window as they always did, and when Huck slid it open, Tom swung in.

"Will you go get Curry? She's walking north down the Jenny Wren road."

"What's she doing a thing like that for?" Huck picked up a shirt and started to pull it on.

Tom didn't know how to answer. They'd never talked about any of this. When it had started, Huck hadn't been particularly interested, but now that he was and they did look at magazines together, they still never spoke about Curry in that way. So for the first time in his life, Tom didn't know what to say to Huck.

"I don't know." He felt like a traitor; he shouldn't be lying to Huck. "You know how girls are."

"No, I don't," Huck answered bluntly. He finished buttoning his shirt and then stuffed the tail into his jeans. "But I know Curry—she doesn't do silly th—" Huck stopped. He gave Tom a hard look. "Yeah, and I guess I know you too." He reached for his keys. "I'll go get her."

Tom felt lousy, and all he could think of was how stupid it was of Huck to bother putting on a regular shirt to go get Curry. She'd certainly seen him in a T-shirt before.

Not much more was ever said. On the way to school the next morning, Curry had looked Tom straight in the eye and said, "We're still friends, but that's it."

Other girls never meant it when they said "still friends," but Curry did, and the three of them went on as they always had until Tom kept finding himself alone in the evenings and finally had to admit that Curry and Huck were probably together, not wanting him. And he wondered if Huck had once felt as left out as he did now.

Of course, there were other girls for Tom. He was desperate to know what it felt like to be with a girl, and there were girls who let him find out. But they were real girls; he had to call them up and make dates with them, pick them up, take them to movies, listen to their chatter. It wasn't like being with regular people, like being with Curry.

He sometimes wondered if Huck were sleeping with her. Huck never talked about what they did, but finally Tom asked him.

It was senior year and, perhaps inevitably, in a locker room. Gym class had been let out early so the boys could shower and dress before a nominally surprise fire drill. They were now all waiting for the drill, lounging on the benches, against the lockers, talking about girls, about who would do what. Questions were asked, names were named. Only Huck and a few others were silent.

Suddenly Tom heard himself speak. "What about you and Curry?" It was a question he would never have asked if he and Huck had been alone.

Huck looked at him. If anyone else had asked, Huck wouldn't have answered. But since it was Tom, he was answering. That was part of the pact. "No," he said simply.

"What's the matter?" someone jeered. "You've been going together two years; doesn't she love you?" "Love" was drawled out mockingly.

"Oh, she'd probably do it if I wanted her to." Huck's voice was even.

"And you don't? You queer or something?"

Huck faced his taunter. "Sure I want it. But not enough to make her do something she doesn't want to."

There was a pause, and Tom swore to himself that he would kill anyone who laughed, but no one spoke, just nervously flicked towels and rattled the locker handles until the fire gong went off.

It was only a few months later, in the spring of senior year, that Tom learned things had changed.

He'd just swung himself into the open window of Huck's room, having seen that his mother's car was gone. Huck wasn't there, and so Tom started toward the living room when he heard Curry's voice.

"I got my period today."

In all the years they'd been friends, for all the

openness among them, this was one thing Curry had never talked about. She never complained about cramps or got coy and said she couldn't go swimming. For a moment Tom couldn't understand why she'd be telling Huck about it now.

He heard a chair squeak as Huck stood up. "You know, Curry," Huck said, "it wouldn't have made a bit of difference to me."

"Well, it would to me," she said flatly. "Good heavens, Huck, what would we have done with a baby?"

"Take care of it. It would be fun."

So when he next saw Curry alone, looking at the mass of golden-yellow hair, at the length of jeans down her legs, he had spoken abruptly. "So you're Huck's now."

Her head swiveled, her expression surprised and then cautious. "No," she answered in a moment. "I'm not anybody's, I never will be, but he and I will probably get married as soon as school is out, if that's what you mean."

It hadn't been what he had meant, not at all.

Chapter Five

Curry James was no fool. She could put one and one together and knew perfectly well that they weren't supposed to equal three. If Tom had been serious last night, she thought as she sat down on her back steps with a cup of coffee Saturday morning, if he really had wanted to have an affair with her, he would have waited for some moment when Huck wasn't prowling about. He must have wanted her to say no.

But why? If he didn't want to sleep with her—which, she supposed, was his right—then why not just keep quiet about it? She certainly didn't go around asking people for things if she wanted them to say no. So why would Tom?—unless being refused was important; unless he wanted to fail, because he felt he deserved to.

She'd seen it among the eighteen-year-olds she took classes with. They got nervous about an exam or a term paper. They worried about doing poorly. But instead of trying their hardest, they did the opposite, procrastinating, delaying, until they had so little time that failure was inevitable.

They were secretly, unconsciously more comfortable when they felt doomed to failure than when they still had time to take the risk involved in trying to do well.

She had thought such behavior just routine growing pains, a part of being poised between adolescence and adulthood. But Tom had not been like that at eighteen, and it seemed possible that he was now.

Well, look at his history. He had come back from Vietnam wounded, physically damaged. He had hated his job, his marriage had fallen apart, his relationship with his father had grown even colder. No wonder he expected to fail. In everything but his current profession, he had.

Tom was a perfectionist. He had to do things right. If he couldn't, he'd rather not do them at all. Failure was better than trying and getting it only half right. And apparently, she was one more thing he wasn't going to try at.

That was the answer to the question she'd posed last night: *if you're so eager to go to bed with someone, why not Tom?*

Because he'll break your heart.

In many ways, Tom was the ideal man for her to have some sort of an affair with. Her date with Colin Wheeler had made that clear. Not only did she find Tom more attractive than other men, but she was comfortable with him. He would fit into her life easily. Oh, sure, he wasn't thrilled with her makeshift way of doing things, but he kept out of matters that weren't any of his business. He hadn't said one more word about the polyurethane on her kitchen floor. Even if he moved in, he wouldn't try to sand it off. He certainly wouldn't try to manage her money, make her decisions, or draw in the loosening rein that she had on Huck. They would rub along together just fine.

The trouble was that Tom wasn't a well-worn, comfortable pair of shoes. Curry knew that there wasn't a lot standing between her and falling in love with him, and if passion and tenderness were added to the affection already felt, she would end up loving him. In this case, she would hand her heart over along with her body.

But the last thing in the world Curry wanted to be doing with the rest of her summer was falling in love with Tom Winchester. If they went along as they were now, being friends, she guessed she'd be all right when he left, but if she loved him, life was going to feel right empty when that house got finished. She'd faced emptiness once, and she didn't much care to jump through that hoop again.

And Tom would leave. Staying would mean he would have to try.

Curry ran her thumb over the white scar on her forefinger. She loved him as a friend; she truly did. She loved having him here; he belonged here just as much as she did. But she wasn't going to give him a chance to break her heart. Sticking together didn't go that far.

She sighed and looked around the backyard, at the basketball hoop on the side of the barn, at the grassy stretch that had once been her grandmother's garden. The last of the wild roses were tumbling over the old wire fence, their pink color fading, but their scent still sweet. The raspberries would be starting to ripen soon. They were all that was left of the garden, and that was because they managed on their own. Curry didn't garden.

"Hello."

It was Tom, coming out of the orchard.

"Hello, yourself."

Now he was standing by her, one foot resting on a step. He glanced up at the sky. "It's going to be a real scorcher."

"We've been lucky so far. It's supposed to rain tomorrow."

"Which will just make it humid."

This is a world-class, thrilling conversation, Curry thought. *Here I lie awake half the night thinking about this man and all the mistakes he has made, all the people he has walked out on, and, yes, thinking, in spite of every scrap of good judgment, how much I wish he were in my bed with me, and when I see him again, we talk about the weather.*

"Would you like some coffee?" Curry offered. "It's already made."

That's supposed to make the conversation more meaningful?

"Sure," Tom answered. "And I'd like to steal your phone for a couple of calls, if that's okay."

But just as they got into the kitchen, the phone asserted itself and rang all on its own. Curry answered.

"Curry, this is Patricia Winchester."

Curry went blank. Patricia who?

Oh, of course. It was Trish, Tom's wife.

Curry glanced over at him as she spoke. "Trish, how are you?"

Tom straightened, looking interested while Curry and Trish exchanged polite greetings and inquiries about one another's children.

"Actually, Curry," Trish said, "I need to talk to Tom. Can you give him a message?"

"He's right here." Curry handed him the receiver and started to leave the kitchen. He frowned at her and pointed to a chair. She sat down, hoping that Trish didn't mind Tom being at her house at a quarter to eight on a Saturday morning.

Curious, she listened to his side of the conversation, which consisted of remarks like "She does?" and "Whatever for?"

"No, of course not. I'd love to see her," he was saying, "but you know what these projects are like, and I haven't even tried to make the place livable. I mean, there's not always hot water and ... I'll tell her ..."

Curry went over to him. "Does Diana want to visit?" she asked softly.

He nodded.

She tugged the phone out of his hand. "Trish, this is Curry again. I'm sorry to be barging in, but if Diana wants to come out to see Tom, she can stay here."

"I'd like to say that I never dreamed you'd offer, but I don't think you'd believe me."

Curry laughed. "It's the obvious solution."

"I'm so glad you feel that way because Diana really does like being with her father, and this is the first time anything like this has been possible."

Curry was surprised. She had never had much contact with Trish, just Christmas cards and a few letters, and she would never have expected this kind of pleasant forthrightness, the lack of insincere "Oh, I can't ask you to do that." Well, Trish had been married to Tom Winchester for sixteen years. That was bound to change a woman some.

"It will be nice," Trish was saying, "for Diana and Huck to get to know one another."

"It will, won't it? It does seem like they are almost cousins, since Tom and Huck's father were like brothers."

Curry said good-bye and turned the phone back over to Tom so he could talk about arrival times and such.

He hung up the phone and turned to her. "This is nice of you. It's a big imposition."

"No, it isn't. How much—" Curry stopped and looked at him suspiciously. "You do want her to come, don't you?"

"Aren't you asking that question about five minutes too late?"

"Tom!" Good Lord, he didn't want to see his daughter; he really didn't.

Every ounce of maternal feeling in Curry's character protested. If she were separated from Huck, she would have done anything, spent any money, imposed on any stranger, to get to her son. Here was a fifteen-year-old girl who, according to her mother, really liked being with her father; why didn't he want to be with her?

Because he wasn't any good at being a father.

He'd said that, calling himself "a lousy father and a worse husband." So he wasn't even going to try.

She didn't know what to say. "Do you find being with Diana a strain?" she asked carefully. Bonnie had said that her ex-husband was now awkward with their girls. "God knows I find being with Huck enough of a strain sometimes."

Tom shook his head. "No, it's just that..."

"What?"

"I don't know...haven't you been in a shopping mall on a Saturday afternoon?"

"A shopping mall on Saturday?" Gleeson did not have a shopping mall. "I suppose so—but what on earth does that have to do with anything?"

"That's where you see them, in shopping malls or restaurants or movies—divorced fathers with their kids. It's just awful to watch them sometimes. They look so stiff, like they don't have anything to say, like they don't know what to do but spend money. I really dread that, that whole divorced father scene."

Oh, terrific, one more label for Tom to worry about—divorced father. "But, Tom, you aren't divorced."

"I know, and that's been my only hope with her. When I see her, we're on her home ground. She can go about her business and we can talk at odd moments. We don't have to sit around staring at each other for hours on end."

"You've really been worried about this, haven't you?"

He nodded. "Trish mentioned at Easter that

Diana was about old enough to travel on her own, and I've been dreading it ever since. What's she supposed to do if she visits me while I'm working—sit around the motel all day?"

If a motel had a pool, a lobby, and vending machines, Curry knew there was no place in the world that any small-town teenager would rather sit around.

"But she's not going to be in a motel. She'll be here. What does she do at home in the summer?"

"I guess she baby-sits a lot; Trish is pretty strict about her allowance. And then she goes to the country club and—"

"The country club?" Curry was amazed. "Tom, do you belong to a country club? You?"

"*I* don't, but Trish and Diana do. All Diana's friends go to the pool there so—"

"I bet it's a family membership."

"Oh, all right. So I belong to a country club." He sounded exasperated. "But it's no big deal, only what you'd expect in Bemidji. They don't exactly host too many celebrity golf tournaments there."

Curry felt guilty. Here he had been talking about something that mattered to him, something that worried him, and she had started teasing him about country clubs. Some kind of friend she was.

"Listen, Tom, it won't be so bad. There will be plenty for her to do. We can let people know that she baby-sits. And Huck will introduce her around. We may never see her again once Huck's friends take a look at her. You know how thrilled they'll be to have a new girl turn up in the middle of the summer."

"I suppose no one knows that better than me."

His tone was odd, and Curry looked at him questioningly.

"Think about it," he prompted. "A new girl turned up in Gleeson a number of summers back, and she, unfortunate woman, ended up as my wife." Tom went over to the counter, opened the cabinet, took a mug off the hook, squinting at it to be sure that it was clean—a gesture that Curry guessed she deserved—and then started to pour himself some coffee. "You know," he said, "I don't think we should make a big deal about Huck and Diana being 'almost cousins.'"

Curry hadn't planned on it. "Why not?"

"I don't know." He seemed a little uncomfortable. "I guess I don't think that they should feel under a lot of pressure to like each other."

Curry had seen pictures of Diana Winchester; Trish sent one each Christmas. Diana might not like Huck, but Huck was going to like Diana.

Still, Tom was right; the only thing that would keep Huck from liking Diana was being told that he had to. The same might be true of her too. But Curry was a little surprised that Tom was so alert to the nuances of adolescent psychology.

Gleeson did not possess anything quite so cosmopolitan as an airport, and the nearest one in Brookings was only served by a little commuter line that Trish didn't want Diana flying on. So Tom had to drive almost ninety miles north to Watertown to pick her up.

He asked Curry if she or Huck wanted to come with him. "It's a long drive."

Since when did long drives bother Tom? He

probably liked driving alone. Undoubtedly, it was the way back, when he wouldn't be alone, that worried him.

"No, we don't," Curry said flatly—although she knew Huck would have been delighted to go. Huck liked going places, even Watertown, South Dakota. "Anyway, it will give you some time alone with Diana. To get reacquainted." *Come on, Tom, at least try.*

He didn't say anything for a moment, and then—"I'm not sure *re*acquainted is the right word. I hardly know her at all."

"You were around when she was a baby and then again when she was a preschooler."

"I don't think it did a lot of good," he said with a shrug. "When she was a baby . . . well, I think I was afraid of her."

"Afraid of her? A baby? Why?"

"You've seen babies, Curry. They're so *small.*"

A high-topped basketball shoe of Huck's was sitting on one of the oak chairs, its dirty white laces trailing almost to the floor. Curry looked at it fondly, remembering the first time she had seen Huck, when he hadn't been that much bigger than his shoe was now.

"And this business of supporting their necks all the time," Tom continued. "By the time I finally got the hang of it, she could do it by herself. She figured it out faster than I did. I never really knew what to do with her . . . babies have this schedule—"

"Huck didn't."

"—and it seemed like every time I wanted to

play with her, it wasn't the right time; it would disrupt her schedule."

Curry guessed that Trish had made the mistake of some young mothers. So surprised and pleased by their own competence at mothering, they held it over their husbands, using the babies almost in a power struggle, saying, "Look, I'm better at this than you."

"Well, she's outgrown all that," Curry tried to reassure him. "She's a teenager now."

"Teenagers are even scarier than babies."

"Well, that's certainly true," Curry admitted. "But you do great with Huck. He thinks the world of you."

"But that's different."

"Why? Because you aren't his parent? Because he isn't a girl?"

"I don't know. He's just Huck."

And as soon as she had a chance to think about it, this worried Curry too. What did he mean "just Huck"?

On one level, he was right. Her son was "just Huck." This name wasn't a nickname for him as it had been for his father. Huck James was her son's full legal name, while carved on that granite monument in Washington, D.C., was the name that commemorated her husband, "Howard E. James, Jr."

Did Tom fully appreciate the difference? Or were there moments when he almost forgot that the Huck he had grown up with was dead? Did he like her son, did he find him easy to be with, because the boy looked so very much like his father?

Even though she had refused to go to the airport, Curry could hardly wait to see Tom's daughter, and as soon as she heard his car turn up the drive, she peered out her kitchen window.

Diana Winchester was tall and slender, seemingly cast out of the same mold that had shaped Tracy Morgan, Huck's abducted girlfriend. Her pale brown hair, streaked almost blond by the sun, was cut like Britain's Diana cut hers; her jeans had a swan on the pocket, her shirt an alligator on the breast. She was very pretty, and Curry was disappointed. She had expected something more distinctive. How could Tom ever have produced such a thoroughly conformist, designer-jeans creature?

Curry's feeling about designer labels was simple. The day Calvin Klein started wearing her name on his cute little behind, she'd start wearing his on hers.

Wiping her hands on the seat of her nameless jeans, Curry went to the porch, holding open the door for them. "Diana, I'm Curry," she said, and as they entered the kitchen, she gestured at Huck, "and this is Huck."

"Hello, Diana, how are you?"

Curry swiveled and stared at him. Huck's manners frequently peaked at muttering hi in someone's general direction. But he had stood up when Tom and Diana had come into the room and was talking like a regular Dale Carnegie graduate.

Curry might be disappointed with the way Diana looked, but Huck certainly wasn't.

Huck and Diana were both so determined to impress each other that the next few minutes were absorbed with adult-seeming social pleasantries, and the two genuine adults, neither of them being the world's prize small-talkers, were awed by their children's social graces.

"School teaches the damnedest things these days," Tom murmured to her. "Could we do that at their age?"

"*You* still can't," Curry pointed out. "But we never met new people; they do."

"How was your flight?" Huck was asking.

"It was fine, thank you. I had to change planes in Minneapolis by myself. Of course, Mother was terribly worried about it, but—"

"She certainly was," Tom interrupted.

"I know." Diana laughed, the politeness in her voice starting to ease into something more natural. "She told me so many different things to do that it made me wish that something would go wrong so that I could rescue myself if I got on the wrong plane or if some weirdo followed me into the bathroom. But everything went fine." Diana seemed disappointed by how easy her solo adventure had turned out to be.

"How is your mother, Diana?" Curry might not be so good at small talk, but she had manners. She'd gone without her supper often enough to get them that she might as well use them once in a while.

"She's very well, Mrs. James."

"Good Lord," Tom cursed impatiently. "Call

her Curry; 'Mrs. James' makes her sound like Huck's mother.''

"But I thought—" Diana broke off, understandably confused.

"Don't listen to him," Curry told her. "I *am* Huck's mother. When Tom says Huck sometimes he means this Huck, sometimes he means his father. It's very confusing, and most of the time you're better off not even trying to figure out who he means, but do call me Curry."

"Okay, Curry." Diana had a warm smile, and her blue eyes were light and sparkling, just like—

Just like Tom's eyes. Of course, they were. This girl, this pleasant, pretty, cheerful girl, was Tom's. His daughter, formed out of his body. How precious that made her.

"Now, that we are talking like normal human beings again," Tom said, oblivious to Curry's tender thoughts, "how *is* your mother?"

"Actually, Dad, she's doing great. She's got a new permanent, it's real curly, like, it's a more natural look than before...."

Curry was sure that even if Tom only saw his wife a few times a year, he was truly interested in her well-being, but she rather doubted that his interest extended to the history of her hairstyles and a description of a recently expanded wardrobe. Nonetheless, only the slightest glassy look betrayed his disinterest to Curry, and if Diana was aware of it, it certainly didn't daunt her.

"What made her do it?" Curry asked, wondering if she ought to chop off her own hair. She'd only been wearing it this way for a few decades.

Diana looked a little confused, and instantly Curry suspected why Trish might have changed her hair and bought more clothes. "Don't tell us anything you aren't supposed to," she said to the girl softly.

Diana shook her head. "No. Mother said it was okay." She turned to Tom. "Dad, she's seeing someone."

Tom's glassy stare vanished. "She is?"

Curry spoke quickly. "That's lovely for her. Who is he? What does he do?"

"His name is Phillip, Phillip Raven. He works in a bank."

"I suppose it is too much to hope," Tom put in, "that he mops the floors at night."

Diana laughed. "No, Dad. He's a vice-president there."

"I should have known."

"Jealous, Tom?" Curry teased in a low voice.

"Not at all. I just thought that it would do Trish good to hang out with more janitors. They're a better sort of people than vice-presidents." He turned back to Diana. "Is he nice? Do you like him?"

"Oh, sure. He's really . . . well, really reliable."

"Reliable? What do you mean?"

"Well, like one time a friend of mine went out with some guy none of us knew, and he started drinking and she got scared and called me."

"Called *you*? Why did she call you?"

"I guess she was more afraid of her parents than she was of him. Anyway, Mother was at bridge club so I called Phillip and he was great. He came over and got me and when we picked up Beth, he didn't lecture her or anything. And he didn't tell her folks; he said that was up to her. He was super."

"You could have called your mother at bridge; she wouldn't have cared."

"Oh, I know. And I would have called her if Phillip hadn't been home—although, of course, none of it would have been necessary if Beth had had the nerve to take his keys from him and drive herself home, that's what I would have done."

"But you don't have a license, do you?" Tom asked.

"I've got a learner's permit, and even if it's illegal, I think I'd be a lot safer driving myself than being out with some drunk. I'm a good driver, Dad. Phillip taught me. Mother said we'd just fight if she tried to."

"Your mother's a wise woman." Curry laughed. She had taught her son how to drive and had not enjoyed it in the least.

But her laugh broke off when she caught sight of Tom. He wasn't looking at anything. His face was blank, but his eyes were flat, unhappy.

She didn't think it bothered him that Trish was seeing Phillip... although maybe it did. But the second half of Diana's offhand report certainly did bother him.

Phillip was operating as her father: being "reliable," rescuing her friends from scrapes, teaching her how to drive. But what could Tom say? "Don't take his keys. Call me. I'll come get you." It would be a long distance call, and Tom would probably have to cross the Rockies if he were to come get her.

He might have been acting all week like he dreaded Diana's visit, but his face right now made one thing clear—this was a man who cared a great deal about his child. He didn't know how to show it, he didn't know what to do, but he cared.

Huck was getting restless. Curry supposed he was remembering the similar little drinking-and-driving escapade he had been a part of last year. He changed the subject. "Did your mother get all nervous before her first date? Mom had a date last week and you'd have thought that she was seeing the President." He was clearly trying to sound very adult.

Diana laughed. "She was in *total* shock." Diana's voice was a little different when she spoke to Huck, a little breathier, as if she found talking to him less easy than talking to her father. Less easy, but a lot more fun. "I kept telling her that, like, I was the one who was supposed to get nervous about dates, not her."

"Do you have a regular boyfriend?" Huck's casual question was undoubtedly carefully calculated.

"Oh, no," Diana said with equally studied airiness. "I date around a lot because, like—"

Curry and Tom fled.

Diana was a model houseguest. Her company manners faded in a day or so, an event which was greatly welcomed by Curry, who sometimes felt like she was living with her grandmother again. But even when she wasn't trying so hard, Diana showed every sign of having been very well brought up.

She didn't expect to be waited on. She was far more tidy than either Curry or Huck—not that Curry and Huck were exactly the fast track in the tidiness competition. She helped in the kitchen automatically and expertly, and she never complained.

Tom needn't have worried about her getting bored. She was incapable of being bored. She loved everything. She loved working in a new kitchen. She loved going to new stores. She loved baby-sitting for new people. She was even misguided enough to love sleeping in a house without air conditioning. "It's so neat—the breeze from the attic fan just whips across you, it feels great. And then in the morning, with the window open, you can hear the birds. I can't at home."

"Is she serious?" Curry asked Tom.

He nodded. "She's usually pretty positive about things."

"Positive? She's not positive; she's crazy."

Her enthusiasm reminded Curry of Huck's father. He had the same sunny temper, the same willingness to be pleased by everything, the same confidence that everything would always be pleasing. That was what Curry had loved the most about him.

Tom stared at her when she said that. "I don't know why she should remind you of Huck, but

Trish is fairly even-tempered; she must get it from her."

Fairly even-tempered? That was an understatement.

And, of course, Diana *loved* being busy, so she started helping Tom and Huck remodel the house. She had never done anything like that, but she learned quickly. Her fine motor skills delighted her father.

"You ought to see her putty a window," he marveled to Curry. "That putty is as perfect as—"

Oh, wonderful, Curry thought, *another perfectionist in my hair.* "Well, you shouldn't be surprised, Tom. She is your kid."

He looked blank for a moment. "Oh, so she is."

So they worked during the day, and in the late afternoons and evenings, they had fun, the sort of fun that Curry hadn't had in years. Spurred on by Diana's "Wouldn't that be great?" they took picnics and went fishing when it was nice, played hearts and staged joke-telling contests when it wasn't. On a dare from Huck, they all climbed the oak tree one night and, from its limbs, watched the moon and listened to the crickets. Their weekends were hot and glorious, and Curry suspected that the only reason they didn't build a raft and all float down the Mississippi together was that the Mississippi was three hundred miles away. If it had been an inch closer, they probably would have.

Tom now ate all his meals with them, and he

and Curry had a few skirmishes over who was going to pay the grocery bill, but in the time-honored fashion of the sensible children they had once been, they broke a wishbone over it, and Tom had won.

One afternoon Curry came into the kitchen and heard the other three talking on the porch.

"I don't mind being with Curry," Diana was saying. "I'm sure she's fine."

"I suppose that since she's my mother and all"—this was from Huck—"I ought to take her."

"Oh, hell"—Tom was laughing—"I've put up with so much from her. Why not a little more?"

Curry James was not used to being thought of as a liability. She went out on the porch. "What's going on? What is it that none of you want me for?"

"We're playing basketball, Mom, and I told them that you weren't any good."

"That was sweet of you."

"But you will play, won't you?" Diana asked. "Oh, please, it would be the four of us. It will be *such* fun."

"Sure she'll play," Tom said calmly. "She's a good sport... or she used to be," he added with a carefully bland look.

Twenty-five years ago Curry had broken an arm proving that she was a good sport. "You know, Tom Winchester, it would serve you right if I were grown-up enough not to care what you thought."

"But you aren't."

She looked around for something to throw at

him, but then decided she ought not to show her form too soon.

Curry wasn't a bad basketball player; she had played with Huck a lot back in the days when his feet were still smaller than hers. She had earned her reputation as a poor player because she had one bad habit—she didn't pay attention. So often she would start thinking about all the other things she was supposed to be doing, and the quality of her play would deteriorate accordingly. Huck would get mad at her, and she'd feel guilty.

When he at last decided that playing alone was better than playing with her, she was almost as grateful as she had been when he had finally figured out how to go to the bathroom by himself.

"I'll play," she said. "And there's an easy way to pick teams. If I am the worst"—if she was going to put the hustle on these three, she might as well do it right—"then I should be with whoever's the best. So who's the best player?"

"Huck," said Tom.

"Tom," said Huck.

"That's crap, Huck," Tom told him. "When did you last shoot baskets?"

"Why, this morning." Huck shot baskets nearly every day of his life. Some people read the Bible; Huck shot baskets.

"Well, I haven't done it in years."

"But you're taller."

"Just until my leg gets gimpy, and then only half of me will be taller."

"Okay," Curry said. "Then Huck gets his

mother. It will be the Jameses against the Winchesters."

"Oh, that will be *great*," the female half of the Winchester team enthused.

"We'll stomp their faces, Mom," said the male James.

"We certainly will," she agreed as they headed out to the barn. "After all, who taught you how to shoot baskets?"

"Mr. Churney in junior high, but only after he had untaught me everything I learned from you."

Diana had been carrying the basketball from the house, and Curry took it from her, tossing it to Huck. He dribbled toward the basket and leaped in the air. The ball arched over the basket and swooshed through the net.

"Isn't that called an assist?" she asked the world at large.

"No," replied Tom, coming up from behind her. "That was still batting practice."

"Come on, Dad," Diana was saying, "let's plan our strategy." The Winchesters moved to the other side of the court to confer. Tom was holding the ball trapped between his arm and hip, his hand dangling loose. Diana started to draw figures in the air, and he was listening to her intently.

"It's pointless," Curry called to them. "We are going to stomp your faces. There's nothing you can do about it."

Without taking his eyes off Diana, Tom flipped his middle finger in Curry's direction.

Huck finished drawing a half-court line in the dirt with his heel. "Okay," he announced, "if you recover the ball, you've got to take it back before you shoot. What that means, Mom, is that—"

Curry listened patiently as he told her that if she got a rebound—an event he clearly did not believe was too likely—she had to bring it back behind the line before charging the basket for a crackerjack slam-dunk. "And don't *carry* it, Mom."

She had sat through countless basketball games in this child's behalf. She had listened to him discourse on strategy and technique. She had been wonderfully sweet and understanding after he had played badly in the game against the Douglass J.V. last year. Why was he talking to her like she was a complete idiot?

Then she understood. The stakes in this game were pretty high for Huck. Diana was wearing a pair of peach-colored basketball shorts trimmed in white piping and a white tank shirt trimmed in peach piping. She and they weren't just Huck's opponents; they were also his audience.

Curry forgave him.

Diana took the ball behind the line and threw it in to Tom. He moved toward the basket, his head down, concentrating on his rusty dribble. But Huck, experienced and alert, was guarding him and in a moment swatted the ball away from him. He pivoted and bounced a pass over to Curry, who was standing over by the hoop, peacefully minding her own business.

Never expecting him to do any such thing, she was surprised and missed the pass. Diana scrambled behind her and Curry then saw the ball whistling toward Tom. He caught it, set, and shot. The ball rolled around the rim and then fell through the net.

He stared at it, disbelieving.

"You aren't supposed to just stand there, Mom," Huck complained.

"All right, I'll move around."

Move around she did, but still the Winchesters made the next shot.

"Listen, Mom, don't throw the ball to where I am, throw it to where I am going."

"Yes, Huck," she said obediently, not wanting to point out that some of their most laborious discussions last year had been over the question of Huck's whereabouts and how much his mother needed to know about them. But it certainly did seem to her that given Huck's habit of ending up in one place when he had every intention in the world of going somewhere else, throwing the basketball to where he was planning on going was simply the worst idea she had ever heard.

It really didn't seem just. Here she and Huck were together day in and day out, here she had fed that slightly freckled face two or three meals every day of its life—and in recent years, four or five—and they couldn't get the basketball from one set of hands to the other.

And those blasted Winchesters, who were virtual strangers to one another—Trish must have pinned a note to Diana's blouse or who knows what Tom would have brought home from the airport—they were playing together like a pair of salt and pepper shakers.

Curry grimaced at her lot in life and then looked

around for something to tie back her hair. Maybe this would go better if she didn't have her hair in her face. She felt a sharp ping on her shoulder.

"Ouch! Huck, that *hurt.*"

"I didn't do a thing," he protested, throwing his hands up. "Honestly, Mom, I didn't."

Tom was looking suspiciously bored, but Curry would be damned before she'd ask him what he had done. She glanced around and noticed a rubber band at her feet.

Oh, great, not only is this man an emotional disaster zone, but he also shoots rubber bands at me.

She gathered up her hair, and as she was looping the rubber band around it, she spoke to the air. "Letting a defenseless child take the blame—tsk, tsk."

Fortunately, Huck was too busy watching Diana take a few practice shots to hear himself referred to as a "defenseless child."

Curry settled down to business and played perfectly well, doing a solid job of guarding Diana and even astonishing the multitudes with some very respectable shooting.

"You were wrong, Huck," Diana exclaimed after Curry had faked a pass to Huck and then laid a sweet one off the backboard. "She's *great.*"

Curry nodded modestly and Tom laughed. "She practiced on church windows."

"That was softball," she reminded him.

"Church windows?" Huck looked interested. "What's he talking about, Mom?"

"Nothing, Huck. He's getting elderly, and he has these spells. Be nice to him."

Tom started searching through his pockets for another rubber band to shoot at her.

Curry couldn't remember when she had had such a good time. She had never played many games as an adult. Things always seemed tough enough without going out of your way to find opponents. But this was marvelous, she and her child playing with Tom and his.

And Tom was clearly loving it too. He was letting Diana captain their little team; he slapped her hands when her strategy worked, made faces at her when it didn't.

They were crouched, heads together, over at the edge of the court, drawing diagrams in the dust. Diana was sitting on the ball. Her coltishly long, splendidly smooth and tanned legs were folded beneath her.

She rose effortlessly. "Let's kill 'em, Dad." Then as all good coaches do, she swatted her father on the rear. He promptly returned the favor.

Huck flushed, and Curry worried that they would lose him. Poor boy, he would probably sell his soul, maybe even his letter jacket, for a five-second encounter between his hand and the backside of Diana's incredibly cute basketball shorts.

Curry took pity on him. "Do you want to change assignments? I'll take Tom, and you can guard Diana."

It was a truly dreadful idea, and Huck agreed to it instantly.

Tom had taken the ball out and when Curry came up and started to wave her arms, trying to block his toss in, he stared at her. "What's this?"

"You're in trouble now, Winchester."

"Am I about to have my face stomped?"

"No, you're going to get your stained glass smashed in."

"Is that supposed to scare me?"

"Let me put it this way. I hope you like the child you have, because you won't be having any more."

"Come on, Dad," Diana called. "Get moving."

He leaned to the side, tossing the ball into her. He tried to move around Curry, but she was determined to block him. She had to foul him to do it, which did not bother her in the least... especially when he didn't call her on it. Naturally this encouraged her to be rather free with her hands and her elbows. She was paying no attention to the ball; she figured Huck could manage Diana on his own.

Apparently not, for in a moment she heard him call "Nice shot." Diana must have made a basket.

Curry stepped away from Tom.

"You play dirty, lady," he told her.

"Then don't you think"—she kept her voice low—"that you should unzip your pants and check to be sure you're still all there?"

He lifted his arms away from his body. "Be my guest."

"If our two kids weren't—"

She was interrupted.

"Huck James, you...you..." It was Diana,

and she was furious. Curry turned to look at her. Her hands were on her hips and her face was flushed.

"What is it, Diana?" Tom asked evenly.

"He let me make that shot, Dad. He *let* me." She wheeled back around, glaring angrily at Huck. "You could have blocked me; you know you could have."

"Oh, come on," Huck scoffed. "You're a *girl*. That's how you're supposed to play with girls."

"Not with me," she snapped. "I'd a lot rather lose than have some *jerk* let me win. You may think I'm a little kid, Huck James, but I'm not." She stormed into the house, with more of an outraged flounce to her basketball shorts than Curry could have managed in a hoop skirt and crinoline.

Huck was red. "Of all the dumb—"

Huck hated being wrong. The only thing he hated more than being wrong was being wrong and having a girl know it.

"Oh, shoot, Mom, but that's the way we play with girls. I mean, when I do anything with Tracy, I always let her do good."

Curry decided this was not the moment to correct his grammar.

Tom was leaning against Curry's car. "Not all girls are the same, Huck."

"Yeah, and I don't understand *any* of them." He charged the basket and sunk a slam-dunk that left the hoop vibrating. It must have made him feel better, because when he had dropped back to earth, he spoke more calmly, seemingly addressing his remark to the barn. "I guess I should go apologize, huh?"

Curry was impressed. "I'm sure Diana would appreciate it."

As he slouched off into the house Curry went over to Tom.

"Can we keep out of this?" he asked hopefully.

"Oh, goodness, yes. Not only can we, but we should."

"I thought they liked each other."

"Of course they like each other." What was he using for a brain? "They're crazy about each other. What do you think this was all about? Haven't you noticed that not one of Huck's friends has called her? I imagine he's sent out smoke signals that she's off limits."

"So it's a matter of—"

"Adolescent hormones? I imagine."

"Oh, terrific." He sighed. "What do we do?"

"Not a blessed thing. At least not yet."

They picked up the basketball and started to walk back to the house.

"Do you know what really depresses me?" Tom said.

"What?"

"I'm pretty sure he was easing up on me too."

"'Oh, shoot, Mom,'" Curry quoted, "'but that's the way we play with old men.'"

Tom lifted his arm as if he were going to swat her rear too, but they were almost at the porch so instead he reached around her and opened the door.

And Curry decided that if he had given her the choice, she would have opened the door herself.

As soon as they went in the house, it was clear that Diana had accepted Huck's apology . . . and it became even clearer a few days later.

The raspberries that now grew wild along the south edge of the orchard were ripe. Huck and Diana had picked a couple of quarts, and after dinner, Tom and Curry had driven into town to take some to her friend Bonnie Crown.

They came home earlier than expected; Bonnie had had a cold. As they were walking toward the house Curry heard Huck, his voice a muffled groan.

"Oh, Diana, please."

"No, Huck, I mean it. Stop it."

Curry grabbed Tom's arm and pulled him back to the car. She opened and then slammed the door much more loudly than before. She walked toward the house, talking to him brightly.

She believed teenagers deserved a minute or so; if they couldn't pry themselves apart and get respectable in that amount of time, then they probably should be walked in on.

The porch was still unlit, but Huck was standing, leaning against one of the supports, his hands in his pockets, and Diana was on the glider, her blouse only slightly rumpled, which meant, of course, she was still far more neatly put together than Curry ever was.

Tom snapped on the light.

"We're back early; Bonnie had a cold," Curry told her uninterested audience.

They looked at her blankly.

She got some help from a surprising source—Tom.

"And you know how summer colds are always the worst." He rolled his eyes at Curry while he enunciated this piece of wisdom.

Curry coughed, trying to swallow her laugh. "Would either of you like a Coke?" she managed to ask after a moment.

Diana and Huck started to speak simultaneously, then stopped, and then started again. Diana began to giggle.

Curry took this for a yes and went into the house.

Tom followed, and in the brighter light of the kitchen, she saw an odd expression on his face, as if he couldn't decide whether all that had been funny or not.

"Well?" she asked.

"Now do we do something?"

"Like what?" Curry was, as always, solidly realistic. "If you know a way to make two teenagers keep their hands off each other, then you should seriously consider running for office in the national PTA."

Tom didn't laugh, and Curry was surprised. This little incident struck her as very routine.

"Look, Tom, he wasn't trying anything that you didn't try with me once. And you heard Diana. She's no wimp; she can take care of herself."

Tom looked at her for a moment and then his expression relaxed. "I guess you're right."

"Hard to admit, isn't it?"

"No, I'll do anything for a woman who tells me my kid's not a wimp." He reached out and tugged at a lock of her hair just as he used to pull her braids. "By the way, I thought you were fixing Cokes."

"Me? Are you kidding? I'm not their waitress."

He laughed, and in a moment, Huck and Diana came into the kitchen and got out the ice and glasses themselves.

"Huck was telling me," Diana said soon, "that there are a lot more raspberries over on the other side of the road."

Talking about raspberries? That's not what we called it. "Yes," Curry said instead. "Huck's grandmother planted them when she lived over there. The house isn't there, but the raspberries still are. We never use them all; it's a shame, considering what raspberries cost in the city."

"I was thinking," Diana mused. "Wouldn't it be fun to make jam?"

Curry bit off a "God, no." She took a breath and said politely, "Jam?"

"I've wanted to try for I don't know how long. The jars always look so great when they're all lined up on the shelf. Do you know how? Is it hard?"

Of course Curry knew how to make jam. She knew how to can tomatoes, preserve peaches, and put up pickles. Until her grandmother died, Curry spent the first half of every summer in the garden and then the second half in the kitchen. Then, as other women were trying all the old-fashioned ways, Curry thankfully abandoned them. She could not imagine that anyone could think weeding a tomato patch *fun*; she'd been forced to do it throughout her childhood. Declaring that if God had wanted her to can her own tomatoes He would not have invented botulism or the Heinz people, she sent her canner and her jar lids down to the cellar, hoping they would get themselves lost forever.

"I haven't had homemade jam in a long time," Tom remarked. "Why don't you make some, Diana? Curry must have jars and such."

Curry could have shot him.

"Oh, Curry, can we? Please." Diana was very excited. "I'll do all the work if you'll just show me how."

"Oh, okay," Curry sighed, "but only if we can—" She immediately swallowed the word *cheat*.

If she was going to do this, she was going to use packaged pectin. It saved what always seemed like hours of cooking time and was thoroughly reliable, so that you were never stuck with a year's worth of what you had to pour on pancakes and call syrup because the jam didn't jell. Of course, it took twice as much sugar that way, but, Curry reasoned, no one ate jam for their health, and if it made Gran roll over in her grave, well, the exercise would probably do the old lady some good.

But as much as she liked her, Curry did not trust Diana one bit. She was, after all, Tom's child. She'd want to do things right. Tell her that something was a shortcut and she wouldn't take it.

But what Diana didn't know wouldn't hurt her, and more important, what Diana *did* know was bound to hurt Curry. So Diana wasn't going to know.

"Okay," Curry repeated, "but only if someone else goes down to the cellar and hunts for the jars. I'm not going near that place."

Chapter Six

And it wasn't so bad. Even Curry, who had decided to get great pleasure out of feeling like a martyr, had to admit that the jam-making wasn't so bad this time.

As soon as she had agreed to it, Diana had immediately seized Huck, dragging him down to the cellar to find the jars. When they returned, considerably more dusty than when they had begun, Diana started loading the jars and lid rings into the dishwasher.

"You know, Curry," she said as she worked, "when we get done with this, I could help you clean out your basement."

"Thank you, no," Curry said swiftly.

"I wouldn't mind. It would be fun."

Curry closed her eyes, faint at other people's unnatural ideas about fun.

"You don't understand, Diana," Tom put in. "Curry doesn't *want* a clean basement."

"I certainly don't. I like having a part of my house that I don't have to keep clean. So I don't want either of you Winchesters near that cellar, and Tom, if you breathe one word about putting up a few shelves down there, I won't ever speak to you again.''

"That is an extremely tempting proposition, madam.''

The next morning while Huck and Diana picked berries, Curry went into town and bought sugar, jar lids, and, glancing over her shoulder to be sure that no one was looking, several packages of Sure-Jell.

And on the second day, they made the jam.

Diana, a Winchester to the core, was true to her word. She did want to do the work. The Sure-Jell instructions made everything very straightforward, and Diana bustled around happily, sterilizing the jars, timing the hard boil, and pouring the hot jam into jars. Curry picked over the fruit and measured the sugar, which were precisely the tasks that she had had at age five. The only difference seemed to be that this time she didn't have to climb on a chair to reach the sugar canister. That and the fact that the kitchen was no longer painted stagnant-pond green with rose decals and maroon linoleum.

And while they worked, just as Gran had told Curry stories about her childhood, about farming in South Dakota in the early part of the century, so too Curry told Diana stories. Tom had never really told her anything about his early years, and now she asked questions about the three of them, about the adventures Curry-Tom-and-Huck had all had together.

"What fun that must have been.'' Diana sighed,

hearing about the time the three of them had tried to build an igloo, which, when it caved in, had nearly suffocated Huck's father.

But as the afternoon wore on, Diana's interest waned, her questions became a little random, and Curry had a feeling that pretty soon they were going to start talking about something she would have never, not ever, discussed with her grandmother.

Diana mentioned something about her mother, and then at last, as she was wiping hot jam off the rims of some jars, she said, "You know, I really like my mother, but there are things I can't talk to her about."

Curry nodded sympathetically as if this were the first time a teenager had ever made such a complaint. What teenager ever thought that her mother understood her?

And suddenly Curry wondered what it would have been like if she herself had had a mother, if her mother hadn't been killed in that car accident when Curry was only two. Gran hadn't seemed to understand Curry at all—not that Curry ever gave her much of a chance. Would her mother have known more about her?

And those difficult years when Curry had been a widow and a mother herself—would they have been easier if she had had a mother of her own? Would Beth Trent have shared some of her daughter's burdens?

Beth Trent—her mother was just a name to Curry; a name, some black-and-white photographs, and a few stories about picnics and such.

She knew nothing of what her mother had been like as a woman. None of them knew anything about their long-dead parents. Cal Winchester had never spoken about his wife, Tom's mother. Myra James had talked a lot about her husband, but Curry now suspected from the fantasies that Myra had created after her son had died, that her stories about the senior Howard James were not an accurate picture of him.

Oh, well, none of that mattered. It was the present that counted, and young Diana Winchester, the grandchild of one of the women in that car accident, was present with something on her mind.

"What sort of things can't you tell your mother about?" Curry asked.

"Oh, just stuff."

Curry knew that in the lexicon of most teenagers, "Oh, just stuff" meant drugs, sex, or both. And it hadn't been drugs that Huck had been trying to give Diana the other night. "Like sex?" she asked calmly.

Diana nodded, not looking at her.

"Do you know all the facts?" Curry was perfectly willing to trot out her lecture on fallopian tubes and testosterone again.

"Oh, sure. Mother gave me some books, and they show us all these movies in school. It's just that, like..."

"You didn't expect to feel the way you do," Curry finished for her. After all, she'd been there.

Diana sighed, clearly relieved that someone had said it. She ran her fingers through her bangs. "Is it wrong to sleep with a guy if you really, really like him?''

Oh, Trish, she's your child; what do you want me to say?

"I don't know if it's wrong in the sense of being wicked," Curry answered carefully, silently apologizing to her son, "but it can be pretty foolish."

"Are you talking about birth control and venereal disease? They tell us about that in school all the time." Clearly what was said in school was not to be entirely believed.

"Well, it's more than that," Curry said, although she did think that that was quite a substantial part of it. "Do you ever read books with s—with love scenes?"

"Sure."

"Do you ever find that after reading one love scene, you skip ahead to find the next one and ignore everything in between?"

Diana blushed, unanswering. Clearly she did.

"It ruins the book, doesn't it? You never get involved in the plot again. Well, relationships can be like that. Once you go to bed together, it can be such fun that you start skipping the in-between parts and spending all of your time in bed. You think you know each other, but you really don't."

Diana washed out the kettle, ready to start the last batch of jam. "Is that what happened to Mother and Dad? Mother says that they are just too different to live together. I've always wondered why they didn't figure that out *before* they got married. Was it because ... well, because ..."

"I don't know about them," Curry lied, not knowing what Trish wanted her daughter to know, "but that happens to a lot of people."

"Did you— I'm sorry." Diana held up her hands, apologizing instantly. "I shouldn't ask that."

"I don't mind. Yes, I did sleep with Huck's father before we were married, but I had known him my whole life and we were sure we wanted to get married."

"Did you ever think it was wrong?"

"I didn't do it until I was sure that it wasn't. That's my advice, wait until you're sure, until you don't have any doubts at all." Curry was starting to feel very schoolmarmish. "Although I suppose you've heard that a million times."

"Not really. Not by someone who's been through it."

We've all been through it; we just don't always tell our daughters.

And as she helped Diana finish the jam, Curry's thoughts drifted back to that afternoon in early spring, nearly two decades ago, when for the first time, she had been sure.

She had loved Huck so—his quick imagination, his unceasing cheerfulness, his plans. She loved hearing him talk, the dreams he would tell her as they would sit together in the dark, their arms wrapped around each other; dreams of what it would be like when they were a little older, when they could get married.

And she loved the way his arms felt around her. It was nothing like it had been with Tom. Huck didn't push; whatever he was doing always seemed as if it were enough to him. When his hand was touching her shoulder, it was as if there were nothing more interesting, more enticing about her, about any girl, than her shoulder. Curry could relax under his caresses, never having to worry that he would do anything she didn't want him to, and with this ease came pleasure for her, a delight she had not known from Tom's touch.

Then the delight became eagerness, urgency, and it was Curry who curled her hand around Huck's and moved it to her breast, her leg, the buttons of her blouse.

For all his self-restraint, Huck longed for her, and as their senior year waxed, then waned, he often pulled away from her, his voice, his body, shaking. "I don't know, Curry, I don't know if I can take this. Sometimes it seems like I can't stop ... I just love you so much."

But he always stopped. Even when Curry was sure that he wouldn't.

One night as they lay side by side, their shirts open to one another's warmth, Huck suddenly, with a strength he never used with her, rolled her onto her back. He moved with her, over her, and his jeans-covered knee forced her legs apart. Then, his eyes never leaving hers, he slowly lowered himself on her.

They were both clothed, and denim pressed against denim, their bodies touching one another in places which even hands had not yet touched. Huck moved, and Curry felt, for the first time, the shape of him.

She would not have stopped him, whatever he might have done. Had his hands gone to the zipper of her jeans, she would have helped him. Had he broken away from her to pull off his own, she would have taken off hers and then welcomed him to her. Had he simply kept moving against her, fully clothed, seeking only his own release, she would have held him, delighting in his pleasure.

But he stopped. Jerking upright and breathing hard, he pulled away from her. "Oh, God, Curry," he moaned, his face in his hands. "Don't ever let me do that again. Please don't ever let me do that again."

She didn't answer; she made no promise.

For the next few weeks Huck was careful. He never touched her below the waist. Even as spring became unseasonably hot and Curry wore cutoffs, he would stare hungrily at her legs, but he never touched them, as if he knew where his hand would go if he did.

And as much as genuine embraces, they satisfied their longing for one another with the very physical horseplay so common to adolescents desperately eager to touch one another. Huck would bend Curry's arm behind her back, not hurting her, but secretly teased, pleased, by the knowledge that he could. She would then twist her leg around his, knocking them both off-balance until they would fall, Huck gladly taking the weight of Curry's body on his. She would struggle upright, sitting on him, holding his wrists down over his head, with him laughing and pushing against her grip. When he would break free, he would in turn flip her onto the ground.

It was all so delicious, and they felt safe, almost as if they were still children romping in innocent play, until one afternoon Huck had her across his lap, holding her, his arm hooked around her neck in something of a half nelson, and as he was trying to stop her from kicking him, his hand, perhaps by chance, perhaps not, landed between her legs.

They both froze, neither sure what to do, both of them longing for this, unsure if it were right, and for a moment, they both pretended that they hadn't noticed.

The spring sun was warm against their arms, and the wild sweet william bloomed a fragrant blue. But nothing, none of the beauties of a prairie in the spring, felt as sweet as the warmth of Huck's hand.

After a moment, the arm linked about Curry's neck curled around her shoulders and Huck bent his head. His kiss was open, and then the movement of the kiss was mirrored by the movement of his hand on her.

He knew nearly nothing about pleasing a girl, and it was only accident that the circular pressure of his fingers against her was in the right place, and the caress maintained its steady, unchanging rhythm quite simply because Huck was too terrified to alter it.

But it felt like nothing Curry had known; she had felt desire, but it had never come in such steady waves, bright pulsing currents spreading out from her young love's touch. She gasped and when she first whimpered with pleasure, Huck, startled, not sure if he had hurt her, moved to take his hand away, and she cried in his ear, "Please, Huck, please don't stop."

He did not, and astonished at his power over her, he held her tightly until he felt a shudder echoing through her, some vibration of pleasure from deep within surging through her until she went limp, burying her face in his chest.

Like anyone raised on a farm, Curry understood reproduction, but what she knew about female sexuality would have danced on the head of a pin. She did not understand what had happened to her.

Huck knew little more, just what he had learned from the magazines he and Tom furtively shared and from what he knew of his own body when he would awaken from a startlingly vivid dream. Although a little embarrassed, he felt the promise to always answer straight obligated him to explain what he knew.

"Then is that," she asked, "how you'd feel if we...?"

He nodded.

They were lying side by side now, and Curry propped herself up on her elbow to look at him.

He lay on his back, his head resting on his hands, his brown eyes warm because he was secretly quite pleased with what he had just done.

How she loved him. There was nothing she wouldn't have done for him, and she wanted him to feel the pleasures of which, until now, she had known little.

She reached out her hand.

They had been talking; Huck had relaxed, but he responded almost instantly to her touch, although undoubtedly, it was more to the idea of her hand on him, for the touch itself was almost too tentative, too soft, to be arousing in itself.

But as his head fell back and his eyes closed, as she knew how she was pleasing him from what she felt beneath the denim of his jeans, she grew more confident, and Huck's breath became ragged and his body moved, his hips rising in nearly involuntary thrusts.

"Curry, you've got to stop," she heard him pant. "Please . . . or I won't be able to . . . I'll have to . . ."

He knocked her hand from him and rolled to his side, away from her, desperately struggling for control.

Quietly and absolutely sure, without wavering or hesitation, Curry slipped out of her cutoffs and lay back down next to him. She let her hand slip down his side, tracing the line of his hip.

"Huck," she whispered, "turn over."

"Curry, no, you don't understand—" But the pressure of her hand on his hip worked where words did not, and Huck rolled toward her, her arms encouraging him, this time her legs opening without his urging.

He pressed himself to her just as he had done before, his desire so blindingly urgent that it was not until his hand found her leg that he realized this part of her was naked beneath him.

He froze, caught in a struggle between his long-held resolve that he would never expect this from her, not until they were married, and his aching desire for what she was so clearly offering. The hesitation lasted only a moment, dissolving as he fumbled frantically with his jeans.

Freed, he moved to her. "Curry, I won't... I just want to touch you. I promise I won't..."

But whatever promise Huck had intended, he did not keep. What his healthy young body found beneath itself was too warm, too invitingly moist to be refused, and once he was within her, he could not leave—not until she felt the boy she loved gasp and thrust deep in her, becoming, at least in his own terms, a man.

Was this what she was waiting for, Curry now asked herself, to be that sure again?

To be as sure with Tom as she had once been with Huck?

But that wasn't possible. It just wasn't.

And it wasn't because of the particular character of the man involved. With any man, there'd be doubts. That was the difference between thirty-six and eighteen. If George Washington turned up on her doorstep, she'd find something to have doubts about.

She and Huck had been so sure that they would spend the rest of their lives together. What they hadn't counted on, what they had never dreamed of, was that after that bright afternoon, Huck's life was to last for only three more years.

You couldn't be sure of anything. Life was so frighteningly random. When a person walked out a door, there was no guarantee that he would make it back.

But against that randomness, against those terrifying accidents, humans had a defense—the love of wife, mother, and sister, the love of woman as friend and neighbor.

Curry knew that people thought her different from other women, and if they meant it well, they were praising her casualness about detail, her flexibility, her merchant's hardheaded pragmatism. And when it was spoken behind her back, it was a criticism of the way she dressed and the way she kept house.

But being a woman meant more than that to her, much more. It meant a warmth of spirit; it meant always being there for others, willing to open your arms when they needed to cry; it meant putting your heart on the line every single day, loving children although they might dart in front of a speeding car, loving men although they would almost certainly leave you a widow in the end.

Curry often made jokes about life being too short; it was her excuse for not having a clean basement, for not using a toning lotion and wearing a light foundation everyday as the magazines said you should. But she, just like any woman widowed young, knew how dreadfully serious that phrase can be.

And life was much, much too short to spend it trying to keep from having your heart broken. Because one of the things that made this short life worth living was that women were willing to risk their hearts.

And, Tom, I've not been willing to do that for you. What kind of woman have I become that protecting myself is more important than loving you?

From her very first greeting—"Well, I'll be crumbed and deep-fried"—she had been quick and glib. She hadn't told him what it meant to see him again. After that night on the steps when he had asked her to have an affair, after she'd spent the night worrying about him, worrying that he felt like a failure, the next morning she'd offered him a cup of coffee because she didn't want to fall in love with him. When he was anxious about seeing Diana, when he dreaded his daughter's visit, she had started teasing him about country clubs.

Yes, they had had fun with their children, and God knows they both needed to have fun. But Tom needed much more than that, and Curry had always been holding back. She had made jokes, let him make jokes.

Why have I been like this? Yes, my life has been difficult. Yes, my heart has been through some long, dry spells, but things haven't been so difficult, so dry, that I should turn hard, that I should worry about being hurt.

And was she really only worried about herself? Wasn't she also punishing Tom? Knowing what he needed, she was withholding it—withholding the understanding, the warmth, refusing to listen to him, because the one time she had longed to talk, when she had needed to talk, he hadn't been there.

Tom had made mistakes; he was a troubled man, deeply unhappy, believing that he had done nothing right except in his work, and Curry, his oldest friend, had not tried to help him.

Tom, we took that oath as children, but it was to last our lives, and as a woman, I have broken it. I have been protecting myself, not wanting your troubles in my life, and you too have wanted to protect me from them. But, Tom, my friend, my dearest friend, I am strong enough, I truly am.

Curry knew that she could endure whatever happened, whatever heartbreak might come. No man alive could make her suffer more than she had already—because the living couldn't possibly hurt as much as the dead.

Chapter Seven

At five fifteen the screen door banged, and in a
moment, Tom and Huck were in the kitchen.

After a quick glance at the twenty-four pints of
dark crimson jam lined up on the counter and the
two rather limp females draped across the oak
chairs, Tom leaned against the doorjamb and
grinned lazily. "Well, what's for supper?"

"Supper?" Diana sat up in surprise, staring at
her father as if he had gone mad.

"Yes, Diana, supper. I mean, the two of you
were home all day while Huck and I were toiling in
the fields; surely you have made dinner."

"The fields, Tom?" Curry queried dryly. "Isn't
that pushing it just a bit?"

"The principle is the same. It's a woman's
job—"

Diana interrupted. "If wanting dinner was a
joke, Dad, it wasn't very funny."

"It better not be a joke," Huck put in. "I'm
hungry."

Curry looked at her son affectionately. "The
nice thing about you, Huck, is that you're so en-

tirely predictable." But she made no move whatsoever to start supper.

"Come on, Huck." Tom laughed. "Let's take these ladies into town for dinner."

"Oh, yes!" Diana hopped up, restored to full energy. "We haven't been to a restaurant since I've been here."

Curry was less enthused, but then she knew a great deal more about Gleeson's restaurants than Diana did. "Only if we go to the truck stop or the taco stand. Their food is the closest to being edible."

"I *adore* Mexican food," Diana exclaimed. And then remembered her manners. "But the truck stop would be fine too."

The taco stand it was.

How like a family we must look, Curry thought when they were all settled into a booth and were busy pulling the wrapping paper off their food. *Mom, Pop, Junior, and Sissy. Some problem with incest in the lower ranks, of course, and Sister's got a home elsewhere.*

But if anything ever happened to Trish, Curry would have welcomed Diana into her home. She would have done that even before she had met the girl.

If I would have raised your daughter, then what wouldn't I do for you?

"Curry, can you grab the hot sauce off that other table?"

Well, she thought as she leaned out of the booth to reach across the aisle, getting Tom a plastic bottle full of taco sauce was not exactly what she had had in mind when she resolved to be a better friend to him, but it would do for a start.

The sauce was farther away than she had expected and she might have crashed onto the floor if Tom hadn't grabbed her arm and reeled her back in.

Huck laughed. "Mom, you would have yelled at me for being too lazy to stand up."

Curry noticed that she was sitting a little closer to Tom than she had been before. "Not 'yelled,'" she told Huck. "I might, however, have issued a gentle reproof."

Tom looked interested. "Tell me, Huck, what are her 'gentle reproofs' like?"

"She asks me if I think I've been acting like a nitwit... but only if I have been," he added loyally.

"Does she cry over you?"

Huck looked revolted. "Lord, no. I'd hate that."

"Isn't that the truth? Huck's mother—"

"Your grandmother, Huck," Curry added the explanatory footnote.

Tom ignored her. "—used to cry for hours if he did something wrong. He always said he'd much prefer it if she just beat him like Dad did me."

Diana gasped. "Grandfather *beat* you?"

"Well, that makes it sound worse than it was, but he did take his belt to me," Tom acknowledged.

"But still..." Diana was shocked. "Do you think that was right?"

"If I thought parents should beat their children, I rather imagine that you, daughter, would be the

one who'd know about it," Tom pointed out.
"But at least my father never did it in anger, and
I'm sure I preferred his belt to Huck's mother's
tears. I'd rather be black-and-blue than wet."

"Why didn't he ground you?" Huck asked.
"That's what Mom did to me last year."

"I don't think he was that eager for so much of
my company."

Curry nodded in sympathy, remembering how
she had wanted to strangle Huck long before his
two-week imprisonment was over, and Cal Winchester hadn't liked Tom nearly as much as she
liked her son.

She wondered why. Impulsively she turned to
Tom. "Why was your father such—"

Tom kicked her, and she shut up. Of course, he
was right. She didn't think Diana and Huck
should be told pretty lies about Grandfather Winchester and Grandmother James, but there was
no need for them to hear their failings as parents,
however many those were, analyzed in detail.

But there was no getting around one thing. Calvin Winchester had been a cold and indifferent
father to Tom. No wonder the boy had turned
into a man who found being a parent difficult.

But it probably wasn't worthwhile asking Tom
why his father had been like that. He wouldn't
know.

It was just before seven when they left. In the
parking lot, Huck and Diana ran into some of his
friends and defected, going back inside with them.
They had brought two cars, guessing that this
might happen.

"Do you want to do something in town?" Tom

asked Curry when they were alone. "It's Tuesday, last chance to see the movie. I think it's a particularly swell one, with a herd of teenagers getting killed at pep rallies and proms."

Curry thought she could live without seeing it. "The school makes Huck go to pep rallies during basketball season. If his life is in danger at them, I don't want to know about it. Let's just go home."

Tom drove silently along the flat blacktop. It was still light out; the long summer day was just beginning to cool. The spring wheat was tall now, starting to ripen and turn golden. The prairie clover had flowered among the wild grass, frosting the green slopes with rose-purple.

And it reminded Tom of the afternoon more than twenty years ago when he had found Curry coming up from her grandmother's garden with tomatoes in her arms. He had taken the tomatoes from her and asked her to go for a drive with him. He didn't remember where they had gone or what excuse they'd made for getting out of the pickup, but he had kissed her that afternoon, the first time he had ever kissed a girl.

Suddenly Tom wanted to be alone with her again. Not that he would kiss her; no, he wouldn't do that. He just wanted to be with her, alone with her again as the afternoon wind faded and the summer light went soft. He turned up the drive to his father's house. "I'll leave the truck here and then walk you home."

The drive was bordered with a thicket of chokecherry trees, the clusters of bitter blackish fruit peeping through the dark, glossy leaves. He drove up the rutted lane slowly, stopping at the familiar buildings: the low hog pen, the white chicken coop, the brick cow barn, and the sloping roof of the frame hay barn.

The door to the hay barn was open.

This was the barn they had so often gathered in. It made Curry's grandmother nervous to have them in her one barn, and the other Winchester barns had been full of animals, but the hay barn had always been quiet, shadowy, and theirs. And now the door was open, a dark square in the red wall.

"Let me get that," he said, "and then I'll see you home."

Of course, Curry could have gone home alone. Or Tom could have closed the door later. But there was something about the open door that called to him, telling him to bring Curry when he came.

The barn door was wide enough for a hay rack and lurched open by sliding along a pole. It was a primitive mechanism, and in a moment Tom understood why the farmer who rented his father's land had left the door open. Something was stuck.

He couldn't see what it was—the door was eight feet high, but with his arms over his head he could easily reach the pole, and with fingers practiced and confident, he began to explore.

Curry moved around him, going inside.

When the door was fixed, when he was ready to close it, he stepped inside to call to her.

Barns don't change. This one was as it had always been this time of year. When haying season was over, the hay would reach all the way to the door, but now the center aisle was clear, the floor dusty and sprinkled with seeds and bits of straw. The golden-brown bales were stacked under the low ceilings that divided the floor from the loft. Light swept in from the door, illuminating the aisle while the rest was in shadows, lit only by occasional shafts filtering through knotholes and cracks in the walls.

The old ladder, just two-by-fours nailed between two posts, was still there, and Curry had climbed up it and was looking in the loft, her feet still on the ladder's rungs.

"It may not be safe up there."

She turned, looking down. A stray sunbeam lit her hair and it was like the fairy tale where straw is spun into gold.

"Oh, Tom, do you remember—"

"Yes."

Why had she asked? Why did she think she needed to ask? Of course he remembered. How could he forget that rainy, hot day when the three of them had cut open their fingers and pledged to be loyal and to be honest. Now there were just two, and he at least had broken both promises to her.

Slowly Curry climbed down the ladder. Tom watched. He couldn't help it. Her jeans were soft and worn. And when she reached the floor and turned, he was standing nearer than he thought he had been. She smelled of sunlight and raspberries.

It wasn't so much that she was beautiful, but that she was she. Curry. And that this place was this place, the barn, where the three of them had promised so much.

His eyes fell from hers, dropping to the light blue shirt that clung to her. If he touched her, he would touch her there first, flattening his hand against her, not to feel her breast, but so that he could feel her heartbeat, the steady, wonderful throb of the human heart, a woman's heart.

If he touched her...

But he couldn't, not in this place, not as the man he had become.

"Let's get out of here." Tom spoke abruptly.

He hardly waited, just hearing her footsteps as she followed him outside; to their backs, the sun was low and their shadows lay before them, long and dark.

He expected her to make a joke; he wanted her to. She had been good about that for the last month or so, getting them out of the murky depths that he kept floundering toward. He would have long since gone sentimental; he would have made a complete fool of himself if she hadn't managed to keep things light. But when she spoke this time, her voice was soft. "Shall we go for a walk?"

He looked at her, surprised, and then shrugged. "Sure, why not?"

The creek that divided their two farms flowed under the blacktop road by means of a concrete culvert. It curved back behind where the little renter's place had once stood, and among a small stand of cottonwoods it joined with another stream, deepening there into a swimming hole. It was to this place that they headed, following the creek, crossing the blacktop at the intersection where Huck's father's house had once been.

It had been a shock when he had first seen the empty lot, when he first learned that the little house where Huck had grown up had been torn down. But it made sense. The place had been poorly built out of shoddy materials, and between repairs and heating bills, Curry must have decided it just wasn't worth the rent it brought—when it was rented. She had let the lot go wild; buttercups and violets must blossom in the spring, and in August the grass would be silvery-gray.

And Huck was gone; it was right that his house should be too.

Curry pointed to where the house had stood. "Are you used to that yet?"

"Not entirely, but I'll get there."

And, of course, they were talking about a great deal more than the missing house.

As in the barn, it was darker within the shade of the trees, and the grass felt clean and cool. It had been a good year for South Dakota and the creek was high, lapping up to the roots of the trees. In bad times, the bank was steep and wide, and Curry and Tom had grown up hearing how, in the thirties, there hadn't been a creek at all, not even a sluggish trickle dampening the dust-covered rocks.

Tom looked around, at how familiar it all seemed, and then suddenly, filled with a boy's energy, he grasped a tree limb and effortlessly chinned himself just as he did in the old days. Dropping lightly to the ground, he said, "It's not changed much back here."

"There's no reason why it should," Curry answered.

There was even a scrap of rope looped around a branch, trailing down a foot or so. "Look"—he pointed at it—"there's the rope from our swing."

Curry's voice was gentle. "No, Tom, that's from Huck's swing, not from ours."

"But—" Oh, of course. The spurt of energy drained away, leaving him weary. It was like the wind chimes. Curry was talking about *this* Huck.

"You're not used to that either, are you?"

What could he say? Huck's face, Huck's name, on someone else? No, he wasn't used to it.

She went on. "Huck, my son, says that you sometimes forget he's not old enough to drink. He's very flattered, but I think it's that you forget who he is; that you think he is his father."

How did she know?

Well, there was certainly no sense in pretending, not if she already understood. "Most of the time," he said slowly, "I have it straight—that he's sixteen and I'm thirty-six. But he's just such a terrific kid, and I like being with him, just like it used to be with Huck... and I guess a part of me still thinks of myself as sixteen... or wishes that I still were." He went over to the edge of the creek, picking up a stone, skipping it across the water's calm surface until it buried itself in the mud of the bank beyond.

"Tom, did you want to make love to me in the barn?"

He started. "What kind of a question is that?"

"Well, did you?"

He shrugged. "Yes."

"Why didn't you?"

Curry, why are you asking me this?

He forced his voice to be light. "Oh, I imagine that sex in the hay is overrated as much as sex on a beach. It would probably be miserably uncomfortable."

Now it's your turn. Keep up the joke. Don't make us talk about this.

But her voice was even. "Did you think that I would say no?"

"Let's just say I wasn't going to give you a chance to."

"Why not?"

Because she should have said no. "I'm not fifteen anymore. I don't expect to get everything that I want."

She shook her head. "It's more than that."

Curry, please stop asking these questions. Please. How can we be together, after all this time, after all I've done wrong . . . after all you've meant to me?

But no, she wouldn't know, she couldn't. Not about that. He had never told her. And surely he owed her an answer, since he sometimes thought he owed her his life.

"Tom, I can tell when you're thinking about Vietnam."

How did she know? How *did* she know?

So tell her.

"It took me exactly two weeks"—his voice was tense, clipped—"to figure out that I had no idea why I was there. We shot at shadows and then went out in the morning to see if there were bodies. In one more week, the whole point became to survive, not fight well for God and country, but just to survive, to make it through that one year alive."

"And you feel guilty about that?"

"I started out to be a good soldier." He regretted the irony in his voice, but he couldn't help it. "And even after I realized I didn't have a clue as to what that meant, I did what I was supposed to. I shot at the shadows, I sandbagged bunkers, I strung up wire, and I carried my wife's picture because that's what good soldiers are supposed to do. But it was never her that I thought about; it was you."

"Tom . . ." Curry had sunk down to the grass, confused, obviously not knowing what this had to do with what had happened in the barn.

He tried to explain. "When it seemed like there was nothing else but that jungle and the uniforms, when everything smelled like diesel or death, when it seemed impossible that there were people still living their usual lives, I'd think of you. I'd work it out so carefully. Just exactly what time it would be in South Dakota, and then figure out what you'd be doing. And it was like a lifeline, the image of you, planting peas or canning tomatoes in all this sunshine. And I'd feel guilty—that I shouldn't be thinking of you, that I should be thinking of Trish . . . and thinking that made you seem so much farther away, and it made it all seem worse."

"But, Tom—"

"And then toward the end, after I found out about Huck...I don't know...I couldn't always remember why I was supposed to survive." Tom knelt down in front of her, and careful not to touch her, just as he had been careful not to touch her when he had taken the tomatoes out of her arms that afternoon so long ago, he picked up a lock of her hair. "I used to look for something this color. It's all I would think about some days, where I could find something the color of your hair. I never could, and sometimes when I was out on patrol, when it would be so easy to get careless, I'd remind myself that I had to be careful, that it was important to stay alive because I had to go on looking for something the color of Curry's hair." He rubbed the curl between his thumb and forefinger. "I never found it, though."

"But you stayed alive."

"Yes—although, I sometimes think I must have been mad."

She shook her head, her eyes glowing with a soft light. "Tom, you came home alive. If that took a little madness, so what?"

"I shouldn't have thought of you in that way. I had no right."

She drew back, surprised. "No right? What are you talking about?"

"You were Huck's wife."

"Tom! That didn't keep me from being your

friend. And Huck wouldn't have cared, not ever.''

No, of course he wouldn't have.

''Oh, Tom, don't you see what you did? By thinking of me as Huck's wife, you just made it all that much harder on yourself. And aren't you still doing it? Isn't that what this is all about? Have you turned me into some sort of symbol of something that you can't have?''

Yes. There was so much, so many things that other men took for granted, that weren't for him, that he couldn't have, that he didn't deserve. A home, a son, a wife's love. South Dakota, her open sky and the clean sweep of her prairies. Yes, these were all things that he couldn't have. And, yes, they all seemed to have to do with Curry.

He felt her touch, her hands resting on his thighs. ''Tom, I'm not sure I understand, but don't do this to me. I don't want to be a symbol of anything. I'm your friend, and I'm a woman, I'm not a symbol.''

But the world around her was green, the wild grasses and the trees. If she were in his arms now, cushioned in the soft clean grass, it would be as if they were both a part of the land, a part of the rich soil.

Tom looked down at Curry's hands, honey-colored against the denim that covered his legs. Her touch was light, and as he watched she began to trace the inseam of his jeans.

Wouldn't it be like coming home? Curry, the land.

Her fingers slid up and down the inside of his

leg, following the ridge of the flat-fell seam, her fingertip brushing where the jeans were the softest, the most worn.

He tried to speak. "Look . . . you'd better stop that." But he found one hand already at the buckle of his belt, and the other in her hair, his fingers lacing through the weight of the golden waves, desire driving him to bring her to his lap, her hair tumbling across his legs. He started to pull her down to him.

She understood. "Is this what you want?"

No, no, of course it wasn't. Not that he didn't like it, but not now, not with her. It would be too furtive, too quick, too incomplete, but . . .

But what? Was he doing it again—deliberately setting out to ruin something for himself? Unable to pull away from her, he had instead started to turn this into the most routine, mechanical exercise so that he could hate himself afterward and so that she could too.

Well, he might deserve that, but she certainly didn't. She deserved a man who was healthy and whole, patient and generous, and what she was getting was him. He heard her voice again. "Is it better for you this way? With your leg and all?"

She deserved better than him, and that knowledge was driving him to his worst. But he'd fallen into that trap too often. This time he wouldn't. Not with Curry. She deserved the best; at least he would try. He hadn't been trying much anymore, not at anything, but he would now. He would for her.

He put his arms around her, drawing her up to

him. "Let me worry about my leg." And brushing her hair from her face, he bent his head, and just as he had twenty years before, he kissed her.

Although she did not think of it at the time, for in fact, Curry *thought* of nothing, giving herself over to physical sensations, later she could not help comparing what it was like to be with Tom to what it had been like with Huck's father.

Sex had been fun for that Huck, astonishing and wonderful fun. He would get happy and excited thinking about it and if they were driving home, he'd sometimes whisper in her ear, telling her about the things they would do together as soon as they got back to their room.

In bed they would romp like puppies, clumsy, happy puppies. Huck talked, sometimes wild, exotic fantasies, sometimes rapturous descriptions of how he felt. The pace was lively, nothing lasted long, they were still too eager. A kiss here, a touch there—there were too many new places still untouched to linger long. There was no need to savor, for there would always be— Oh, how confidently they had believed in the future—a next time.

But Tom made love to her as if it were the only time that he ever would.

At first, in the moment she felt his fingers in her hair, his hand guiding her head downward, she thought, she dreaded, that he was going to be quick and selfish.

She would have done it, but she would have hated it. Not so much the act itself—although she

had never done that for a man—but for what it
revealed about him. He wasn't selfish; he was capable of great generosity, but for a moment, he
had seemed determined to be everything insensi-
tive and indifferent, as if he believed himself to be
that sort of man—the sort of man who cared only
about himself, only about his own survival.

But that moment had passed, and once Tom
took her in his arms, she learned of a pleasure
quite different from what had come from her husband's exuberant, inexperienced caresses. Tom
went slowly; he savored each bit of her, his caresses lasting and treasuring, his sensitive fingertips learning each changing texture. Just as she
had seen his hands, brown and strong, linger on
newly sanded wood, loving the velvety smoothness, so now he had stroked her from shoulder to
thigh, over the swell of her breast, the curve of
her hip, again and again until she was lost in sensation.

And unlike Huck, he spoke only to murmur
her name or words too low, too inarticulate to be
understood, muffled against her as they were.
Only once did she understand him, did she need
to understand him; only when he finally moved
over her, having waited until he had been certain
of her pleasure, when he was poised above her,
one hand against the soft grass, holding his weight
off her, as she felt the first strong pressure against
her, her body first opening to his, he went still,
passion trembling through him, and he spoke.
"Oh, Curry, is it really you?"

Surely Huck had loved her more. Surely her

long-dead husband had loved her with a simple, uncomplicated love that Tom was no longer capable of. But still, however odd, it mattered more to Tom that he was with her than it had ever mattered to Huck.

For Huck, sex and Curry had been one. He had never slept with another woman, and he never intended to. He had no idea what sex would be like if the woman were not she, and he had no plans to find out.

But Tom knew. He'd been with women whom he had hardly known; he had been with women for whom he cared little. He knew, beyond anything even Huck's quick imagination could have grasped, just how precious it was to be with a woman that mattered. And she mattered to him.

Oh, Curry, is it really you? That had been deeper than Huck's astonishment that sex's delicious naughtiness was now permissible. Tom looked down on her face, realizing that these warm depths were hers, with a surprised awe that had nothing to do with inexperience, an awe that gained its richness, in fact, from experience. Tom had long believed that this kind of meaning was no longer possible for him, that it was no longer possible for him to care this much. Discovering how wrong he had been brought a rapture and joy that eclipsed any merely physical pleasure.

"I feel like a kid again."

Afterward, when they lay side by side, satisfaction enveloping them like a heavy velvet drape, Tom had suddenly pulled at Curry's hand.

"Tom, no, I can't move." But she had allowed him to pull her up, and in a moment found herself dragged, sputtering and splashing, into the cool creek.

It had been years since Curry had been swimming naked, and the rush of the water over her breasts was delicious. They romped as they had as children, ducking each other, playing tag, smearing mud. At last they draped themselves on the grassy bank, hoping to dry in the twilight before putting on their clothes. That was when Tom announced that he felt like a boy again.

"Except," Curry pointed out, "it isn't our *parents* that we'll have to keep this from, but our kids."

Tom grimaced. "They won't go weird and Oedipal on us, will they?"

"No...at least, I *hope* not. No, I think it's just that given what's going on between the two of them, it would make it a lot harder if they know that we're sleeping together."

"I don't see that we are *sleeping* together," Tom said. "I have this feeling that my bed is going to feel a bit on the lonely side tonight."

"You know what I mean."

He nodded in agreement. "Then this will be like being kids again. I'll probably start groping you in dark hallways."

Then something occurred to Curry. "But, Tom, if we plan on keeping this up, then we do need to be more adult about birth control. I know it seems like I'm too old to be worried about getting pregnant, but I'm not."

Curry was so occupied trying to remember when her last period was—she didn't keep track, not finding the ups and downs of her menstrual cycle to be particularly interesting information—that it was a moment before she realized that Tom had sat up, a tight, blank look on his face.

Oh, Tom, don't be unhappy, not now; let's laugh and—

She stopped herself. *You knew that he was troubled. You knew he had problems. You knew this wasn't going to be easy.*

"Tom, what is it? What's wrong?"

"Don't you know I would have protected you if there had been any threat to you at all?"

"I don't understand."

"I've had a vasectomy."

"Oh."

It made sense; of course it did. Curry didn't know if he slept with Trish when he saw her, but surely they wouldn't want more children, not with their marriage in the coma that it was in, and Tom's other encounters were of the most casual. A vasectomy was logical, perfectly logical.

No, no, it wasn't. Maybe for other people, for city people, but not for people brought up around here. Curry wasn't sure why. Perhaps it was all the topsoil that had blown away in the thirties. It was gone, and there was no getting it back. Fall plowing and those dry, bitter winds had blown it away, leaving the land less rich, less fertile. People who knew about that didn't do it to themselves.

Unless they hated themselves.

Tom, my love, do you hate yourself so?

"Why did you do it?" she asked, hoping there was no anguish in her voice.

She braced herself for his answer; whatever it was, she'd listen and go on loving.

It took him a long time to answer. He didn't want to, that was clear, but she knew he would.

At last he spoke. "When I got back, I was wounded and it took a while before...anyway, about a year later, Trish got pregnant. She was happy about it, she really was, but me, I could hardly face the thought. I was working in that lumbermill, and I just couldn't stand it. I felt so trapped and confused, I thought I was going mad...and another baby seemed like one more hold over me."

"Did she have an abortion?" Surely he hadn't made his wife do that.

"Trish? An abortion? God, no. She had a miscarriage, and the fetus...well, it was a mess. Even if she had carried it to term, it would never have survived."

The fetus...well, it was a mess. Suddenly everything was achingly, miserably clear to Curry—just as clear as it had been that day when the green Chevy had turned up the drive; she had seen that car, and she had known right away that those men were here to tell her about Huck. And now...children with birth defects; she knew what that meant too. In a moment he would start talking about cancer of the soft tissues. Agent Orange. It had to be.

Almost everyone she cared about. Why not him too? "Oh, I just move in the wrong circles, that's all," she had told Colin Wheeler.

And so Curry waited, miserable and still; just as she had waited for the men to get out of that green car, she waited to hear Tom tell her that he was dying.

He must have understood her look; he was taking her hand, gripping it tightly and shaking his head.

Shaking his head. She was sick with relief.

"No, it wasn't Agent Orange. Trish's doctor looked into that, but I was never near the stuff. This was just one of those things that can happen to anyone."

Curry buried her face in his shoulder, in the strong, wonderful warmth of his shoulder. Tom wasn't dying. He really wasn't. "Then why..."

"Because I still felt responsible. All these crazy things were happening to me—Huck, my leg, the job, the baby, and I felt so sure that they would go on happening, and that there was nothing I could do about it."

"Like in a dry spell when there's nothing you can do to make it rain."

He sighed. "That's exactly how I felt...until I realized that this was one thing I could do something about; this would be one bad thing that would never happen again. Getting a vasectomy made me feel like I had some control over all that was happening."

"Destroying part of yourself made you feel like you were in control of things?"

"Believe it or not, it made me feel better. I'd never do it again...although, I guess a vasectomy is a once in a lifetime thrill."

"Do you regret it? Have you ever tried to have it reversed?"

He shrugged. "I'm a pretty poor father to Diana; this just kept me from doing the same for someone else. Psychologically, emotionally, I seem incapable of being any kind of a father; this just makes it biological as well."

Curry ached for him, that he could say that, think that, about himself. "Tom—"

"Anyway," he interrupted, "the bottom line is that if you want more babies, you aren't getting them from me."

She shook her head. "I don't want more children."

"But you're a terrific parent."

"Thank you, but that's not the point. Oh, once I would have loved to have another baby. If Huck's father had lived, we probably would have had four or five. Or if I had met someone ten years ago."

"You're thirty-six. That's not too old to have a baby."

"Not physically, no. But I do not want to do the baby-toddler scene again. Even if, God forbid, something happened to Huck, I wouldn't want another baby. Not at this point in my life. I like teenagers; I think they are fascinating. That's why I want to teach high school. If I need to cluck around in a maternal way every so often, I'm sure there will be students who need to be clucked after. Or I could get involved in foster care. There're plenty of children out there who need to be loved."

Babies are easy to love. Anyone can love a baby. Life's harder part is loving the rest; a senile grandmother; a teenager, sullen and confused; and a man like you.

But, Tom, my friend, my dearest friend, I do love you.

Chapter Eight

It was hard to find time to be alone. For the next few days Huck and Diana seemed so often underfoot that they might as well have been inquisitive little two-year-olds, and when they did disappear—undoubtedly to engage in some behavior rather beyond the repertoire of the average toddler—there was no telling when they might suddenly return.

Finally at supper one evening, Huck spoke. "Diana and I are going in to see the movie. Is that—" He broke off.

Curry understood. He'd been about to ask if that was all right. Generally Huck didn't mind asking permission, but he would be fried before he'd do any such thing in front of Diana.

"I hope you have a good time," she replied. If he couldn't bring himself to ask permission, she wasn't going to humiliate him by giving it.

"Why don't you shove off, then?" Tom said. "I'll do your KP for you, Diana."

"Oh, no," replied his strong-minded daughter. "If we all help, it won't take a minute."

"At least she didn't say it would be *fun*," Curry said to Tom as she took his plate from him.

"The fun starts when they leave."

His voice was low, and Curry was deeply grateful that Huck and Diana were sufficiently fogged in by adolescence that they didn't notice the sparkle in Tom's blue eyes.

As soon as Huck's car was gone Curry turned to Tom. He was leaning against the counter, his arms folded, his smile warm and lazy.

"Well?" she asked.

"I have a headache," he announced.

"You don't either."

"That's true," he admitted. "This is revenge for when we were kids. You wouldn't let me put my hand under your shirt then, so I'm certainly not letting you put yours under mine now." He settled the collar of his shirt primly and tried hard to look outraged.

Curry laughed. "Fine. It wasn't your *shirt* I was interested in anyway."

"Come here," he growled, but as he drew her to him, he went on. "Maybe we should go over to my house just in case the kids come home early."

That made sense. "Let me get my shoes." Curry leaned over, looking under the table. "If I can find them, that is."

"Listen, you don't need to wear shoes for me. I'm weird, but not *that* weird."

In a few minutes they were at Tom's old house. Curry started to open the door, but the latch didn't move and then she noticed Tom pulling his keys from his pocket.

"You lock the house? Whatever for?" Curry never locked hers. "There's nothing in it."

"My tools."

"I beg your pardon," she drawled.

"Well, I don't know about you, but I am rather glad that this door is usually locked. If we get any unexpected visitors, they won't be surprised to find they can't get in."

"Good point." Curry stepped inside. "Wait a minute, Tom. This house *is* empty. Where are we going to—"

"What's wrong? You scared of a few splinters?"

"Yes."

"I've got a bed upstairs, you goat. Get on up there." He pushed her toward the stairs.

But at the landing, she stopped. "Wait a minute. This is not romantic enough."

"Romantic? Curry, this is South Dakota. What do you expect?"

"I expect a little gallantry. I think that the appropriate decorum at times like this is for you to carry me up the stairs."

"I'm not carrying you up the stairs. You can walk."

"Then I'm not going."

"Hey, I don't care. I've never made love in a stairwell before, but there's always a first time." Tom's hands dropped to his belt and he approached her menacingly.

But instead of flattening her against the wall, he suddenly ducked and Curry felt herself being swung up and over his shoulder in a fireman's carry. Her bare feet dangled in front of him and her long hair swept down in back almost to his knees.

"Wait a minute," she protested as the blood rushed to her head. "This isn't how Clark Gable did it in *Gone With the Wind*."

"Well, maybe not," Tom returned as he started up the stairs. "But frankly, my dear, I don't give a damn."

"My God, what literacy. You're a regular Bartlett's."

"I just read the comic book."

Whether it was a romantic way of being carried or not, Curry had to admit the view from where she was was really rather nice. And as long as she was back here, she might as well take advantage of it.

"What are you doing?" Tom demanded.

"Just picking your pocket," she replied, and rather than make a liar of herself, she proceeded to do so—even if larceny had not been her original intention.

Trying to hold her head up, she opened his wallet and calmly—or rather as calmly as a person can when she is upside down—began looking through it. He had very little of the clutter most people have in their wallets, just a Minnesota driver's license, an AAA card, a telephone credit card, Diana's school picture, and an astonishing amount of cash.

"Good God, Tom, you carry a lot of money."

"I don't use credit cards."

"Can't they take your citizenship away from you for that?"

"Probably. But they'll never be able to find me. Credit card companies can find people better than the government can."

"That's sure true," Curry agreed as she slipped the wallet back into his pocket, taking her own sweet time about doing it too.

Tom kicked open the door to his room with his foot and tossed Curry across the bed, or rather across what he was using as a bed.

"You call this a bed?" It was a thin, but firm foam mattress on a low platform, covered with a double sleeping bag. Actually, it was surprisingly comfortable.

"If you don't like it, leave," he returned. "The door's open."

"No, it's not. It's locked."

"Well, then, you're stuck here, and you might as well make the best of it." Tom dropped down beside her and pulled her into his arms.

And within just a very few minutes Curry was thinking that if all men were like Tom, she really ought to move to a state that had a professional football team.

"You doing all right?" Tom asked her about an hour later.

Curry nodded, snuggling her cheek into his warm shoulder. "Do you know what the nicest part of this is?"

"That I'll still respect you in the morning?"

"No, I don't care about that. What's really wonderful is that there is not a blessed thing I'm supposed to be doing."

He nudged her forehead with his chin until her head dropped back and he could look at her. "I suppose you're talking about a bit more than the fact that the dinner dishes are already done."

"I've always been so busy. Having a store is really numbing; there's always stuff to do. And then looking after Huck and Gran and Myra. I felt like I had two thousand lists running through my head all the time. And after I sold the store, I started school. These last few weeks are the first time since before Huck was born that I haven't had millions of things to do."

"I hate to criticize you," Tom said. "God knows you've done a better job with your life than I've done with mine; but it does seem like maybe you should have taken more vacation time."

"We certainly should have traveled. I'm sorry Huck hasn't seen more."

"It's *you* I'm talking about. You're the one who needed time off."

He was probably right, Curry sighed. It was lovely to have fun again; it felt like years since she had been as loose and free-spirited as she had been with him this summer. During all those years before he had come, she'd had to deny part of herself, that part that wasn't brisk and decisive, the part that had fun, the part that felt.

But Tom was helping her find it again.

Oh, how I am going to miss this when you go.

"Do you ever think about the old days?" she asked suddenly.

"I try not to."

"Why not?" She propped herself up on her

elbow, looking down at him. She might as well ask. "Because it hurts too much to remember Huck?"

"That's part of it," he said slowly. "But also because...well, when you look back as an adult, you start wondering if things were really as they seemed."

Curry frowned. "What are you talking about? You aren't talking about the three of us, are you? What about us wasn't as it seemed?"

"Didn't you ever wonder why we were all so close, so much closer than kids usually are?"

"I've never really thought about it, but I suppose it's that none of us got enough love and support from the adults in our lives so we gave it to each other."

"Doesn't that seem sad?"

"Not particularly. Of course, it was tragic about our folks getting killed, your mother, Huck's father, both of mine; that's terribly sad, and that your dad was cold and Gran so rigid, well, that's sad too, but the fact that three children stuck together because they needed each other, that's not sad. That's pretty wonderful."

Tom didn't say anything.

"You know," she went on, "the other day, for the first time in years, I wondered about what it would have been like to have had a mother. That's what I mean about having always been too busy; I've never taken the time to think about things like that. I don't think I've been reflective enough."

"Well, I've been reflective enough for the both

of us," he said almost bitterly. "And, believe me, there's no percentage in it. None at all."

"That's probably because you only reflect on the things you've done wrong."

Tom looked at her, surprised. "I don't know," he said slowly. "Maybe you're right."

Of course, with there being only one picture show in Gleeson, it wasn't often that Huck and Diana were as safely entombed as they had been that evening. But whenever the two teenagers went into town, their parents crept off, being thankful that because of his overdeveloped fondness for his tools, Tom had made a habit of locking his door.

One Friday afternoon he returned from doing some errands in town. As he came into her kitchen he tossed Curry a grin and, opening the refrigerator, took out a beer. Just as he was opening it, he stopped, looking at her with his blue eyes sparkling. "I don't hear the patter of little feet. Is it possible that we're alone?"

"If you're talking about Diana and Huck"— Huck's feet were anything but little—"they're down by the creek, but they could be back at any time."

"Hell, this is a joke," he grumbled. "Here they are sneaking off for precisely the same reason we want to sneak off. Don't you think we could work out some kind of deal not to disturb each other for a couple of hours?"

"Fine. You can be the negotiator for our side."

"Terrific. What am I supposed to say? Tell

Huck that I want some privacy so I can do all sorts of strange things to his mother and if he even thinks of doing a single one of them to my daughter, I'll shoot him?''

"I imagine you're just a little late on the 'thinking' part, and as for the doing, Diana is saying no, and that will stop Huck much better than anything you could say. But, Tom, it's not fair to them to leave them alone too much.''

"Fair to them? Who cares about them? This isn't fair to me." But Tom laughed and pulled Curry into his lap. "I'm not so sure I like being a grown-up.'' She was wearing a pair of Huck's outgrown jeans, and because she had a waist that neither her son nor his jeans had, the jeans gaped in back invitingly. Tom slipped his hand in.

"If we weren't grown-ups,'' she pointed out, "I'd rip your arm out of its socket for doing that.''

He gave her a warm squeeze and was starting to kiss her when the phone on the kitchen wall rang.

"If you'd be so kind as to get your hands out of my pants, Tom Winchester, I'd answer the phone.''

Instead of releasing her, Tom tilted the chair backward—at great peril to both humans and chair—snared the receiver off the hook, negotiated a landing that all three survived, and then stuck the phone under her ear.

"Hello.'' Curry was a little breathless.

"Curry, this is Patricia Winchester.'' Curry instantly slid off Tom's lap. "Can I speak to Diana?''

"I'm sorry, Trish. She's down by the creek. I'll go get her and have her call you right away.''

Curry waited for Trish to say that it wasn't urgent, but the other woman did not, instead thanking her and then almost hesitantly asking if Tom was around.

"Just a second." Curry passed the phone to Tom and went out to get Diana, being careful to call her name loudly before entering the cottonwood grove.

Surprisingly Tom was still on the phone when they got back, and he handed the receiver to Diana. "Your mother's got some news for you."

He took Curry's arm, steering her out to the porch. She looked up at him inquiringly.

"I'm being divorced."

Curry blinked. "That's a surprise."

"It shouldn't be. Most people think she should have done it years ago."

"Why now? The banker?"

"Apparently. Without Diana around, they've been spending more time together, and he finally gave her an ultimatum—divorce me and marry him, or he would walk." Tom's voice had been flat and then it picked up its usual teasing. "I offered to be incredibly mean to her if she needed grounds for the divorce."

"That was very obliging of you, I'm sure, but I don't suppose grounds will be a problem."

"Hardly," Tom scoffed. "I think she's got every one in the book, except that I've never knocked her around—mental cruelty, desertion, adultery—"

"What a lovely opinion you have of yourself," Curry remarked. *Why do you have to make a joke of*

it? If it doesn't feel funny, if it hurts, you can say so.
"But the divorce will be pretty straightforward,
won't it? Except for the country club membership, of course."

"Actually, we will fight over the money."

"You will?" This seemed surprising.

"Lord, yes. I will want her to pick me clean, and
she's already said she doesn't want anything except the one house... not even for Diana."

Curry sat down on the picnic bench. Tom's
voice had gone flat over those last four words:
"not even for Diana."

She didn't know how much Tom minded that
Trish wanted to divorce him and marry someone
else. She suspected that he didn't know either.
Whatever feelings he still had for Trish, whatever
remaining affection, passion, or possessiveness,
were probably overwhelmed by his feelings for
Diana.

Did he feel like he was being pushed out of his
daughter's life? He might not have been a model
father, but she was the only child he would ever
have, and he was closer to her now than he had
ever been.

Did he feel that he learned of the joys of being a
father only to have them taken away?

Diana stepped out on the porch gingerly. Tom
stood up and Curry could tell he was trying hard
to look like his usual easygoing self. He held out
his arm, wrapping it around her shoulders when
she came to him. "Are you happy, baby?"

"Oh, yes, Dad." She peered up at him from
under her bangs. "Do you mind?"

Curry saw his arm tighten around the girl. "No, sweetheart, I only want what's best for the two of you." He brushed aside her hair and kissed her forehead. "Now, do you have time to sit down and tell me all about it or would you rather not?"

"Now's fine." And Diana sat down on the glider, tucking her legs under her, and began to talk, telling them about Phillip, not just how "reliable" he was, but how she and Trish had met him, about what he had given her for her birthday.

As Diana talked away Curry wondered if this was one difference between sons and daughters. Although Huck did, in the end, tell her most everything, he did so in part because he didn't notice he was. If told to sit right down and tell all, he sat right down and didn't.

It was interesting to hear Diana talk, and Curry didn't quite trust Tom to encourage her, so she asked a question. "Are you surprised that they want to get married?"

"Not really. I mean, like . . ." She turned back to Tom. "Dad, when I was little, I used to hope that you and Mother would work things out, that we'd be like other families."

"Diana—" Tom didn't seem to know what to say. "I—"

"Of course you felt that way," Curry put in. Bonnie Crown had said her girls still wanted her to remarry their father. "It's natural."

"You know, it's hard to see your parents like they are real people and all, who change and stuff, but Mother has been so much happier since Phillip started coming around. Even I could see that. And you—"

"Me?" Tom frowned. "What about me?"

"You're different here. When you come visit us at home, you're real quiet all the time."

"I don't mean to be."

"Well, you are; you must be happier here than you are at home."

Although her voice did not have the least bit of resentment in it, Tom spoke quickly. "I hope you don't think that has anything to do with the way I feel about you."

She looked at him blankly. "Why would it? Anyway, the two of you really are happier apart; even I can see that. I know that Mother's been telling me this for about ten years, but I guess it takes that long for things to sink in." Diana rapped her knuckles on her head as if she expected it to be made of wood.

Tom didn't smile. "Don't worry about your mother and me. The important question is what will make you happy. Will you mind living with this Phillip character?"

She laughed and shook her head. "He has a videocassette recorder. How could I mind that?"

"Be serious. He'll be your stepfather; is that going to be all right?"

"Oh, of course. I mean, I can't imagine why it wouldn't be."

Tom asked her a few similar questions in which the word *stepfather* kept recurring, but Diana was constitutionally incapable of imagining that anything would not work out just wonderfully well, so finally Tom gave up. "Just remember," he said at last, "it's not going to change the way I feel about you."

"That goes double for me."

Tom cleared his throat, and it was a moment before he spoke again. "Your mother says she doesn't want any money. If I send you some, will you spend it?"

"I'll do anything for you, Dad."

"You're a wonderful daughter, Diana," he said dryly.

Her tone was exactly the same. "I try my best."

Jokes again, Curry thought. But at least the joke had come a lot later than she expected.

Not surprisingly, Diana wanted to be home with her mother. Curry knew that the girl felt a little caught between her interest in Huck and her desire to share her mother's happiness, and Curry thought it said a lot about Diana's character that her mother won.

She did have to stay a few more days, since her round-trip ticket was some special fare that only allowed her to fly Monday through Thursday. Tom told her to go home whenever she wanted, but she refused to let him pay the difference, and Curry enjoyed the process of Tom being defeated by a simply repeated "No, I am not going to let you do that."

"Men should never have daughters," he complained to Curry. "It's just not a fair fight when your opponent is fifteen, pretty, and yours."

Sunday afternoon, the day before Diana was to

leave, Curry had Bonnie Crown and her two girls over. Diana had baby-sat for Bonnie a few times when one of the girls was going to be home alone, and they had liked her. Moreover, Curry worried that a Winchester-James party was likely to get a little morose. She was going to miss Diana; Tom just might feel like this was the last time he had with her before signing her over to a stepfather; and Huck was entirely capable of persuading himself that Diana's leaving was the end of his world, just as he had been blankly miserable for a full forty-five minutes after Tracy Morgan had left for art camp.

They decided to have a picnic, and Tom and Huck carried the picnic table off the porch. Diana made a raspberry pie, and Huck picked sweet corn and tomatoes from the farmer down the road who rented Curry's land and willingly supplied her with all the vegetables she refused to grow herself.

Curry gritted her teeth and actually fried the chicken again, and in a burst of domesticity, she even made up a batch of yeast dough—although she waited until Diana was well out of range and dumped everything in the Cuisinart, which she had won in some paint-selling promotion a couple of years ago.

Of course, when Diana returned, she was crushed that Curry had not let her help knead the dough. "It would have been fun," she said.

"It sure was," Curry returned. Curry loved the sound of the Cuisinart thumping the ball of dough around, comparing it, as she did, to the memory of her grandmother's voice: "Now, girl, was that really a full ten minutes? You have to develop that gluten."

But Curry took pity on Diana. "You can make it out into rolls," she offered magnanimously.

The afternoon was as pleasant as it could be— hot, windy, and bright. After they ate, Tom and Huck rigged up the badminton net that Bonnie had brought and the four younger members started to play.

"Those are nice girls you've got there, Bonnie." Tom dropped down onto the picnic bench beside Curry.

"They've certainly got good taste in men," Curry added. Stacy's and Jamie's adoration of Huck was apparent to everyone, except the young god himself.

"Diana is something special too," Bonnie told Tom.

"Thanks," he replied, "but I can't take any credit for that. It's all her mother's doing."

"Don't be modest." And when Tom grimaced, Bonnie went on. "No, I'm not just saying that. She wouldn't be that way with you if...Oh, Curry, tell him."

"I'm not sure what you're talking about," Curry had to admit.

Bonnie was not used to understanding things better than other people, but clearly she thought that these two were missing the obvious. "Diana is an assured, self-confident girl, and—"

"But you have to give Trish credit for that," Tom interrupted.

Bonnie ignored him. "And one thing that girl is very sure of is that you love her."

Tom started, clearly surprised, and it took him a moment to recover his usual bland expression. "Go on," he said evenly.

"Look, I've got two daughters who aren't sure that their father loves them, and they are just in knots when they're around him. They're like pathetic little puppies; they'll just do anything to please him. Stacy's even started flirting with him in this desperate unconscious effort to get his approval."

Tom grimaced. "I don't want her jumping through hoops trying to please me. Particularly that one."

"She doesn't. Because she knows you love her."

"I do, but I've got no idea how she knows it. It's not exactly like I've been around a lot."

"And I don't suppose you have the world's closest father-daughter relationship—she wouldn't be so happy about this banker if you did—but given the enormous difficulties of your situation, things are awfully good. Of course, I couldn't know what it is, but you've done something very right, Tom."

Tom cleared his throat and stared out across the field. It was a moment before he spoke. "You can't know how pretty that is to hear."

Bonnie shook her head. "It's not 'pretty.' It's true. There's a lot I don't know about, but the effect of divorce on young girls is my current specialty."

Tom's eyes turned to Curry's.

"She's giving it to you straight," she told him. "Believe her."

Bonnie was right. Diana respected Tom, she loved him, she knew that he loved her—a lot of live-in fathers couldn't say as much.

In every way, Tom had had the most difficult of all fatherhoods. His own father had almost ignored him, so he had no role model as to how to be a father. He had been absent during those delicious years when Diana learned to walk and talk, he had come home wounded, and those first few years back had been ridden with his hatred of his job, his basic incompatibility with Trish, and the nightmare of that miscarriage. Then he had left, and it was another man who taught his daughter to drive, who knew which albums she wanted for her birthday.

But still, despite all that, when Diana had every reason to feel abandoned and unloved, she did not. When Tom had hurried to assure her that his unease, his quietness, when he was in Bemidji had nothing to do with his feelings for her, she had looked at him blankly. It had never occurred to her that it might. Diana knew that he loved her.

Why didn't you notice?

Curry was horrified at herself. She who thought she loved him, who thought herself his dearest friend, who would have done nearly anything for him, she hadn't noticed. It had taken the most casual acquaintance to say the words he had so needed to hear.

Why?

And then it came to her. She had done Tom a

terrible disservice, something nearly unforgivable.

She had believed him.

He had ridden into town, not as the hometown boy who'd made good, but as the tall stranger with a black hat and a mysterious stain in his past.

And he had put that black hat on himself.

Tom hated labels. "Historic preservationist." "Vietnam vet." His lips had tightened and his eyes had gone flat. He didn't want labels hung on him, compartmentalizing him, saying he was something that he was not. He had great doubts about himself, a fear that if someone called him something, he might just become that.

But he had festooned himself with labels of his own making. *"A lousy father and a worse husband."* Those labels were just as false, as simplistic, as any other.

"Psychologically, emotionally, I seem incapable of being any kind of a father; this just makes it biological as well."

Again and again Tom had criticized himself, and when he had, Curry had believed him.

But none of it was true.

Of course, his marriage had failed, but that wasn't his fault alone. Just because Trish had a domestic temperament, a calm and cheerful manner, didn't mean that she was blameless. She had probably made as little effort to meet Tom's needs as he had to meet hers.

And Trish probably knew that. Few women, if they believed themselves completely the victim, could hide their resentment from their children.

Trish didn't resent Tom—at least not much or at least not anymore. That said a lot.

And as a father—how could Curry have missed the signs that now seemed so obvious? From the very beginning she had assumed he was an inadequate parent, but nearly every piece of evidence was to the contrary.

Yes, he hadn't wanted Diana to come, and yes, he hadn't wanted to be alone with her when he had picked her up at the airport. But things had changed since then.

Tom loved being with Diana, that was clear. He enjoyed playing basketball with her, he enjoyed working with her. He had praised her work on the house openly and sincerely, letting her know that he was proud of her. Curry herself, as hard as she tried, knew that she didn't always praise Huck enough.

And just the other day, when Diana was telling them about Phillip, Curry had been afraid that Tom would not encourage her to go on talking. How wrong that was. Diana was open with Tom. Maybe she couldn't talk to him about sex, but it seemed she could talk to him about everything else.

Bonnie had seen it. Tom had been doing something very right and he had been doing it right for years.

In the early part of June Curry had worried that Tom was not seeing Huck and her clearly. He occasionally confused the two Hucks, and he had trouble adjusting to Curry as being mother and businesswoman. But that wasn't the problem. The problem was that he didn't see himself clearly.

Tom didn't believe in himself. He thought of himself as a failure, a wounded man with much more wrong with him than the still-damaged muscles and nerves of his leg.

Oh, Tom, how have you failed? You have a daughter who loves you, a wife who is divorcing you with fond regret. And you are the hometown boy who made good. None of us around here pay any attention to your professional success because we don't understand how good you are, but no one in Gleeson has earned the kind of national recognition that you have.

Yes, you are damaged physically; you have a wound in your leg and now you can't have children. But that wound, that one malformed fetus, are things that happened to you, things that were done to you; don't make them into symbols of some deeper failing. They aren't.

Curry stood up, shaken, slowly clearing the table, scraping the chicken bones and corn cobs onto one of the plates.

And, Tom, why can't I talk to you like this? My thoughts have poetry, eloquence, but when I speak, I am crisp, glib, and offhand.

Curry had always thought of herself as an open person, as blunt and forthright.

But no. I always say what's on my mind, yet I never speak of what's in my heart. People know what I think, but never what I feel. Not even you, Tom.

Is it because there's always been so much doing, so much daily bustle in my life, doing things for Huck, and then for Gran, and later for Myra? So much day-

to-day ins and outs, running the store, getting Huck to school, Gran to bed, Myra to the doctor, that there was never time to say the things that mattered, to say the things that counted?

I started listening to you, Tom, that evening by the creek. As your friend and your lover. I have done that, I've let you talk, but I haven't spoken. I haven't said all that you need to hear.

Have I even told you that I love you?

But Curry said nothing to Tom, neither that evening nor the next morning. She just kissed Diana and told her to come back any time, perhaps next summer, "even if your father's not here."

Diana was sweet. Curry was sure that she and Huck had said—if *said* was the right word—some private farewells the night before, but when she turned to him, she lost her usual poise.

"Huck, I..."

He put his arm around her shoulders—although he had never touched her in front of Curry or Tom before. "Now, listen, when all those lawyers sit down to figure out what to do with you, tell them that the Jameses want visitation rights too."

"Visitation rights!" Tom sounded startled.

Diana laughed shakily. "You know that Mother will let me see Dad anytime."

And Curry knew that to be right. The greatest threat to father and daughter was not Phillip, but Tom himself...if Tom were to decide, in advance, that things would not work, if he refused to try.

"Come on, sweetheart," Tom was saying gently. "We've got to get going."

Huck kissed her and, with gallantry that astonished his mother, opened the car door for her.

But Diana turned. "Curry?"

"Yes?"

"I don't know how to say this, but..."

"Tell me."

"A couple of years ago everybody at school started calling each other by their middle names, it was really dumb, but they were doing it, and I felt strange about mine, and Mother said I could say it was Jane if I wanted a real girl's name, but—"

"I don't get it," Huck interrupted. "What is your middle name?"

"The same as Dad's. James."

"Oh, that's right," Curry remembered. She looked at Tom, wishing she could say more. "Huck was so pleased when we got her birth announcement."

"I was?" Huck was surprised.

"No, not you. Your father." For once Curry had made the mistake. "Although, come to think of it, you enjoyed the birth announcement as much as we did. You ate it."

"No wonder he eats so much now, Curry," Tom put in, "if you only fed him paper when he was a baby. But, Diana, what was the point of your story?"

"Well, it was just that Mother said I could change my middle name, but she told me how much your friends—Curry, and Huck's father—had always meant to you, so I didn't change it, but

I still didn't like it." Diana took a breath and turned to Huck and Curry. "But I just wanted you to know that I do like it now and that I'm proud to have it as a part of my name."

For a moment, looking at this girl, her blue eyes—Tom's blue eyes—sparkling with tears, Curry was afraid that she was going to cry too, and it took a moment of scurried farewells before she could be sure of her composure.

That night as she set the table she automatically picked up four forks and then had to put one back. It was like when Huck's father had left for Vietnam; it had taken awhile to remember not to set a place for him.

In fact, she should have put back two forks. Although he should have had plenty of time to get back from Watertown, Tom didn't show up for supper.

Huck was restless and Curry sent him into town to meet up with his friends, and then the house seemed achingly empty.

I'm not a schoolgirl who must sit at home and wait until her boyfriend calls. I wasn't like that when I was younger; I'm certainly not going to do it now.

Tom was sitting on the front steps when Curry came around the corner of his father's house. He again had some small piece of wood across his knees, but he was leaning back on his elbows, staring across the road to the fields beyond.

"Ah, Curry, how did you know I was over here moping?"

"I didn't." She sank down next to him. "But I was over there moping."

He smiled but said nothing.

"We missed you at supper."

"I thought you and Huck might like some time alone."

She shook her head. "One thing a sixteen-year-old never admits to is wanting to be with his mother."

"I certainly wouldn't know anything about that."

They were both quiet. The sunflowers by the barn would blossom in another week or so; the rough stems were tall. It had been a good year; there'd been enough rain.

Would it be a good year for the two of them too?

There was so much she wanted to say to him, so much he needed to hear. She didn't know where to start.

"Did Diana get off all right?" *Oh, wonderful, that's just exactly what you want to say.*

Tom nodded.

"I'm going to miss her," she said.

"Tell me about it."

Well, all right, I will. "I'm sure I would have loved her whatever she was like just because she is yours."

Tom looked up, startled by the sincerity in her voice, but when he said nothing, she went on. "But after a while, that almost didn't matter. She's so bright, so enthusiastic; she's one of those people who will always be happy, because whatever happens to her, she will be determined to be happy. I think the world needs people like that."

Tom nodded. "She's always been like that.

Even when she was a little kid. When I got back from...from Nam, that used to fascinate me, how cheerful and eager she always was.''

Suddenly he straightened. "You know, if any of what Bonnie was saying was true, it's probably because of that.''

"I'm not sure that I follow you.''

"I've always loved her. I'm sure of that now. But for a long time I didn't really understand my feelings for her"—Curry didn't find that too surprising, not knowing his own father as she did—"and all I could really say to myself was that she was interesting.''

"Interesting? That seems like an odd thing to think about your child.''

"Well, maybe. Part of it might be that I wasn't around all the time, and when I'd come home, well, Trish already knew everything about her, but I wouldn't, so she'd get to tell me what her dolls were up to and things like that. And I found it interesting.''

Curry thought of all the times when she had had to force herself to listen to a very young Huck talk on and on about things she already knew—"You know what, Mommy?"—how she would sometimes, in her anxiousness about all the things that she had to get done, simply tune him out. "Well, it's no wonder that she can talk so well to you now.''

"Can she?" He looked surprised.

"Good heavens, yes. None of the teenagers I know are as articulate and open with their parents as she is with you.''

"Really? That's odd. I assumed—''

"You automatically assumed that everybody else was doing a lot better than you were."

"I suppose I don't have anything to compare it to. Except for Huck now, she's the only teenager I know."

"Do you realize that even if things aren't ideal, you've not been such a dreadful father after all?"

"That's kind of a new one to wrap my mind around, but if it's true, I owe it all to—" He stopped.

"To what?"

He stood up. "Not to clean living, that's for sure." He put out his hand to pull her up. "Come in and see the house, you haven't looked around in weeks."

Certain that he had ended the discussion, Curry allowed him to pull her up, but she wondered what he had been about to say. What or who could he possibly owe it all to? Certainly not his father or to Trish. Oh, well, he didn't seem to want to tell her, and her experience with a son had taught her that confidence can't be forced.

It was true that she hadn't looked over the improvements on the house. With Tom paying Huck, she didn't want her son to think she was checking up on how he did his job. And when she had been over alone with Tom...well, she had simply paid no attention to the house.

Curry was astonished. They were so far along. All the rewiring and plumbing was done, the new bathrooms were in place, the new kitchen appliances and cabinets were installed, and the double-glazed windows were in. The bathrooms weren't tiled, the new plaster work wasn't sanded yet, the layers of linoleum hadn't been ripped up, but the house was almost done.

"I had no idea," she marveled.

"It was all that help. Huck is strong and he works hard, and Diana's patience for detail is like—"

"Yours," she finished for him.

He shrugged, but he was smiling. "Do you think it will sell?"

"Like everything in South Dakota, it depends on the crops. You know that, Tom."

"You don't sound optimistic."

"I don't? If this weather holds and the grain prices don't drop, everyone is going to be painting their hearts out next spring."

But the dismal tone in Curry's voice had nothing at all to do with the crops. It was quite simply that when Tom finished the house, he would leave.

Chapter Nine

Curry started hating hearing about the house, about Sears getting the tile in, about Tom choosing a stain for the floors. And she heard a great deal about it; without Diana around, Curry had the full benefit of Huck's confidences and they were entirely centered around the house.

One morning she was coming out of her bedroom, about to go downstairs, when she heard Huck call to her.

She turned. The bathroom door was open, and he was standing at the sink, shirtless and shaving.

"What is it, Huck?"

The sight of him shaving still startled her sometimes. He had to shave almost every day now, and it reminded her how close to being grown up he was.

He leaned toward the mirror and stuck his jaw out as he finished stroking off the last bits of shaving cream. "You remember when we were talking about Joe Oates last year?"

Curry nodded—although she had no idea which conversation about Joe he was referring to. Joe was a classmate of Huck's; he was a guard on the basketball team.

Huck rinsed off the razor, shaking the drops of water off the head. He then bent to the towel rack, wiping off his face without bothering to unfold the towel. "You know how you said that maybe one of the reasons Joe was sometimes better than me was because he was hungrier, because he had to get a basketball scholarship to go to college and I didn't?"

Curry nodded again. Joe Oates was much more driven than Huck; he worked harder because he had more to work for.

"Is that still right? Not about Joe, but about there being money for me to go to college?"

"Yes, Huck. It's the money that your father earned for you."

"Is there a lot of it? Enough for more than college?"

"More than college?" Curry didn't know what he was talking about. If he wanted a van or if he wanted to travel for a year or so, something that he thought she was going to disapprove of, his manner would be much more defiant than it was.

"Well, Tom says..." Huck stopped, a little self-conscious.

'Tom says what?"

"That if you want to be an architect, you've got to—"

"An architect?" Huck? An architect?

"Is that so weird?" Now he was adequately defensive.

"No," Curry said quickly, "goodness, no. I just

didn't know that you were even thinking about it."

Huck relaxed. "I wasn't. But in school whenever they pass out what you ought to be because of your tests scores and all, *architect* is always on my list. I guess because math is such a breeze for me and because I do so well on those silly fold-up-this-box tests."

"The spatial reasoning skills tests."

"That's right. Anyway, I never thought about it because, I mean, I didn't really know what they did. Even when they were putting up the college building, I didn't connect that with architects. Pretty dumb of me."

"You were only nine." When the single building that housed the community college had been erected, Curry and Huck had had to go check on its progress nearly every day, an interest that did not originate with Curry.

"But then, once I started working with Tom," Huck continued, "it started to make sense. I wouldn't want to fix up old buildings like he does; I'd rather plan new ones. But Tom says that to be an architect, you have to go to graduate school"—Huck worked his way through the two words slowly as if they were a new concept—"after college."

"Don't let worries about money stop you. There's enough." Curry had no idea what architecture school cost—if that was the right word for it—but even if it cost as much as medical school, there'd be enough money. She'd make sure of it. She could always go back to selling paint. No, maybe she'd do carpets this time; the markup on carpets was wicked, and Gleeson didn't have a carpet store, just special orders from the department store or Sears. You could pick up roll ends in Sioux Falls; major costs would be shipping and inventory...

"Well, I just wondered, that's all." Huck picked his shirt off the radiator and started to pull it on. The phone rang. "Do you want me to get that?" Clearly he considered this conversation over.

"No, I will." Reluctantly she turned back to her room; she would have rather continued talking to Huck.

She was pleased with what he had said, more pleased than he would ever know. Even if nothing came of it, even if he changed his mind, at least he had an interest now. She had seen enough of this town to know how restless the older boys got. Again and again it was the ones who had some direction, some motivation, who made it through the last two years of high school without getting into trouble. Now Huck had something that would help him through these difficult times, and Tom had helped him find it.

Oh, Tom, bless you. Just when he needed a man the most, you came. You were here for him when his father could not be.

Curry sat on her bed and picked up the phone. "Hello."

"Hello," a polite female voice said, "I have a call for Mr. Winchester. Is he there?"

"No," Curry answered unthinkingly. "I'm afraid he's retired and moved to Florida, but I can—"

"Retired!" The voice was a great deal less polite. "Ah ... can you hold the line?"

In a moment a man's voice was in her ear. "This is Dade Caldwell. What's this about Winchester retiring?" He was upset.

Curry was hard pressed to see how anything about Cal Winchester's retiring could possibly be such a blow. He hadn't been a bad representative for the seed company, but still ... "He retired last fall, and—"

"Last fall? But he swore—"

What an idiot she was. "Mr. Winchester" meant one person to her, but it was a name shared by another. She was getting as bad as the younger Mr. Winchester. "Are you talking about *Tom* Winchester?"

"Of course. Thomas J. Winchester."

"I thought you meant his father," Curry apologized, feeling like a bit of an idiot. "Tom's not here at the moment, but I can give him a message."

The man recited a phone number that Curry obediently wrote down on the top of the Kleenex box. "Now, will you please try and get him to call back. He never returns calls."

Curry wasn't surprised. "I'll do my best."

As she hung up, looking for something more reliable to copy the number down on, she noticed the 504 area code. She had no idea where 504 was.

Impulsively she picked up the phone and dialed a single digit.

"Operator, may I help you?"

"Marge, this is Curry James. Can you tell me where area code 504 is?"

"Just a second... it's Louisiana, the eastern part."

Louisiana? Curry thanked Marge and hung up. Why would anyone in Louisiana call Tom? Curry knew nothing about Louisiana—she could go from one year to the next without thinking about that state—which was okay; people in Louisiana probably went their whole lives without thinking about South Dakota.

Huck was on his way over to Tom's so she sent the message with him, but Tom didn't come back until late afternoon.

"You're sure not in a hurry to return the call," she commented.

He shrugged. "He's been after me for more than a year; another couple of hours aren't going to hurt."

"A year? What is he? A process server? A debt collector?"

"No, he's got this staircase that needs work."

"And he's waiting a *year* for you to come fix his stairs?"

"This isn't just any set of stairs, it's made of chestnut with this amazing serpentine railing. An absolute beauty and she's shot full of termite damage," Tom said as he dialed. "And quite frankly, if I were him, I wouldn't let anybody put their hands on her but me."

At least he was confident about something.

Tom tucked the phone under his chin and leaned back against the counter, straightening

when he got an answer. "Caldwell, this is
Winchester... I found some chestnut planks sitting in a barn in Iowa; God only knows how they
got there, but we're all set now... No, you ar-
range the shipping... about a week or ten days,
I'd say... No, just pay me when I'm done...
Look, if I said I'll be there in a week, I'll be there
in a week."

A week! Tom was leaving in a week.

He was hanging up the phone. "The only thing I
don't like about my work is having to deal with rich
people; they're just intolerable. I'm going to take
up mobile home repairs—you get nicer people in
mobile homes."

His voice seemed very far away.

"You'll be done with your father's house in a
week?"

Oh, Tom, how can you go?

"Sure. With Huck and Diana, things went a lot
faster than I ever expected. And I'm just going to
hire someone to paint. Labor's so cheap right now
that it really doesn't make sense for me to do it
myself, and I suppose you'll know who can do it
right."

Why was he talking about paint? Curry had
talked about paint six days a week for thirteen
years, and she thought it the most boring subject
ever invented.

"And then you'll be going."

"Sure, there's this—" Tom stopped and looked
at her for a moment, but before he could say anything, the screen door slammed and then Huck
appeared in the kitchen.

"Who's going somewhere?"

"Tom's leaving in a week."

Huck grimaced. "I was hoping you'd stay the summer, but I guess the house is almost done and all. Where are you going? Back to Bemidji?"

"No, New Orleans."

New Orleans! Curry had seen pictures of New Orleans. It had these narrow streets and wrought iron balconies; it looked like it was on a different planet than South Dakota.

Huck seemed to think so too, and he was eagerly asking questions about the city.

Tom laughed. "I don't know any of that. Why don't you just come with me and see for yourself?"

Huck stared at him. "You aren't serious, are you?"

"Sure I am. Why not? You aren't doing much around here, the store doesn't really need you, and I could use a second pair of hands. You could see New Orleans, see where the Mississippi has taken all the topsoil."

Huck was red with longing, but he knew he was not a free man. For this, he needed permission. "Oh, Mom, can I?" he pleaded. "Please let me go."

Curry was hesitant. "We'll—"

"Don't say we'll talk about it later. What's to talk about? I'll be all right; you know I will be."

Curry didn't know that, not in the least. Her knowledge of New Orleans was limited to the song "The House of the Rising Sun," and that wasn't particularly reassuring.

"I'll look out for him," Tom promised.

Well, he would be with Tom; if she couldn't trust Tom to return her child safely, who could she trust? And Huck needed to travel; as long as she had the money for it, he had a right to see more of the world than eastern South Dakota.

"You'll have to swear to me," she said, "that one of you will look at the calendar every day, and if it's Labor Day, Huck had better be on his way to the airport. I've got to take trigonometry next year and I'm not doing it without him around."

It took Huck a moment to realize what she had said, then he shouted and shot one hand in the air just as he did on the basketball court. He hugged her enthusiastically. "You're a brick, Mom, a real brick."

"Thank you, darling," she returned dryly. But Curry was pleased. Huck had not voluntarily embraced her in years.

He started chattering, asking Tom all about New Orleans and what they would be doing. As Tom started to draw a picture of the staircase on the cover of the phone book, Curry drifted out to the porch.

She was not going to feel sorry for herself, she just wasn't. So Tom was leaving and taking Huck with him. She had known all along that Tom would go, and Huck would be back after a few weeks.

She'd be alone. She'd be down to one fork on the table, so what? Huck was going off to college year after next anyway. She'd known that would happen. That's why she had sold the paint store and gone back to school. That's why she wanted to teach, to fill the void that Huck's growing up would leave. This next month would just be a dress rehearsal for what would happen later. What was the big deal?

Huck came charging out on the porch. "Can I go tell the guys, Mom?"

"Of course."

Tom had followed Huck and as the screen door banged behind the boy, he sat down next to Curry on the glider. He put his arm across her shoulders.

"It was good of you to ask him," she said. "He's thrilled."

"He is, isn't he?" Tom looked pleased. "And it was good of you to let him go."

He's growing up. I can't expect him to be around here forever. And right now maybe he needs to be with you more than he needs to be with me.

But she wasn't going to think about that. Deliberately she changed the subject. "I guess he's talked to you about this business of wanting to be an architect. What do you think?"

"That it might be the thing for him. He does like buildings and he's probably got too much imagination, too many ideas of his own, to be satisfied as a general contractor."

"We know where he got the imagination from."

Tom shook his head. "He's different from his father. His imagination is more visual, and he's a lot more practical, which is probably something you're to blame for, madam."

Curry shrugged. Life hadn't given her much

choice but to be practical. "How much is this going to cost? Is it as much as medical school?"

"Lord, no. Not even by half. Listen, if it's a problem, I can—"

"That's a relief," she interrupted. "I wasn't looking forward to selling carpets."

"Selling carpets? What are you talking about?"

As Curry told him, she thought about the sentence she'd interrupted. Tom almost certainly had been about to offer to help with Huck's tuition. She ran her thumb over the scar on her forefinger. Was that what the promise had become? Money? He would leave, but he'd send money?

"Curry, you're incredible." Tom laughed when she finished.

"No, I'm not. Money's easy; a person can always make money. It's the rest that's the hard part."

Why had she said that?

She started to stand up, but the arm around her shoulders tightened and Tom held her there. "What do you mean—the rest is the hard part?"

"Nothing. I was just talking."

"No, you weren't."

She didn't answer, but when he pulled her closer, she let her cheek rest against the soft blue cotton of his work shirt. "It's not like you to be worried," he said.

Oh, no. I worry. I get scared. I just don't have anyone to show it to, that's all.

He went on. "If you're worried about being alone next month, then—"

"Worried about being alone?" She sat up. "Me? Why should I be worried about that?"

Hey, I'm a pro at this. People leave me all the time.

Her parents, her grandmother, Huck's father, everyone that she'd ever cared about—except Tom and Huck. They were just going to New Orleans. This ought to be easy.

But it wasn't.

"What I was about to say," Tom went on calmly, "was why don't you come with us? School's over; you don't have a crop or livestock to worry about. So come."

Go with them? With Tom and Huck to New Orleans? This was the adventure Huck had dreamed of.

No, it was *Huck's father* who used to plan the adventures, and they were the dreams of childhood. She and Tom were no longer children.

She shrugged his arm off her shoulders. "No, thanks. South Dakota is no picnic in August; can you imagine what New Orleans would be like?"

He looked at her for a long moment. "Don't joke."

"Me? Don't joke? You're a fine one to say that."

But what else am I supposed to do? Do you want the truth, Tom? That I think I can make it when you go, that I think that I can go on being myself, good old Curry James, as tough as prairie grass, as solid as a grain elevator. But if we go to New Orleans together, with its music, its bright confetti and strange flowers, I don't know how I can come back here alone.

I don't want to be like this. I wish I could be different. I wish I didn't feel like I have to protect myself, like I have to circle the wagons because the Indians are coming, but without you here . . .

She found herself at the edge of the porch, looking out across the drive to the red barn.

Tom, I need you. I've only thought about how you need me because of all that troubles you. I've not thought about how I need you because of all that's wrong, that's limited, about me.

She felt his hands close around her shoulders.

"Is it that you don't want Huck to know about us?" he asked.

"What?" She felt dazed, confused.

"We don't have to go to New Orleans as lovers if that would make you uncomfortable around Huck. I'd just like you to be there; it wouldn't matter if we didn't share a room."

"No, no, it's not that," she said, not really sure what she was saying. "He doesn't run my life. If there were a man who was going to be part of my life, I wouldn't mind if Huck knew—"

Tom's hands fell off her shoulders.

Curry charged on. "But I don't want him thinking I take on lovers for a temporary good time."

The afternoon light was hot through the mesh of the screen porch. The air outside looked still. Curry felt sick.

She hadn't meant that. *If there were a man who was going to be part of my life . . .* This one was. If she never saw or spoke to him again, he would still be part of her life. He always had been; he always would be.

She'd said that because she'd been trying to punish him, to hurt him because he had hurt her.

Well, she had succeeded. His face was blank, expressionless, but his eyes said everything that he never would.

"Oh, Tom, I didn't mean—"

He was shaking his head, not listening to her. "Surely you know that if there were any woman I could make a promise to, it would be you. But I can't; I wouldn't believe myself."

He was so sure he'd fail that he wouldn't even try.

"And it's not just you," he went on. "It wouldn't be fair to Huck, to promise him that I could ... could be a stepfather to him."

Stepfather? Curry stared at him. What was this about stepfathers? Who had ever breathed a word about that?

"Maybe Trish's banker has it in for him to be a stepfather," he was saying, "but I know that I don't."

Why did he think that? What did he think was involved? He had only spent half the summer providing Huck with a role model; he was willing to pay for his education; he had just committed himself to spending nearly a month with him, supervising him through all the temptations and dangers of a city like New Orleans. Curry knew plenty of fathers who would go peaked at the thought of that. But Tom had offered willingly, readily, cheerfully.

And this was a man who said he would be a bad stepfather?

That simply did not make sense. Unless *step-father* was another one of Tom's labels, another word he couldn't, for some reason, stand to apply to himself. Or was it another one of those things he wouldn't even attempt to try?

Oh, God, what *else* was wrong with him?

Chapter Ten

Curry looked at the thermometer nailed to the side of the porch. Ninety-two degrees. The sun was glaring against the side of the barn with August-white light. She leaned against her car and then jerked away. The metal was hot, biting.

Tom had put the camper back on his pickup, and he was putting Huck's suitcase and knapsack in.

"Is that it?" he asked.

"What do you mean 'is that it?'" Huck called back. He was so excited he could hardly stand it. "Mom made me take a ton of stuff; I'll never use it all."

Left to his own devices, Huck would have taken a pair of cutoffs and a basketball.

"Then I guess we're ready."

Curry came forward. "Good-bye, Huck."

"Bye, Mom." He let her hug and kiss him. "Do you want me to write?"

"I'd love it."

"I'll see what I can do." He grinned at her and then went around to the front of the truck, leaving her alone with Tom.

"You have Caldwell's address and phone number?"

"Yes."

Tom's blue work shirt was unbuttoned. His hands were in his pockets, and the shirt sleeves rippled in the wind, molding against the muscles of his arms.

"Well, then..." He wasn't looking at her; his blue eyes were turned toward the fields, squinting in the sun. He didn't know what to say.

She didn't either.

"I'll look after him, Curry. You know I will."

"I know."

She looked down at her feet. They were bare, peeping out beneath the hem of her jeans. She traced a line in the dirt with her toe.

"Well, then—"

"Oh, Tom..." *How can you go?*

He pulled her to him. His chest was warm against her cheek, and she could feel the strength of his arms and his legs. He lifted her chin and kissed her, long and hard.

"Good-bye, Curry."

"Good-bye, Tom."

There wasn't anything else to say.

She went around to the front of the truck. Huck was already in, the window rolled down.

She put her hand on his arm. "You wear your seatbelt, now."

"Oh, Mom, I always do."

She heard the door on the other side open, then close. She didn't look at Tom; she couldn't bear to.

The truck started and she stepped away.

"Is it okay if I clean your room?" This was to Huck.

"What would you want to do a thing like that for?"

"Is it okay?"

"Sure."

The truck backed out, turned, and headed down the drive. Curry went around to the front of the house and watched as it turned from the lane onto the blacktop. It dipped down into a little hollow and then reappeared at the rise, smaller now, disappearing, the red shape becoming a black dot and then nothing.

She sank down on her front steps alone.

There had been times when Curry had ached to be alone. She'd come home from the store, tired of the chatter, sick to death of being nice to her customers, and Gran or Myra, after a long day alone, would want to talk, would want her to talk, expecting her to pass on every bit of news that had come into the store. "Now, who *else* came in?"

Huck would get jabbering fits, going on endlessly, telling her some pointless schoolboy joke. "Don't you get it, Mom? I can tell it again."

And she would long for some quiet, for everyone to go away.

Well, everyone was gone now.

There was nothing she needed to be doing. Not one thing from now until time to register for the fall semester. No paint cans to count, no papers to write, no son to feed. She could sit here on the steps, with nothing to do, no one to account to, just the Dakota sunshine on her face and arms and the wind in her hair. The goldenrod had blossomed and the meadowlarks were singing from the cottonwoods. It was a quiet world, quiet, peaceful, empty.

And you're wasting time feeling sorry for yourself.

Curry stood up briskly, dusting off her hands on the seat of her jeans. She went back around the house, into the kitchen. Quickly, before she could stop to think, to cry, she pulled the plug on the refrigerator and sprayed oven cleaner into the oven. Defrosting the freezer and cleaning the oven were among her favorite activities, right up there with plucking her eyebrows and shooting herself in the foot. But if she got the oven clean, at least she could put the battery back in the smoke detector.

Curry worked hard, scrubbing out her kitchen into the late evening. She hated every instant of it. When she was done, her hair stuck to her forehead and neck in sweaty mats, and her fingertips were shriveled from the ice, the water, and the Brillo pads.

She showered and as she lay in bed, waiting to fall asleep, the attic fan pulling a powerful breeze through her open window, she missed Tom more than she thought she could stand.

Oh, Curry, come on. You can take anything.

The next morning she started on Huck's room. He was right, she did't know why she wanted to clean it, but it seemed like the thing to do.

She went through his drawers, sorting out the torn T-shirts, the socks with holes in them, the too-small jeans. She moved all his shoes off the floor of the closet and mopped it. She shoved all the furniture to the center of the room and scrubbed the baseboards—something that Huck was sure to care about just terribly. And then Curry decided that as long as everything was moved around, she might as well repaint the room, so she went down to her basement to see what paint she had and to find drop cloths and brushes.

Six times a week for thirteen years, Curry had told people to clean their paint brushes well, but she did not practice what she preached, and her own brushes were rock solid.

She would have to go into town.

As she was trying to get a brush through her hair, the phone rang.

Breathless, she rushed to answer. It might be . . .

"Mrs. James? This is Tracy."

Curry blinked. What a surprise this was. Tracy Morgan, Huck's girlfriend . . . or rather Huck's girlfriend from last year. Curry hadn't thought about her in weeks, and she suspected that Huck hadn't either.

"Welcome home. How was your summer?"

"It was great, really terrific."

They chatted about that for a moment, and then Tracy asked hesitantly, "Is Huck there?"

"Oh, Tracy, I'm afraid he's not. He's gone to New Orleans with a friend of his father's."

"New Orleans?" The girl was quiet for a moment. "But that's so *far*."

Well, yeah, I thought so too. "But he'll be back just before school starts."

"I guess I'll see him then."

Given the size of their high school—to say nothing of the size of Huck himself—Curry was certain that Tracy would see Huck in school. Beyond that she could make no promises. She said good-bye to Tracy and went into town.

Gleeson was bustling—at least by its own standards. The crops had all come in at nearly record levels. It had been a good year.

Jeff Ransom straightened when Curry walked into the paint store. He came around the counter quickly.

"I need some paint," she said right away. She didn't want him to think she was in here after her money. "I'm painting my boy's room."

"Oh, that's right. I heard he was off to Louisiana."

"He left yesterday."

"He went with Tom Winchester, didn't he?"

Curry nodded and drifted over to the display of color chips, looking at them as if she cared what color Huck's room was.

Jeff followed her. "Winchester sure knows his stuff, doesn't he? He was in here one day when George Toggin was and he figured out what they should do to get paint to stay on that brick of theirs. In fact, George and I were just saying this morning that it was too bad he didn't stay. He would have added a lot to the town."

I don't need this. I don't need to hear that people think Tom should have stayed.

Jeff went right on. "At least we don't have to worry about him putting us all out of business."

"That's hardly a danger. Tom's no business-man."

"No, but you are. That's what we were all saying at the Merchants' Association meeting last week, that if Curry James and Tom Winchester put their heads together, the rest of us could just close down tomorrow."

Oh, Jeff, don't, please don't . . . "Well, he never planned on staying. He was just here to redo his father's house."

"I hear that the Jenkinses went in to the real-tor's first thing this morning. Apparently, his wife's folks would help them with a downpay-ment."

"Chad Jenkins? That would be good if they de-cided to buy the place. I'd like having little kids living nearby." Curry hardly knew what she was saying.

"Those twins are something, aren't they?"

Two days ago, Tom, just two days ago, we were down by the creek, the water rushing, the grass soft, and you were strong and alive, your body with mine. And now I'm in a paint store, talking about other people's kids, other people's downpayments.

Is this my life? Is this all there is?

Curry got her paint and walked almost blindly toward her car, not seeing anyone, not speaking.

She felt like the world was stretched thin. The sun glittered against the parking meters, the shop doors closed with sharp clicks, car engines chugged and coughed. But none of it seemed real.

"Curry . . . Curry!"

Tom was real, and he was gone.

"Curry!" A hand closed on her arm and she turned. It was Bonnie.

"Curry, are you okay?"

Curry took a breath. "Goodness, yes, I'm fine." *Good old Curry James, she's always fine.*

Bonnie tilted her head sympathetically. "Do you miss Huck?"

Yes, him too.

But she didn't want to talk about it. What was the point in feeling sorry for herself? She pointed at the package Bonnie was carrying, one of the big green sacks from Betty Lou's fabric store. "What a lot of fabric you've got. You're going to be sewing from now until doomsday."

"Just Labor Day, I hope." Bonnie laughed. "Back-to-school clothes. You're lucky Huck's a boy."

"Are you kidding? If Huck were a girl, he'd have stopped growing by now."

"But if he were a girl, he might care about what he wore."

"That's true." Huck didn't care what he wore— just as long as he looked exactly like his friends. So a few times a year, Curry sat down in front of him with a tape measure and the Sears catalog. She measured him, figured out his size, and then re-ordered the same styles he had just grown out of. They'd have to do it as soon as he got home.

Back-to-school clothes . . . the Sears catalog . . . Yes, this is it. This is my life.

"Curry?"

Curry blinked. "What?"

"You looked like you were a million miles away."

Not a million, they aren't that far. "Sorry. It's just odd not having Huck around. I don't know what to do in town now that there's no reason to buy out the grocery store."

"Let's have some coffee, then."

They went into the bakery. There were so many people in town, feeling the ease of this year's good crops, that all the tables were full.

"Do you mind waiting?" Bonnie asked.

Usually Curry did, but not today. What difference did it make?

In a few minutes they got a table in the back corner. Janelle, the waitress, came over right away.

"I heard your boy went down to New Orleans. How long is he gone for?"

"He'll be back before school starts."

"Three weeks? That's a long time."

"Not long enough to get his room clean."

Janelle smiled briefly. "And I suppose he took Tom Winchester with him?"

"He did."

Janelle looked at Curry long and hard, and then she set down her pot and turned to face the room. "Anybody need anything?" she called. "I'm taking a break, so speak up now."

A few men called for their checks and Janelle whipped them off her pad. In a moment she came back and sat down at the table with Bonnie and Curry.

"This is a classy place," Bonnie commented.

"Isn't it, though? But customers are like kids—once you start giving in, they start expecting it." Janelle pulled a pack of cigarettes out of the pocket of her white apron, offered it to Curry and Bonnie, and then shook one out for herself. She lit it. "Ain't easy when men leave, is it?"

"No."

Curry and Janelle weren't close friends. Back in those early days, when they'd first been widows, they'd been scrambling so hard to bring up their kids, neither had had time for friendships. But Janelle had known in an instant what Jeff Ransom at the paint store hadn't, what even Bonnie hadn't realized: that Tom hadn't just left Gleeson, he'd left Curry.

"How did you know?" Curry asked.

"Oh, honey . . . back when they were building the college, one of the contractors up from Sioux Falls . . . Hell, I knew he wasn't staying and I knew he'd never ask me to go with him, not with my two kids, but you know how it is."

"I know."

"Well, it will be awful for a while. You just have to face that."

"But, Janelle, we've lost our husbands. This can't be as bad as that."

"Probably not, but it's a different sort of hurting. Because he's still out there, walking around. You can make yourself silly with hope; we couldn't do that the first time. That's the hard part, learning not to hope."

"I don't think that's my problem."

"Just plain, dumb misery?"

"Close enough."

"Do you want some unasked-for advice?" Janelle flicked the ashes off her cigarette.

"Sure."

"We were kids when our husbands died. We're not anymore. So give yourself your breathing space. You need time to wind down. Curry, you are a doer; I am too, but don't try to lose yourself in doing." Janelle gestured down at the paint can and sack of brushes that sat at Curry's feet. "Remember him. Talk about him. Don't pretend that it doesn't hurt. Then you can take up with your doing again."

"It seems self-indulgent."

"Honey, you're thirty-six, you're alone. That's not bad, but if you aren't going to indulge yourself, who is?"

"You've got a point."

"Of course I have." Janelle smiled and stubbed out her cigarette. "But don't hope, that's what will make you crazy." She stood up and, in a rustle of apron and uniform, was gone.

Bonnie had been quiet throughout and now she spoke. "Curry ... I had no idea—"

"That Tom and I were lovers?" How good it felt to say that aloud, to let someone know that it had happened.

"And so it's not just Huck you miss?"

"That's right."

"Listen, I don't know a lot about this. It sounds to me like Janelle is right, that you should talk it out. And if you need someone to listen, I'm here."

When Curry didn't say anything, Bonnie went on. "Remember I was there the day he came. There was ... I don't know, such warmth between the two of you, like you'd been friends forever and ever."

"We have been." *Oh, Tom...* Curry had to bite her lip, turn her face to the wall.

Curry had never had a close woman friend before Bonnie. When she was a girl, Huck and Tom had been enough. She didn't need anyone to giggle with as long as she had them. And then after she had lost them, she hadn't had time for friends at all. Never before had she looked across a coffee cup and seen another woman's eyes soft and waiting. And Curry was tempted.

But what was the point? Who would ever understand?

Bonnie touched her hand. "I had to divorce a man I still loved. I felt like no one would understand, and maybe no one ever did. But I have a sister in Fort Wayne ... my phone bills were unbelievable, but it helped."

Curry didn't have a sister. Right now, it felt like she didn't have anyone.

No, she had a friend.

And so, at a formica-covered table, tucked in behind the glass cases of cupcakes and peanut brittle, slowly, haltingly, Curry spoke. She talked about Tom—not about their childhood, but about being an adult with him. She spoke of June and July, how it had been, how she had felt with him, what it had been like to splash and to play, to relax, to know the warmth of his smile, the strength of his form, how she felt like a different person when she was with him, how she was the sort of person she wanted to be when she was with him.

Bonnie shook her head. "How odd ... you've always seemed so self-contained, so whole, like you don't need anyone."

"I need him."

"Is Janelle right? Is there really no chance that he'll ever be back?"

"Bonnie, I didn't see him for fifteen years and I can only guess as to why. But whatever was keeping him away didn't get solved just because I went to bed with him."

They were both silent, thinking. The people at the next table got up and left. Then in a moment they heard a cough and the rustle of bags and packages.

"Can I join you?" It was Nancy Triplett. Her daughter Megan was in Huck's class.

Bonnie glanced at Curry, and Curry spoke quickly. "Sure, but we're about to leave."

"I only have a minute, but I did need to talk to you." Nancy started rummaging in her purse, a roomy straw bag. But before she found what she was looking for, she stopped and looked up. "I hear Huck's out of town."

"Yes," Curry said for what seemed the hundredth time. "He's gone to New Orleans with a friend of his father's." *With the man I love.*

"That was Tom Winchester, wasn't it?"

"Did you know him?" Tony Triplett was a hometown boy, but like Bonnie, Nancy had come in from the outside.

"No, but of course Tony did. He saw him downtown sometimes and asked him to dinner, but he said he had a lot of work. I guess he never saw many people except you."

"Well, he was busy," Curry explained. "And his daughter was here. He wanted to spend time with her."

"That's not the way I heard it—"

Curry went stiff. Dear God, it wasn't all over town, was it?

"—it wasn't *Tom* that Diana was spending her time with."

Curry breathed. "That's true. She and Huck did have a thing going."

"When does he get back?"

"I doubt that he's coming back."

"Curry!" Nancy was shocked.

"I think," Bonnie put in gently, "that she was asking about Huck."

"Oh, Lord," Curry apologized, "of course Huck's coming back. Who would feed him except his mother? He'll be back the day before school starts."

"Meg and her friends are all dying to know if Huck and Tracy Morgan are still 'a couple.'"

"I haven't a clue." Curry tried to stay out of Huck's love life.

"I think my Meg would be pleased if Huck were fancy-free."

"I'm sure I'll be the last to know."

"Isn't that the truth?" Then Nancy seemed to remember why she had sat down and she started rummaging through her bag again. She pulled out a fistful of papers and lists. "We're trying to raise money for new band uniforms this year. We're having an auction and a white elephant sale. Since Huck's on the basketball team, I thought maybe you'd make some calls to get stores to donate things."

"I liked it better when I was one of the stores that got called."

"But you'll do it, won't you?"

"Oh, sure."

"Then here's your list. Now, don't let Betty Lou Toggin give you remnants; hold out for a needlepoint kit or good scissors or something, and—"

Curry took the list.

Life goes on.

Chapter Eleven

Tom was putting away his tools. He kept most of them in a heavy gauge steel mechanic's chest, the kind with casters and about a million little drawers, and, of course, every tool went back every night to exactly the place it had been the night before. Huck couldn't imagine being able to remember what went in each drawer, but Tom certainly managed it.

Huck had swept the floor, sorted the scrap lumber, and brought the tools over to Tom, but he didn't help put them away. Back home when he had first started working with Tom and thought that this nightly tidying up was a real pain, Mom had told him to bear with Tom; getting his tools lined up all nice and neat in just the right drawer probably made him happy. Huck had thought that anyone who was happy about a neat line of tools was a bit short on things to be happy about, but he put up with it, and by now, of course, he was used to it.

Tom slipped his chisels into their leather sheaths and unbuckled his tool belt, taking out the scraper he didn't think he'd use again. He put it away and then turned to Huck.

"What do you want to do tonight...besides eat, of course?"

"We can work if you want." Apparently, when Tom was on the road, he usually worked in the evening, but they hadn't worked one single evening in this whole week that they'd been in New Orleans. Huck didn't want to work—especially as they had already cleaned up—but he thought he ought to offer to spend the evening pounding old nails straight.

Tom smiled and shook his head. "You think I'm willing to pay you overtime? No way. Where do you want to go? The French Quarter?"

"You don't mind?"

"Not a bit."

They'd already been to the French Quarter, the old part of New Orleans, twice in the last week, but Huck liked it a lot. He wasn't so sure that Tom did. The place was pretty touristy—there were more T-shirt shops than anything else—but it was so different from anything at home.

Tom had said that part of the reason for the difference—beyond the fact that New Orleans was a city and Gleeson just a little turkey of a town—was that New Orleans was the least American of American cities because it had been ruled by both the French and the Spanish for a while. Well, whatever the reason, it was great and Huck was sure that coming here was the best thing that had ever happened to him. Working on the staircase was pretty interesting, and everything else was great. The buildings were great, the food was great; in fact, this entire trip was perfect, or at least it would be if there weren't quite so many nails that needed straightening, and if it were basketball season and New Orleans still had a team . . . and if Tom didn't feel like he had to apologize for him all the time.

It was strange, but Tom hated it whenever waitresses or motel clerks thought that they were related. It seemed like a natural enough mistake, and Huck didn't think that it was any big deal.

But not Tom. He always had to correct people. "Here's your son's Coke," a waitress might say, and Tom would say, "He's not mine. He's the son of some friends." Every single time he would say that, like he would wither up and die if these absolute strangers thought the two of them were related. It made Huck feel like he had hoof-and-mouth disease or something. "The son of a friend." Some honor.

Huck didn't know why it bugged him so much. He usually hated it when men called him "son." It was always part of that whole "poor, fatherless boy" routine, which was a song and dance he figured he could live without.

He kept telling himself to forget it. Tom was great about everything else. On the way down from South Dakota he had let Huck drive as much as he wanted to, and he had never turned down the car radio like Mom always did. Sure, he didn't say much, but when he did, it was always interesting. He'd start talking about something, and it would be so interesting that it would take you a while to realize that it was history like they teach in school.

And now that they were in New Orleans, Tom never told him what to do—except when they were working. In fact, when they weren't working, he usually let Huck decide what they'd do, which was why they were heading toward the French Quarter again.

Huck just liked walking around there. Bourbon Street was noisy and dirty, but he didn't care. There were always a ton of other people, and he liked the way you had to pick your way through the crowd. Downtown Gleeson was never that crowded, not even close.

And there was the music. Walking down the sidewalk, you could hear music in the bars, real live bands playing jazz. Maybe they weren't the finest musicians who ever lived, but they were a hell of a lot more exciting than a jukebox with the AM Top Forty, which was what passed for music back home.

Then sometimes a door to a certain kind of bar would swing open, and you could see the girls who danced there. If there was anything like *that* in Gleeson, he certainly didn't know about it.

Huck tried hard to be cool about not stopping to gawk at the doors to the topless bars like so many other guys were doing, but, of course, Tom noticed everything and in a couple more blocks, he stopped at a place with a red neon sign that said "The FunTime ReView." "Do you want to go in?"

Huck didn't know what to say. He felt like he

wasn't supposed to want to go in, but he did. The girls just wore these little tassels on top and just the skimpiest things on the bottom—G-strings he guessed they were called. Tammy Webster's swimming suit had enough fabric to cover ten of these girls, and he had thought he was going to *die* when he saw her for the first time this summer. Hell, yes, he wanted to go in.

Tom was holding open the door.

It was really dark inside; most of the light came from the spotlights shining on the girls. Huck looked at one of them and then looked away. He followed Tom to a table. It was sure different from looking at magazines.

A waitress came up; she had her clothes on, but her black blouse was really low-cut and clingy. It was showing more of her than most girls had to show. She stood super close to Tom, almost touching him. If he'd moved his head, he would have brushed against her breast. But he didn't.

"What can I bring you all?" she asked.

"Two dark beers, please."

That was strange.

Usually when they went into a bar, Tom just said, "What will you have, Huck?" Of course he wanted a beer. He drank, and Tom knew it. But Mom didn't like him to, and Tom knew that too. So Huck had decided not to push his luck and had always ordered Cokes.

But in a place like this . . . well, he wouldn't want to look all wimpy, ordering a Coke.

The beers came; they were dark, almost thick. He tasted his. He wasn't sure that he liked it.

"Do you like dark beer?" Tom asked.

"I don't think I've had it before."

"I wondered."

He bet that Tom did that deliberately, ordered a beer that he wouldn't like. Well, he'd rather have a beer that he couldn't drink than a Coke that he could. Tom must understand things like that.

Anyway, he wasn't here for the beer. The music was good. It was just on tape, but it had a heavy bass and a solid driving beat, the kind of rhythm that surged through you, that made you feel powerful and alive, that you felt... well, just everywhere.

At last Huck looked at the girls. There were three of them, each dancing on her own little pedestal. Two were blondes, and the other girl, the one nearest them, had dark hair. He thought she was the prettiest. Her costume—what there was of it—was red, with sequins on the bottom. The spotlight sparkled off the little triangle down in front, and just one strand of sequins ran around her hip and then disappeared. You could tell she was a little warm. Her skin was all rosy and moist and the spotlight glowed against her stomach, her legs, her shoulders, her breasts... there was just so much of her to look at. She looked great. She really did.

"It's a pretty hot night for this kind of work," he heard Tom say.

Huck looked over at him. He was sitting back, his chair away from the table, his legs crossed, all calm and relaxed, like this was nothing.

"You make it sound like they are working construction."

"Construction pays better, I imagine."

Huck looked back at the dark-haired girl. She was dancing with her shoulders back; he wondered how the tassels stayed on.

Only Tom would think of it that way, as if they were just working a regular job. But he guessed he was right; they were working, getting paid to dance like this.

Huck glanced around the room. Even though it was so dark, you could see it wasn't a very nice place to work. Pretty crummy, in fact. The floors were just boards, littered with stuff that no one had bothered to pick up—used matchbooks and a lot of wadded-up napkins that were little white splotches in the dark. Great place when the used napkins were the cleanest thing around. The tables were little, but not too close together. That was okay, it wasn't like you'd ever want to *talk* to anybody you'd met in a place like this.

"How old are the girls?" He didn't know why he asked Tom that, just for something to say. "Can you tell?" Huck never could.

"About thirty, I'd say."

Thirty! That was so *old*.

"But the one near us"—Tom gestured at the dark-haired one—"she's a lot younger, early twenties, but she's had a baby."

"She has? How can you tell?"

"Look at her stomach—those little white lines on either side are stretch marks. Some women get them when they are pregnant."

"They do?" He was probably sounding like a moron here, but he didn't know this.

"It's because their skin has to stretch so much when the baby's growing. It doesn't always happen; your mo—"

Tom stopped and Huck wondered if he had been about to say something about Mom. Then he thought about this girl dancing being someone's mother too. She wasn't wearing a wedding ring; maybe she hadn't been married when she had her baby and was having to work here.

He looked at her face, which he hadn't paid a lot of attention to before. She was smiling, but it didn't look like she meant it. Maybe this was "The FunTime ReView," but she sure wasn't having any fun.

And that took all the fun out of watching her.

It wasn't supposed to be like this. He had always guessed that topless dancers were nymphos or something, who really got off on being naked in front of people. But maybe this one was just an ordinary girl who had to stand up there and let guys ogle her stretch marks because she needed the money. It seemed sad.

And, you know, once you stopped looking at their bodies, you realized that they didn't dance very well. Lots of the girls at school danced better.

"You ready to go?" Tom asked—even though he had hardly drunk any of his beer.

"Yeah, I guess I am."

Tom didn't say anything until they were out on the sidewalk. Everything seemed hot and noisy. They walked for a bit. It was like a carnival. People

were buying cotton candy and T-shirts: "My
Grandparents Went to New Orleans and All They
Brought Me Was This Dumb Shirt." He had seen
the same shirt on a little kid earlier, only his
grandparents had been sailing on the S.S. Some-
thing-or-other. Talk about dumb.

Too bad they didn't have a "My Son Went to
New Orleans..." shirt so he could get it for Mom.
She'd get a kick out of it. In fact, she'd probably
wear it.

Huck wondered what she'd think of all this. It
was so different from South Dakota. She was
probably back at home, doing all the usual stuff,
reading or taking the dishwasher apart, while he
was down here, going to topless bars. It seemed
weird.

"Do you want to stop on the way back to Caldwell's"—Tom's voice broke into his thoughts—
"and get something to eat?"

Huck shrugged. "Sure. Why not?"

They left the French Quarter and stopped at a
lunch-counter café-type place that had a couple of
cop cars parked out in front of it. Tom always
looked for cop cars when he was hungry. "Don't
believe that thing about truckers knowing where to
eat," he had said. "Trucker food isn't bad, but the
cops are the ones who really know the local food."

Great. When he got home, maybe he'd have to
write a "What I Did on My Summer Vacation"
paper. *On my summer vacation this summer, I
learned that cops know where to eat and that it's no
fun watching naked ladies when they aren't having
fun.* That should thrill Mrs. Delancy.

It was late enough that a delivery man was loading up the sidewalk vending machine with the first edition of the morning papers, and Tom stopped to wait until he could get one. Huck went on into the restaurant. There were some video games, and he played a couple of rounds of Galaxy Shot. But, like the video games in the French Quarter, it had been rigged to be harder than the ones at home, and he didn't win like he should have.

It was tough being away from home. Worth it, but tough.

He went over to the table where Tom was sitting. The waitress was there, talking to him. Huck pulled out a chair, and she looked at him, surprised. She glanced back at Tom. "I didn't know your boy was with you."

Here it comes . . . let's have a drumroll . . . Here's Tom Winchester with his world-famous—

"He's not mine. He's the son of a friend."

The audience cheers madly. "Encore," they cry, "encore." Huck slumped down in his chair and opened his menu.

"But he's with you?" the waitress asked.

"Yes, we're working together."

"That must be real nice."

But she sure didn't sound like she thought it was real nice.

She took their order and left. Tom passed him the sports page, but none of the box scores were in it yet.

He guessed this business about "the son of some friends" bothered him so much because he really did admire Tom a lot. He'd like to be like

him. He was so good at what he did. Like this
staircase. After one look at it, Huck figured they
might as well set to it with crowbars. The thing
looked hopeless. But Tom had known exactly
what to do, and they were rebuilding the sucker.
Huck wondered if he would ever be that good at
anything.

And in so many other ways, he'd like to be like
Tom. Just this evening, he was so cool about
everything, not rubbing up against that waitress's
black blouse like anyone else would have, just
looking at the dancers like they were regular
people he felt sort of sorry for, ignoring the fact
that they didn't have any clothes on.

"You know a lot about girls, don't you?" Huck
heard himself say.

"Not about girls, I don't know anything about
girls. But I know a bit about women."

"That's what I meant."

"Was there something you wanted to know?"

"Not really."

That wasn't true. There was so much he wanted
to know. What it felt like, what you said, how
you knew if a girl really wanted to and when she
was just leading you on. But he guessed asking
wouldn't help.

"I haven't been faithful to Diana's mother, if
that's what you're asking."

Oh. He didn't know if he had been asking that
or not. Well, yeah, he guessed he had been.

It was no surprise when you thought about it.
Diana had said that Tom wasn't in Bemidji very
often at all. Just a couple of times a year.

And grown women really seemed to like Tom. All the time checkout counter ladies or waitresses would smile and start passing the time of day with him, real friendly-like. Huck had just thought people in New Orleans were friendly, but maybe it was—

Oh, God, what an idiot he was, what a complete and total idiot. No wonder this waitress tonight wasn't thrilled that Tom had some jerkwater kid hanging around.

"Listen, Tom," he spoke really fast; he wanted to apologize. "You know how if you go into a restaurant ahead of me, the waitress sometimes will start talking to you and then quits when I come up?"

Tom glanced at him. "Yes?"

"Why didn't you tell me to get lost?"

It took Tom a minute to understand and then he shook his head with a little laugh. "First of all, it's not like every woman who says good morning is planning on falling into bed with me, and second... Huck, you are never going to believe this, not ever, but maybe I'd rather be with you than one of them."

Huck frowned. He liked Tom, he really did, more than he liked anyone, but if Diana turned up... "You're just saying that."

"No, I'm not. Things change as you get older. And one thing is that sex gets less important."

Huck guessed that his disbelief showed on his face, for Tom smiled and went on. "It's partly a biological thing, hormone levels and all that. And also it's not a mystery anymore. One thing about being reasonably experienced is that you know sex is not always wonderful."

"It's not?" God, how couldn't it be wonderful?

"No, sometimes it's very routine. And sometimes it's—Oh, Lord," Tom interrupted himself, "you don't want my advice."

Was he ever wrong there. "No, go on... I mean, if you want to and all."

Tom looked at him for a second. "The mistake we make—we men, that is—is that we force the woman to do all the deciding. Just because a woman is willing... that's not enough of a reason to sleep with her. Sometimes you'll really regret it."

Huck would be happy just to have a chance to regret it.

"I think I've only loved one woman," Tom was saying, "and being with others just doesn't compare to that. You can do the same things, and it just doesn't feel the same, not like when you know her and love her, when nothing in the world, except maybe your child, is more important to you than her. After that..."

Tom's voice trailed off, and Huck didn't know what to say.

But it did seem too bad if Tom felt that way about Diana's mother, that they were getting a divorce. Everybody—Mom, Diana, everybody—had said that the divorce was a good thing, but they must not have ever heard Tom sound so wistful.

It didn't make any sense; none of it did. If Tom

loved Diana's mom so much, why didn't he see her more? And if he was so wild about spending time with Huck, why did he go around telling the whole world that they were nearly strangers?

The waitress brought their burgers and Huck reached for the ketchup. He had to bang the bottom of the bottle, and then a whole wad of the stuff gushed out all at once. It always happened that way.

And then suddenly he blurted it out. "How come it gives you the creeps everytime people think we're related?"

Tom put down his burger without taking a bite. "It doesn't give me the creeps."

"Then why do you always tell people that we aren't?"

"Because it's the truth."

"So? What difference does that make?"

Tom smiled. "You sound like your mother."

"No, I don't. She's really big on the truth."

Tom laughed. "But she has a sense of proportion about these things."

"I don't get it."

"She'd probably say that since we won't ever see any of these people again, they could think you and I were sisters, for all she'd care."

"Sisters?" Oh, he was joking. "Well, she's right, isn't she?"

"She usually is."

"Then if you agree with her, why do you keep telling people that I'm not your kid?" Huck turned and looked out the café's big front window. The streetlight glittered against the red finish of Tom's pickup. "You aren't ashamed of me or something?"

Tom's cup clattered in the saucer. "No, Huck, God, no. Whatever gave you that idea?"

Tom was leaning forward, this funny, worried, grown-up looking expression on his face.

Huck shrugged. "I don't know; it's just that you make such a big deal all the time about me being 'the son of a friend,' like I'm some random nobody."

"Some random...Oh, Huck, no." Now Tom looked away, through the plate glass out to the parking lot. When he turned back, he looked sort of tired and real serious.

"I don't like doing things that I'm bad at," he said slowly.

What did that have to do with anything?

"And when I've hurt people," he went on, "I never know what to do, I never know how to stop hurting them—Diana, her mother, and yours too."

Mom? How has he hurt Mom?

"So I usually don't do anything, I just leave, but this time...listen, Huck, you've just got to understand this; it's really important to me that you do."

Huck didn't know what to say. "Okay."

Tom took a breath. "I've only had two real friends in my life. Just two. Your mother and your father. That you are their son makes you just about—" He broke off, took a drink of water, and started again. "I don't know if you will understand this or not, but because you are 'the son of some friends' and because those friends are who they are, that makes you every bit as important to me as Diana is, and she is my own."

This was embarrassing. Nice but embarrassing.

And Tom kept going. "I know you don't remember Huck—your father, that is. But he meant the world to me, he really did. I know he's dead, but he's still my friend, and when people think I'm your father, well, I feel like I'm grabbing the credit that really belongs to him."

"Credit? For me? I'm not a credit to anyone."

Tom shook his head. "Oh, no. You're wrong there. He'd be so proud of you, Huck. You just can't know how proud he'd be."

Huck squirmed a little. So Tom didn't think he was a blot on the face of the earth. That was neat.

Huck thought he ought to say something, but he didn't quite know what. "I wouldn't mind if we were . . . well, related. I mean, I'm not related to anyone."

"Except your mother."

"Oh, well, sure. But mothers don't count."

"Not so in my book," Tom said right away. "Your mother counts more than anyone."

They didn't go back to the French Quarter at night, just once during the day to look at the buildings. In the evenings after supper they went to other parts of town or played basketball.

Tom's game was improving a lot since they had played with Mom and Diana this summer. His shooting still wasn't as accurate as Huck's, but his concentration was super. In the early part of a game Huck would have to play as hard as he ever had, but then Tom's leg would get tired and weak. The muscles and nerves had been all shot up, he had said, and they were almost all right, but only almost.

"That's too bad," Huck had answered.

"Other guys got hurt worse."

And Huck could tell that Tom was thinking about his dad.

It was funny, but he never thought about his dad. When he was a kid, it used to bug him sometimes that he didn't have one, but he was used to it, and anyway he only thought about it when the other guys would have these terrible fights with their fathers, and then he'd figure that he wasn't missing much.

But Tom thought about his father all the time. And it was clear that he still missed him a lot. That was sort of scary, that anything could go on hurting that long.

Caldwell's house, the one they were working on, was in a neighborhood called the Garden District, which had a lot of huge old houses. The Caldwells weren't home, and he and Tom were staying in a little building out back, which Tom said was a place where back in the old days the young bachelors of the family—guys about his age—could live with more freedom than if they were in the house. It sounded like a terrific idea to Huck. A couple of the houses in the Garden District still had them.

There was one house in the neighborhood that Tom really wanted to poke around in. You could tell, as he kept talking about it, about how the guy who owned it really cared about doing things right, how he reused all the old nails even though he was putting in air conditioning and more bathrooms. Tom would get off on something like that.

But it wasn't open to the public.

So they just kept driving past it. One time Tom got out of the truck and went to the iron railings just to look at the outside. The house was another one of those big white-columned numbers—Greek Revival, Huck now knew to call them—but Tom clearly thought it something special.

Tom rocked back on his heels. "It sure is tempting to go up and ring the bell." But then he turned away and started back to the truck. He wasn't going to do it.

Which seemed crazy. Why didn't he at least try if he wanted to go in so badly?

And he claimed he was Diana Winchester's father. She would try anything.

Huck called to him. "'It would, like, be fun.'"

Tom turned. "You aren't quoting my daughter, by chance?"

"Who, me?" Huck acted innocent. "I never quote anyone. I don't know how. Except that I had to learn part of *The Merchant of Venice* last year. I can quote that. Would you like to hear it? 'The quality of mercy is not strain'd,— It droppeth as the—'"

"Oh, shut up."

"'—gentle rain from heaven— Upon the place beneath:—'"

This was great, Huck thought as he chanted

away. This had been his guaranteed, surefire way to drive Mom crazy last year. She said they'd all had to memorize the exact same passage when they were in school, and she had hated it. And it was working just as well on Tom.

"'—it is twice bless'd;— It blesseth him that gives—'"

"She'd do it, wouldn't she?" Tom interrupted.

"Diana? Go knock on some stranger's door and ask to be shown around their house like she's casing it for grand larceny? Of course she would. And they'd let her in too."

"But she's prettier than we are."

Well, that was unanswerable. Diana was prettier than everybody. Where was he? "'—and him that takes:— 'Tis the mightiest in the mightiest; it becomes—'"

Tom said the sort of word that Huck had never heard him say. "Is the alternative listening to you quote Shakespeare all afternoon?"

"'—The throned monarch better than his crown;— His sceptre shows the force of—'"

Tom started off down the drive. "I just don't want people thinking I've been outmanned by my own daughter."

Huck was relieved; he wasn't sure that he remembered much more. He whistled, stopping Tom. "Come back here. We need to make plans."

"What? That you'll faint and I'll rush in while they are distracted?"

"We could try that. Or we could just try looking respectable."

"How the hell are we going to pull that one off?"

This was just super; Huck was having a terrific time. "We could tuck in our shirts; that ought to do it."

Tom looked at him in awe as he started to stuff his shirt into his jeans. "What a person of great resources you are."

"I know," Huck said modestly.

At first it was kind of awkward. A maid answered the door, which was enough to silence Huck until Judgment Day and beyond. But Tom did okay. Then the lady who lived there called her husband to see if it was all right. The husband recognized Tom's name and was so excited about Tom's being there that he took off work just to show him around the house.

"Someone said you were in town," the man said right off. "I don't know Dade Caldwell, and I've been wondering if I'd have the nerve to come over and introduce myself."

Huck was impressed. Here this guy had enough money to have this house and a maid and a swimming pool, and he'd been trying to work up the nerve to introduce himself to *Tom*. He should try and remember to tell that to Mom. She liked hearing things like that.

Then the man gestured to him. "Is this your son?"

Huck braced himself.

"No," said Tom . . . just as Huck had known he would. "No such luck, but he works with me, and he's a good friend."

No such luck . . . a good friend. Huck had this really horrible feeling that he was blushing like some girl.

Of course, Tom was interested in *everything,* but just when Huck was thinking it might be more fun to go back to Caldwell's and straighten some nails, the people's daughter showed up with one of her friends. They were fourteen, about to start ninth grade, and were really impressed that he was a junior and was on the basketball team. Huck liked that.

The family asked them to stay for supper. Huck was a little afraid that the maid might serve dinner; he wasn't sure he could handle that. *On my summer vacation this summer, I learned that cops know where to eat, that topless dancers are nice, ordinary folks, and that the scariest things on earth are rich people's maids.* But fortunately this family ate like normal human beings.

As they were leaving, the man spoke to Tom. "I don't know when I'll get to the ballroom up on the third floor, but I'd really like you involved."

"I'd like that," Tom answered. You could tell that he wasn't just being polite.

"It won't be for a couple of years. How can I get in touch with you? Can I have your card?"

Needless to say, Tom didn't have a card. "In fact, I don't even have an address at the moment." He sounded a little like he was apologizing. "My ex-wife's getting remarried. I used to have her forward everything, but I don't know if she'll want to do that now."

"Why don't you use our address?" Huck put in. "Mom can forward stuff to you. She'll always know where you are, won't she?"

Tom looked at him, a long, funny look. "Yes,"

he said slowly. "I guess she will." And he rattled off the South Dakota address, getting the zip code right and everything. "Be sure it's 'Care of Curry James'; otherwise it might get forwarded to my father, down in Florida."

"What's so funny?" Tom asked him as soon as they were walking down the drive.

Huck hadn't laughed or anything. "It's not funny, just weird. I never think of Mr. Winchester as being your father."

"Well, he is."

"Why don't you have your mail sent to him?"

"Because he doesn't always know where I am."

That sounded even more weird, but, now that Huck thought about it, Cal Winchester had always kept to himself. He never seemed to mind if Huck played in his barns, but he hardly ever spoke to him. His having moved to Florida last year hadn't made a scrap of difference in Huck's life, except that Mom had made him go over and check on the house a lot. That was what he'd been doing when he first met Tom.

"I'm glad we went in," Tom said as he unlocked the truck.

"Me too. I had fun."

"And Diana would have been proud of us. Let's not discount the importance of that."

Huck hadn't been about to. "She probably could have pulled off a faint on the front steps that would have gotten us invited to stay for a week."

Tom didn't say anything, but Huck could tell he liked hearing about Diana. It was funny. Of course, he hadn't thought about it at the time, but in the weeks he had been working with Tom before Diana had come to South Dakota, Tom had hardly ever talked about her. But he did a lot now, at least a lot for Tom.

Finally Tom spoke. "You know, I thought about calling her, asking her if she wanted to come down for the weekend."

"You what? You thought about asking her?" How great that could have been.

"Yes, there's a couple of plantations up the Mississippi that take in overnight guests. You can sleep in a four-poster bed, have breakfast on the veranda, all that antebellum gracious living. I didn't think you'd care about it, but Diana might have."

"She would have *loved* it. Why didn't you call her?"

"I don't know. I didn't think she'd want to come."

Huck stared at him. "That's crazy. Just crazy. She hasn't traveled much more than I have—and she loves doing new stuff, especially this *Gone With the Wind* business, girls really go for that."

"I guess they do." Tom was speaking sort of slow.

"I'll bet she'd be furious if you told her you were thinking about asking her to come down and then didn't. I mean, she was saying how glad she was that you and her mom finally thought she was old enough to travel on her own."

Tom didn't say anything.

Huck was almost irritated with Tom. Here he

had had a wonderful idea, about the best idea he had ever had, and he just sat on it.

They were at Caldwell's now. Tom turned the truck off, but he didn't get out. After a moment, he spoke. "I'm not perfect, Huck."

What were you supposed to say to a remark like that?

Tom ran his hand around the steering wheel. "I realize you're disappointed that I didn't call Diana."

What was this? Sure, he was disappointed, but why was Tom apologizing to *him*? Tom was just as disappointed as he was.

He was sorry Tom felt bad. He didn't think about grown-ups feeling bad. Mom never seemed to.

Huck wanted to say something to make Tom feel better, but he wasn't quite sure what. "It would have been great to have her here, but, you know, this wasn't so bad. I mean, just the two of us, you and me... well, I'm having a really good time. It would have been fun to have Diana here, but it wouldn't have been *better,* if you know what I mean. It would have been different if it weren't just the two of us."

And as he said it, he realized how true it was.

Tom was staring out the windshield, and he went on for a minute or so, and then he looked at Huck, his face really serious. "I do know what you mean, maybe even better than you do."

"What do you mean by that?"

Tom shook his head. "You ask a lot of questions."

If anyone else would have said that, Huck would have been hurt.

Tom had already gotten out of the truck and was walking across the drive. Huck caught up with him. "I ask them because you always answer."

"You mean I bring this on myself?"

"Yes, most grown-ups hedge around all the time, but you give it to me straight."

Tom gave him another one of those funny looks. "I guess I have to with you."

"With me? How am I different from anyone else?"

"Haven't you looked in the mirror lately?"

"The mirror? What does that have to do with anything?"

Tom shrugged. "You know you look a lot like your father, don't you?"

"People tell me that." Huck had never paid much attention when they did. He didn't see that it mattered one way or another. But maybe he was wrong. "Does that make a difference?"

Tom held out his left hand, extending the forefinger. There was a thin, white scar across the tip. "Don't you know the story behind that?"

"Should I?"

"Doesn't it look familiar?"

Huck had no idea what Tom was talking about.

"Your mother's hand," Tom prompted. "Don't you remember what your mother's hand looks like?"

Huck squinted, trying to picture it. It was hard to remember something as familiar as your mother's hand. "Oh, yeah," he said slowly. "She's got a scar like that."

And Tom explained it to him, how the three of them, Curry, Tom, and Huck, had sworn a blood oath to "stick together and answer straight."

"So you sort of feel that since you promised to answer straight to him, you have to be straight with me because we look so much alike?"

"At first, yes. And then later— Look, don't be offended by this, but it seemed like maybe you needed a man you could be straight with."

Why should he be offended? It was sure true. "Mom's great, but it's not the same as being with you."

"Then if you have questions, ask me."

"I have been."

Chapter Twelve

"I guess it's about time, Huck."

It was Labor Day, and the airline ticket agent was calling for people to board Huck's flight. Huck stood up. He didn't quite know what to say. These three weeks with Tom had been so terrific.

Tom didn't know what to say either. He cleared his throat and put out his hand. "It's hard to say good-bye to you, Huck. I hope you know that. It's like—"

"Like saying good-bye to my father again?"

Tom didn't say anything for a moment. "Actually, I never did say good-bye to your father."

He looked really sad, but before Huck could think of what to say, Tom went on. "No, Huck, you aren't just a substitute for him. It is unnerving that you look so much like the way I remember him, but I'd think you were great whatever you looked like, whoever your parents were."

"Oh."

Tom gripped his hand tightly and squeezed his shoulder. For a moment Huck thought Tom was going to hug him.

It would have been okay.

And if Tom found it hard to say good-bye, Mom found it hard to say hello. She hugged him hard and when she stepped away, she was blinking and looking a little vague. For an awful moment Huck thought that she was going to cry, which would *not* have been okay. He had never seen her cry, and he didn't want to start now.

But in a second or so she was herself again, all cheerful and brisk. As they drove home they talked about New Orleans. She had read a couple of books on it while he was gone and she seemed to know more about it than he did, even though he was the one who had been there. He felt like he had already told her everything on the phone or in postcards—at least everything he was going to tell her—but she didn't seem to mind hearing it again. And he liked talking about it.

"Mom, you just wouldn't believe how great it was to be with Tom."

"Oh, I believe it." She started running the tip of her left forefinger along her jeans. She must be thinking about when she had been a kid, when she and Tom and his dad had all been together, Huck thought.

It must have been hard on her when his father died. He'd never really thought about it from her point of view. When he was little, he'd sometimes think that it wasn't fair that he didn't have a dad like most of the other guys did, but it had never occurred to him that she didn't have a husband. She had probably loved his father a lot;

it must have been really rough when he didn't come back.

"Mom, did you say good-bye to my father?"

She was surprised. "Why, of course, I did."

"Tom says he didn't."

"Oh." She thought a little. "Well, in that way, I didn't either. I'm afraid none of us had much sense back then. It didn't occur to us that anything would actually happen to either of them, that they wouldn't come back home."

"I don't remember him, you know . . . my dad, that is."

"I know that. And it's nothing to feel guilty about . . ."

She was unbelievable sometimes, how she knew what you were feeling even before you did yourself.

She was still talking. ". . . I don't remember my parents either."

This was getting heavy. "Well, that gives us something in common, doesn't it?"

She laughed and they talked about New Orleans the rest of the way home.

As soon as they were up in his room he opened his suitcase and handed her a package, wrapped in white tissue paper.

"What's this?" she asked.

"What does it look like? I brought you a present."

"You *what*?"

It was no wonder she was surprised. He usually got her something for Christmas, but he never remembered her birthday, not since Grandma

Myra had died and there hadn't been anyone to remind him. He would have liked to have remembered it, but he didn't.

But bringing her something from New Orleans had been his own idea; Tom had helped him pick it out—he had said that shopping for women was the hardest thing a man had to do.

He hoped she liked it. It wasn't a T-shirt, but a leather purse, a shoulder bag, handmade by this guy who sold them in this park in front of some church, Jackson Square, or something. Tom had said it was a good idea; in fact, he had gotten a little clutch-type thing for Diana from the same man. And if Tom approved of someone's workmanship, it had to be good.

She was ripping off the wrapping. "A purse! Oh, Huck, I've needed a new purse for ages; mine's almost a fire hazard. And this one is just beautiful."

She was opening it up, smelling the leather, trying it on her shoulder; you could tell she really did like it. He was glad she was happy with it—as mothers went, she wasn't so bad.

"Tom said that I probably shouldn't get you one with a lot of different pockets and dividers because you'd never remember which pocket you put anything in, and you'd have to look through every single one."

"That's sure true."

"And anyway, those were a lot more expensive."

She laughed and kissed him again. "I'm so glad you're home."

"Well, yeah, I guess I am too." And it was almost true.

She stepped away. "What do you think about your room?"

"My room? What about it?"

"Huck! Doesn't it look different?"

He glanced around. Now that he thought about it, it was different. The furniture and books and stuff were all his, but it did look different. It took him a minute to figure out why.

The place was *clean*; it was incredibly clean.

"Did you do this, Mom?"

She laughed. "It is a little out of character, isn't it?"

That was for sure. "Did you paint it?" She nodded. "What did you do that for? Did you want to rent it out? Were you hoping I wasn't coming back?"

"Huck!"

Her voice was sharp, sharper than he had ever heard it, and she was pale. A minute ago she'd been laughing. Now she was all pale and sick-looking. What had he said?

"Mom, what's wrong?"

She ignored him, starting to take things out of the suitcase. "Are all these clothes dirty?"

Just because at the airport he didn't want to have her cry all over him didn't mean that he was a little kid she had to hide stuff from.

"Look, Mom, if something's wrong, I have a right to know."

Where did he pick that one up? Since when did he have the right to know squat around here? She'd probably laugh.

But she didn't. Instead she sat down on the bed, clutching one of his shirts. She stared out across the room for a minute and then looked up at him. "About your not coming back...I guess I really was worried about that."

"What are you talking about? Why wouldn't I come back? I mean, where would I go?"

"It was completely irrational."

Huck shook his head. Grown-ups sure could be confusing. It was too weird for him.

No, no, maybe it wasn't. It was taking forever to sink in, but he was finally starting to get a handle on this one. It mattered to both of them, both Mom and Tom, that he looked so much like his dad.

His father had gone off to *war*, for heaven's sake; he'd just gone off to New Orleans with Tom, but still... "Were you worried that I wasn't coming back because my father didn't?"

She sighed. "Oh, Huck, I suppose so. I didn't quite realize it until right now, but I guess I was."

"Well, I'm back, Mom." Huck sat down next to her and awkwardly touched her arm. "I'm back, and I'll always come back. You know that." And he decided that if she really did want to cry, he could probably take it.

Fortunately, she didn't. She just patted his leg a couple of times, and then in a second, made a joke. "Are you always going to bring this much laundry?"

"Why do you think I have to come home? Who else would do my laundry?"

Which was an incredibly stupid thing to say, because right away she took it into her head that maybe he should start doing his own laundry this year.

Huck ate supper, went to bed, and then the next morning, bingo, he had to put on a decent shirt and rummage around for a spiral notebook and a pen. School was starting.

Living so far out in the country, he got one of the few student places in the school parking lot, and he was hardly out of his car before the guys started flocking up, asking him about New Orleans.

"What was it like? Did you have a good time?"

"It was wild. I mean, you wouldn't *believe* it. The music—"

A soft voice interrupted. "Huck?" He felt a light touch on his arm.

He turned, looked down. It was Tracy.

Oh, Lord. He hadn't thought about her in *months*. He hadn't sent her a postcard from New Orleans or anything.

But she looked really pretty. Her hair was lighter and shorter than it had been in June. She had on a new blouse, not quite pink and not quite purple, but somewhere in between.

Tracy's dad owned a clothing store, and everyone was always complimenting Tracy on her clothes. Huck had liked that last year, that he was going out with a girl who dressed better than everyone else. He didn't really know why everyone thought she dressed so well, but he liked it that everyone did.

The guys drifted off as they always did when a

girl came up. She was looking at him, her face turned up. She seemed to expect him to kiss her, so he did, not a real kiss, just a little brush across her cheek. Only the greasers really got into it in front of everybody.

"I was hoping you'd call last night."

It had never occurred to him; it hadn't even crossed his mind. He felt bad. "My plane"—that sounded good: *my* plane—"came into Watertown, so we got home too late." That was a lie. "But I knew I'd see you today." Which wasn't incredibly accurate either. This wasn't going great. "Here, give me your books; let's go on in."

Tracy just had one spiral, but she handed it over.

And looked impressed while she did it. After all, he'd never carried her books before. At the beginning of the year last year, when he was just an idiot sophomore, he'd seen some of the seniors carrying girls' books. At first he'd thought it was weird; a girl had to be a super weakling if she couldn't carry two spirals and a crummy English book. Then he decided it was pretty cool, and when he first started going out with Tracy, he'd wanted to, but hadn't known how to bring it up. Then he forgot.

But he'd handled it fine. *Here, give me your books*—like it was real routine. Was he ever glad not to be a sophomore anymore.

"You're taller," she was saying.

Huck glanced down at her. The top of her head was just a little above his shoulder now. Diana was taller than she was.

"Well, you're prettier."

As he held open the door for her it occurred to him that Tracy would have heard about Diana. There was no way she wouldn't have; he had taken Diana with him everywhere this past summer, everyone had met her. He guessed that Tracy would say something about it sooner or later. Probably sooner.

Too bad that Tom made such a big deal about their not being related. Huck thought this afternoon might be a lot easier if he could say that Diana was his cousin or something.

As soon as they were in the building Tracy started waving and saying hi to people. Sometimes he thought that was why Tracy and her friends came to school, just to say hi to people in the halls.

Right away Julie Michaels came up. She was a senior, the head cheerleader. She had another senior cheerleader with her. Tracy was one of the two juniors who had made a squad; that's why they were talking to her.

"What a *great* blouse, Tracy." Then Julie turned to him. "Are you going to be playing basketball this year, Huck?"

If a senior cheerleader had spoken to him on the first day of school last year, the janitors would still be scraping him up off the floors—"Oh, look, this must be another piece of the James kid."

But if Tom could look at a naked lady as if she were a normal human being, then Huck guessed he could talk to a senior cheerleader as if she were one too.

"Actually, Julie, I'd heard you'd been dropped

from the squad, and I figured that if you weren't going to cheer, I wasn't going to play."

"Oh, Huck." And Julie Michaels, who had half the senior class in love with her, *Julie Michaels* actually blushed.

"Well, if you're still on the squad, I guess I'll play."

This was great, not being a sophomore anymore.

As soon as Julie and the other cheerleader left, Meg Triplett came up. "Did you tell Huck about the party?" she asked Tracy.

"What party?" he asked. He liked Meg. She was quiet and really terrible at math, although she was always the best in the class in English. He'd seen her once in the library last year just about to cry because she was so confused by some proof in geometry, and he had helped her. If he hadn't been going with Tracy, he would have asked her out.

"I'm having one on Saturday. Can you make it?"

"I don't know why not. I'll—" He stopped. That was wrong. He'd be going with Tracy. "Sure, we'll be there."

Was he crazy or did Tracy look relieved?

Classes went by quickly; since it was the first day, they were only half as long as usual. The teachers passed out the books and told you about all the great stuff you'd get to learn that year. Tracy had cheerleading practice in the afternoon, so Huck swore on everything sacred to him that he would call her that night and then met up with the guys at the A&W stand.

There were twelve, maybe fifteen of them. Some of them were sitting on a picnic table, their feet swinging against the benches. A couple of others were leaning against the cars. Everyone was in jeans, polo shirts, and running shoes.

These were Huck's friends. They ran track or played on one of the teams. They had cars, and they dated. They were the jocks, and in the afternoons, the A&W was theirs. The greasers hung out in front of the drugstore, and the wimps... well, Huck guessed they all went home and wrote computer programs. That's the way this town worked.

People were all talking about the summer. The guys who'd been away were bragging, and the guys who hadn't were complaining.

Huck ordered a chili dog and went over and leaned against Joe Oates's beat-up Dart. The talk about summers dried up. Every guy there knew that Huck had had the best summer of any of them. First, there'd been Diana, and if she hadn't been enough, then there was New Orleans.

"How does your brother like the Navy?" he asked Joe.

"Okay, I guess. He says it's not what he expected, though."

"Yeah, that's what Tom said about the Army."

"Tom? Isn't that Diana's father?"

Huck nodded.

"And you call him Tom?"

Huck could just imagine what Tom would do if he called him "Mr. Winchester."

Steve Pierce leaned back from one of the tables. "Are you still going with Tracy?"

Hardly a surprising question. "She seems to think so, and that's good enough for me."

Todd Estes slid down off the hood of a VW Rabbit. "You really think you're hot stuff, don't you?"

Huck ignored him. Estes was always on his case. Mom said it was because Todd was competing with him, but that was crazy. This wasn't how you competed.

But Todd went right on. "This guy you went to New Orleans with, I mean, so what? He's a friend of your mom's, right?"

Huck hated this. "Yes, but—"

"So it would just be like going somewhere with your uncle," Todd sneered, "and what's so great about that?"

That did it. "I suppose your uncle takes you to topless bars?"

Silence. Absolute silence.

You could tell that everyone was about to die with curiosity. Maybe half of these guys had gone all the way with girls—although at least three of them had only been with Dixie Parker and that hardly counted—but they were just as impressed as everyone else.

"A topless bar?" Joe asked at last. "He took you to a topless bar? With girls?"

"Sure, with girls. It wouldn't be much of a thrill if there'd been guys dancing."

"What was it like?"

"What do you think? It was—" Huck stopped. He looked at everybody, waiting, listening.

What was wrong with him? He'd been about to tell them how terrific it had been, when it hadn't been at all. It had been awful.

He thought he knew why Tom had taken him there, and it wasn't so that he could come home and brag about it.

"Actually—" Huck looked away from everybody, over toward the Texaco station across the street. The attendant was putting gas into a red pickup. "Actually, it was sort of sad. They were real pretty and all, but they were a lot older than I thought they'd be and they didn't look like they liked being there. They were just there because they couldn't get other jobs. It wasn't much fun."

Nobody said anything, and Huck wadded up the wrapping of his chili dog and went over to the green trash barrel. Usually he just threw his trash in from wherever he was sitting. They all did, seeing who made it, who missed. He almost never missed.

He really wished that he hadn't brought up going to that bar. He had been showing off, that's all. It would be all over the earth tomorrow. Mom would find out and get mad at him or be ticked off with Tom for taking him. And everybody at school would probably think he was queer or something because he found it boring.

As Huck drove to school the next morning he braced himself for endless razzing. Having the entire student body memorize a Shakespeare speech about the "quality of mercy" hadn't done a bit of good; the place was merciless.

"Hey, James, who *cares* if they want to be there?"

"If *I* had been there, they'd have wanted to be there"—this from a guy who could hardly get dates.

A couple of seniors kept asking him how old too old was.

But it wasn't nearly as bad as he had expected. Everybody was still laying into Steve for having blown out the electrical system of his van when he was trying to install new speakers.

On Friday morning Coach stopped him as he was going into the locker room to suit up.

"Can you come in my office for a minute, Huck?"

Oh, man, this was it. If you were on the team, you were supposed to be a fine American boy. Huck had already heard this lecture once, last year when the cops had stopped them after they'd been drinking. Coach had really come down hard on him, talking about his not having a father—like what he'd done was worse than the other guys, because they had fathers to come to the police station, and his mother had had to come. When she had found out about that, Mom had been mad. She said what he'd done was stupid, dangerous, illegal, etc., etc., but no more stupid, dangerous, illegal, etc., etc. than when the guys with fathers did it.

But that time Coach had called him "James,"

real crisp and militarylike. The "Huck" was a good sign. At least, he hoped it was.

"I hear you're getting a bit of ribbing this week."

Huck sighed. "Yes, sir."

"And I bet you wonder what they are saying behind your back."

Huck felt sick. He didn't even want to *think* about that.

"Well, they aren't saying anything."

"What?"

"Oh, people are telling the story, but no one's teasing you. Not behind your back, only to your face."

"They're not?" If Coach was saying it, it must be true. He and the shop teacher were the only ones who had a clue as to what was really going on among the guys.

"You may feel like you made a fool of yourself, but you didn't. Not at all. Your stock's gone up a lot around here this week. People are impressed that you had the guts to tell the truth."

Huck did not know what to say, but he sure was glad to hear this.

"I've been in places like that—"

"You have?" Huck was astonished. Coach? In a topless bar? Grown-ups were amazing sometimes.

"I fought in Korea," Coach said like that explained it. "I had the same reaction as you did and although I was older than you, I wasn't man enough to admit it."

Huck shrugged, surprised, embarrassed.

Of course, Coach couldn't leave well enough alone and he did go on for a while more, being a little preachy about always telling the truth.

The thing that bothered Huck was that if Coach knew, Mom had to. She just had to. She always knew everything. It came from having had the store; she said news went around town just as fast as it did around school. But she didn't say anything to him about this business, and he appreciated that. She was surprising sometimes.

The other surprising thing was that Tracy hadn't said anything about Diana. Not one word. Of course, she knew. The whole world would have told her, but apparently she had decided to act like it hadn't happened. It seemed pretty hypocritical, but Huck had to admit that he was relieved.

But when he picked her up for Meg Triplett's party, she seemed a little nervous and jumpy, just like she had last spring before cheerleader tryouts, and he figured that she had decided to break up with him. He certainly deserved it for having gone around with Diana all summer.

And he wasn't sure that he minded either. Now that calling girls didn't make him as nervous as it had this time last year, he thought it might be fun to date around. Of course, you didn't get as much that way, but he guessed he could live with that for a while. Diana hadn't let him do hardly anything, but it had still been fun to be with her.

Meg's party was okay, but only okay. Her parents were home, so there were just Cokes and other soft drinks and the lights were a lot brighter than Huck thought they needed to be. The girls talked about Homecoming; the guys talked about sports and cars. But finally somebody turned the lights off, and they started dancing.

Well, if Tracy was breaking up with him, she was certainly going about it in a strange way. She linked her arms around his neck, which she didn't usually do, so he could put both arms around her. She rested her cheek against his chest. She couldn't reach his shoulder anymore.

It felt good having her this close. More than good. He tightened his arms.

"You're getting so strong," she said softly.

That wasn't the half of it. Strong wasn't all he was getting. "I wish we were alone," he whispered into her hair.

She leaned back a little, looking up at him. "Let's just not be the first to leave, okay?"

As soon as two other couples had left, they went too. Huck felt sort of sorry for Meg. It must be tough, giving a party and having people leave early because they wanted to go make out. But Tracy had never been this affectionate; he had to leave.

He opened the car door for her, and then went around to his side and got in. "Do you want to go somewhere and talk for a while?"

That's what everybody always said, "Go somewhere and talk," although when he had said that to Diana this summer, she had laughed.

"Talk, Huck? If we wanted to *talk*, we could stay right here."

But Tracy wasn't like that. She just smiled and said that they hadn't talked for a long time.

That was for sure.

"But, Huck, is there somewhere we could... well, really be alone?"

She had a point. The Jenny Wren road would be well attended tonight, and on Monday morning everyone would know which cars had been there and for how long. "My mom's not home." She was having dinner with her friend Bonnie and someone named Janelle. "We could go there and listen to some music."

Once they were home he took her into the front room. There was just a radio there, but his stereo was in his bedroom, and even as affectionate as Tracy was being, he didn't dare suggest *that*.

He didn't bother with the lights, just tuned in the radio and then pulled her down on the sofa. He put his arms around her and started kissing her. She let her mouth go open. He stroked his hands across her back for a while and then slid one in to touch her breast.

She felt great, soft and warm—better than last spring—more like she didn't have a bra on, although she did, as he had felt the elastic across her back. He squeezed her lightly—he was always afraid of hurting a girl—and it really was like she didn't have anything on under her blouse. He could feel her nipple growing hard. He knew that that happened to girls, but he'd never been able to feel it before, and he rubbed his hand lightly over it. Just this little nothing movement, the tip of her breast tracing tiny circles in his palm, and it was all he could think about, just the way that felt. And looking at her face, her eyes closed, he knew that she liked it too.

"Come on, Trace, let's lie down."

He thought she might say no; last year, she wouldn't even get in the backseat with him, but she let him take her hand and help her down to the floor.

They were near the window, and the moonlight shone on her. Her shirt, yellow and soft, was a little crumpled where his hand had been. He lay next to her on his side, kissing her, both hands on her breasts, one leg over hers. He was careful only to let their legs touch, although he was aching to do more. His leg started to move against hers, up and down, the denim of his jeans against her skirt, and there was friction and warmth and rhythm, the same rhythm pulsing through everything—his hand, his kiss, his leg, through her, through him.

This is what it's like. But it must go on and on, getting better and better . . .

"Huck!" Tracy gasped, like she was trying to stop him. And so he stopped, resting his forehead against hers, breathing hard.

It was a minute or so before he could speak. "I didn't hurt you, did I?"

She shook her head. "I just got a little scared, that's all. It was silly."

No, it wasn't. She was right to be scared. Hell, *he* was scared. But he wasn't about to admit it. "You don't have to be scared with me, Tracy, you know that. I'll never do anything you don't want me to. I wouldn't, I won't."

"I know that. I trust you, Huck, I really do."

He leaned down to kiss her. He meant it just to be a little kiss, a "that's all, folks" sort of kiss, but when he felt her tongue brush against his mouth, suddenly everything was starting up again.

This was insane. *Okay, James, this is where nice boys and girls stop. Stand up and tell her she's crazy to trust you for another second.*

But he couldn't stop, he just couldn't.

"Let's keep going...please, Trace, let's keep going...we don't have to go all the way..."

And when he started to unbutton her blouse, she didn't stop him.

She was really beautiful, lying there in the moonlight. And her bra was like nothing he'd ever seen, it looked so incredibly great. All of it, the straps and everything, was of this strange shimmery fabric that was both light blue and transparent at the same time. He could see everything, how the tips of her breasts were dark and pink, how her nipples were aroused. And it was better, a million times better, than anything you could ever see in a bar.

"Do you like it, Huck? Isn't it pretty?"

"God, it's—" He swallowed. He couldn't speak.

He curved his hands around her. Her skin seemed to shine through the pale, shimmering bra. He liked the way his hands looked against her—his hands, all tan and strong, so clearly a guy's hands, against what was so clearly a girl. And then he moved his thumbs, letting them pass lightly over her nipples. She sighed, and her eyes closed.

Between her breasts was the clasp; it wasn't

around behind her back, hard to reach, impossible to unfasten. She wouldn't have worn it unless she meant for him to undo it. He was sure.

And it opened like in a dream, easy and smooth, and he slid it off over her breasts, feeling, for the first time, how warm she really was. She sat up a little, and he slipped her blouse and everything over her shoulders. From her waist up, she had nothing on.

He started to pull his shirt out of his jeans.

She looked up at him questioningly.

"Just my shirt, Tracy. I'll just take off my shirt."

He tugged it over his head and threw it off to the side. She reached up and smoothed his hair. He pulled her to him.

She winced.

"What is it? What's wrong?"

"Your belt buckle. It's cold."

He paused. "I can take it off."

"Oh, Huck..."

She didn't seem sure, but she didn't say no. So Huck unbuckled his belt and slowly looking at her the whole time, pulled it free from the loops of his jeans. He threw it aside.

He lay back down beside her, and he put his arms around her, trembling, almost afraid that he would crush her, he wanted to hold her so tightly.

He was moving lightly against her, and her breasts were brushing against his chest. She seemed to press closer toward him. "Do you like it, Tracy? Do you like doing this, us being like this?"

"Do you?"

How could she ask? God, of course he did. She should feel what she was doing to him. He was—

In the past, he had always been careful not to embarrass her when they hugged or after they'd been dancing a slow dance for a while. He had always moved away a little. He hadn't wanted her to think he was some kind of animal—although, sometimes he felt like enough of one.

And though he had never gone this far with her before, he knew he wasn't an animal. This was the way that guys . . . that *men* were supposed to feel. So he crushed her to him, tight, all the way down. He was kissing her hard, and she was kissing him back. He rolled over with her; she was on her back, underneath him, just as it would be if they were actually . . .

When was she going to stop him?

He was moving against her, starting to feel frantic, desperate. He had to get his jeans off—they felt so tight, so confining. He wanted to feel his legs against hers, or even if he was just against her skirt, this soft, soft skirt she wore, that would be enough.

When *was* she going to stop him?

Oh, Tracy, you'd better do it soon, or I'll . . .

He could hardly breathe. His eyes squeezed shut, and his heart was pounding just like he'd run a million laps. Then he felt her legs move and he was closer to her still, his body right up against hers, touching, moving.

He couldn't take it much longer.

And then he knew. He knew he didn't have to take it. She wasn't going to stop him. He had to make love to her, and she was going to let him. He needed to finish this with her, and she was going to let him.

And all his questions, all his wonderings about how you did it, who said what, who went where, vanished. He knew what was to happen. Just a few more clothes and then she'd lie back, letting her legs open for him. He'd move between them and then soon, very, very soon, he'd be inside her, making love to her.

He drew back, quickly unsnapping his jeans, not fumbling like he always thought he would, but easy and sure. As he started to slide down his zipper he looked down at her, wondering if she was watching, wondering if she wanted to see him as much as he wanted to see her.

And then he stopped.

She had a blank look on her face, and he thought of the dancer, the one down in New Orleans with the dark hair and the red sequins and the baby.

"It's okay, Huck, really it is."

But it wasn't. Something had happened. She didn't want it anymore. She had a while ago, she said she did, but she didn't now. She was willing, she was going to let him do this to her, but she didn't want it.

The dark-haired girl had had to be there, dancing in sequins and tassels to support her baby. But Tracy didn't have to do this. He'd never make her do it, not ever. So why did she think she had to?

Did she think it would give her some kind of hold over him?

Well, it would have. If he went through with this, he would do anything she asked of him. He'd have to.

The mistake we make is that we force the woman to do all the deciding. He remembered Tom saying that.

And it was sure true. He hadn't decided to do this; Tracy had—no wonder she'd been nervous and jumpy.

Just because a woman is willing . . . that's not enough of a reason to sleep with her.

He didn't love Tracy, not the way it had sounded like Tom had loved Diana's mother. Maybe at sixteen you couldn't love someone that much. He didn't know.

His heart was drumming so hard in his ears that he could hardly hear or think. Every part of his body was craving for release. But Huck zipped his jeans.

"Tracy, no. We aren't going to."

She stared at him, unbelieving. "Huck!"

"We'd make love if we took our clothes off. You know we would. I couldn't help it; I'd have to. And we talked about it last year, we decided we wouldn't . . ."

God, he hadn't even *thought* about birth control. He might have gone ahead and made love to her without it. He could have made her pregnant . . . what a mess that could have been. And even if she hadn't gotten pregnant, it would have been instant death if Mom ever found out he'd been so dumb.

Tracy turned all red, looking like he had humiliated her somehow. She pulled down her skirt and grabbed for her top. "But *you* were the one who wanted it. It was you; I was just willing to do it for you because you wanted it so much." She was angry with him, furious.

"But, Tracy—"

"I just hate you, Huck James. I really do."

And she didn't say one word to him all the way home in the car, she just sat way over by the door, staring out the window.

Girls!

Chapter Thirteen

Curry woke up to the rhythmic slap and thud of Huck's basketball. She glanced at the clock. It was six thirty, early for him to be up on a Sunday.

But, she guessed, young Mr. James could not have slept particularly well last night.

She had heard them. She had come in a little after eleven, surprised that Huck's car had been there.

As she passed through the dining room on the way to the stairs, she heard some music in the front room and had smiled to herself. She had seen how many cars were pulled off the side of the Jenny Wren road. That would have been why Tracy and Huck had decided to come here. She didn't mind their using the front room; it was just a good thing that neither one of them had dust allergies. Then she had heard Tracy—

"It's okay, Huck, really it is."

Curry had halted, unsure of what to do.

On one hand, she was a realist. If Tracy were willing, then there was precious little Curry could do to stop the two of them from making love.

Sure, she could interrupt them now, but what was the point? There was always tomorrow.

On the other hand, she was a mother. She thought it a mistake for Tracy and Huck to do this; they were too young, they didn't have that much in common, Huck certainly wasn't in love with the girl. So Curry wasn't going to stand by while it happened in her own home.

Even if she simply postponed what was inevitable, it would give Huck a chance to prepare himself. He knew all about birth control, he believed in it, but, as far as Curry knew, he did not carry condoms in his wallet.

Well, he probably would after tonight.

Condoms in his wallet...her little baby was grown up...

She turned back toward the kitchen to start slamming doors and banging pots, and then she had heard her baby say, "Tracy, no. We aren't going to."

She could hardly believe it. Huck had chosen not to. Tracy was willing, and he had said no. Even his father hadn't been able to do that. But this Huck, her son, had done it.

Curry had gone upstairs. Huck James did not need his mother on this one.

She got out of bed now and tugged on jeans and a shirt. She went downstairs, through the kitchen, and then outside.

Huck was playing so hard that he didn't notice her. She dropped down on the steps to watch him.

Curry supposed that she was terribly prejudiced, but she thought he looked wonderful. He had already pulled off his shirt and the sheen of perspiration on his skin glowed in the morning light. The hair on his legs was golden and each week, it seemed, the soft mat on his chest grew thicker. She was so proud of him.

And so very glad he had come home.

She hadn't known it, but she really had been assuming that he would not. So many other people had left and never come home.

He had changed while he was gone; there was a different air about him. He was more confident, less doubting; he no longer spent every moment wondering if he was making a fool of himself. But however changed, he had still come home. This would go on happening. He would go away, to college, to a home and family of his own; he would change, he would need her less—but he would always come back. She would always know where he was; he would never vanish.

She had decided to take up teaching because she was worried about the "empty nest." But Huck wasn't a bird. Yes, he would fly away, but he wouldn't forget the way back.

Curry stood up. "Do you want—" That was a waste, asking him if he wanted breakfast. He hadn't changed that much. "How many eggs do you want?"

He held up three fingers, and Curry went in to start frying bacon.

He appeared sooner than she expected. He dropped into a chair in all his sweaty glory, waiting for his breakfast.

"Mom?"

"Yes?"

"Do you know Meg Triplett?"

That was about as much a waste as asking if Huck wanted breakfast. Curry knew everyone. "Sure," she answered anyway. "Her dad was in my class, and I know her mother."

"I'm thinking of asking her to Homecoming."

"That sounds fine."

If Huck had said he was thinking of asking Pope John Paul II to Homecoming, Curry would have said that it sounded fine and not to forget to order a pretty corsage for His Holiness.

"I guess I should talk to Tracy first."

"I guess you should."

Curry's forbearance was rewarded as Huck continued. "I don't know, Mom. She's real nice, but everytime she's nice . . . I don't know . . . there are strings attached."

Oh. She was being "real nice" last night, but there wouldn't have just been strings; there would have been ropes, chains, and cables. And Huck had had the sense to realize it.

Curry felt sorry for Tracy. She lived under so much pressure, all the popular girls did. There were so many ordeals for them: they had to do well in cheerleader tryouts, they had to be finalists in Homecoming Queen elections, they had to have dates for every dance, they always had to dress well, be friendly, and get good grades. Everything the popular girls did was so visible, and everyone else was always waiting for them to stumble. It was no wonder that Tracy had tried to secure Huck in the only way she knew how.

There was much Curry wanted to say to him, but she fried his eggs in silence. A mother's advice was usually the last thing a sixteen-year-old boy admitted to wanting.

On the other hand, Huck wasn't entirely a boy anymore.

She put his plate in front of him and, after pouring herself some coffee, sat down too.

"Do you want some unasked-for advice, Huck?" She remembered Janelle asking her that once, right after Tom had left. She didn't know if the adolescent psychologists would agree with doing it this way, but Curry would put her money on a good waitress over a psychologist every time.

Huck didn't answer or stop eating, but he did look up at her like he was willing to listen.

"Huck, have you ever heard Tom say anything bad about Diana's mother even though they are getting a divorce?" Curry knew that the current magic word in Huck's life had three letters and began with a *T*.

He thought. "No, I guess I haven't."

"Wouldn't you be uncomfortable hearing it if he did?"

"Yeah, I guess."

"Then maybe you should be careful about what you say about Tracy."

"Oh." It was taking Huck a moment to see the parallel.

"You may think she's clingy, but maybe that wouldn't bother other boys." Curry felt pretty sure that some boys would not object to this particular brand of clinginess at all. "And anyway,

she may change." Indeed, Curry suspected that
Tracy would never again try what she had at-
tempted last night, and she hoped that Huck
never told a soul what happened. But that was so
much to expect of a boy his age.

"But what should I say?" Huck asked. "People
are going to ask why we broke up—girls as well as
guys."

"Just say that your interests have gone in different directions."

"Interests gone in different directions..." Huck
sat up. "Hey, I like that. 'Our interests have gone in
different directions,'" he repeated with dignity.
"That's good, Mom, real good."

"Thank you."

Huck stood up, clearly ready to conquer the
world of divergent interests. But, halfway to the
door, he stopped and turned. For a moment
he looked twelve again. "What if someone asks
what interests?"

Curry tried not to laugh. "Just look mysterious."

Huck managed to survive breaking up with Tracy
as well as he could be expected to. The session
with her was not pleasant—at least that's what
Curry gathered; Huck had given no details of it.
But his "changing interests" strategy seemed to
be working well.

"I look mysterious a lot," he reported happily.

Curry could not imagine anyone less capable of
looking mysterious than her son, but she did not
say so.

"I thought about what Tom does," he went on. "Every time anyone mentions Diana's mother, he says something nice about her, so every time Tracy's name comes up, I say something nice about her. I'm saying nicer stuff about her now than I ever did when we were going out."

Huck clearly believed himself to be acting like a gentleman of finest water and he was no end pleased with himself.

"Does she have a date for Homecoming?"

"Joe is taking her. He says it doesn't matter if her interests have changed, because he doesn't have any."

Huck had asked Meg Triplett for Homecoming, but he was also going out with some other girls. Curry thought that that was probably very healthy.

He seemed set to have a good year. His teachers had told Curry that his having a professional goal, this new interest in architecture, was making a difference in how hard he was working, and they were pleased—although they weren't nearly as pleased as his mother, of course.

So he was doing fine. For her own part, Curry guessed that even if she weren't fine, she was okay. Chad and Molly Jenkins had moved into Tom's old house with their family, a little first-grader and a pair of four-year-old twins. They were good people, they loved the house, and Curry liked having neighbors again.

Her classes were going smoothly. Her math teacher was terrible, but the young gentleman she was living with was more willing to help than he had been last year.

European history was harder than American history had been; it seemed alien, harder to relate to, but she still loved it. She could see why Colin Wheeler had made her choose, as Tom had put it, between him as a man and him as a teacher. It would be awkward, when she sat around the cafeteria with the other students, complaining about how much work he assigned if she were sleeping with him. What would she say? "I can't go home with you tonight; I've got too much history to read. You've got a choice: my body tonight or my paper Monday morning. You can't have both."

Anyway, Curry didn't want Colin Wheeler's body. Not when she still remembered Tom's.

She was surprised by how long this winding down was taking. She'd lost that stretched-out feeling, she no longer felt that the world around her wasn't real, but here it was the middle of October, and she still felt fragile.

And Janelle was right. This business of him still walking around did make it harder. He was in Illinois now. He'd called when he left New Orleans, but he'd called on a Wednesday and that was when she had her evening class.

"He sounded disappointed," Huck reported. "He thought your class would be on Thursday, like in the summer."

"There was no reason for him to think that."

"He said you could call if you had anything to tell him."

But she didn't call him. What would be the point? Wouldn't talking to him only make it worse?

Then they got a letter for him.

Huck had brought in the mail and was flipping through it. "Look, here's something for Tom."

Curry had been making supper. She glanced over Huck's shoulder. "That's not for Tom. What's wrong with you, Huck? Can't you read? That's for Mr. Thomas J. Winchestee. We don't know anybody named Winchestee."

"I wonder what it is."

It didn't look personal. "Open it," she told him.

"Really?"

"Sure. I don't know about this Winchestee fellow, but Tom certainly wouldn't care."

Curry turned back to the hamburgers she was making.

"Look, Mom." Huck sounded excited. "This is great! Tom just won a vacation."

"What? A vacation?"

"Yeah, a three-day weekend on the beach in North Carolina—the 'sun-kissed white sands'" he read.

Life certainly wasn't fair. Here Tom traveled all the time and she never went anywhere, and he was the one winning vacations on sun-kissed white sands. She wiped her hands and took the letter from Huck.

She looked at it for a moment. It was one of those computerized letters printed on cheap paper with a blurry dot matrix printer. Every so often Tom's name—or rather Holiday Resorts' version of Tom's name—was inserted into the text. "You, Mr. Thomas J. Winchestee, are entitled to . . ." She handed the letter back to Huck. "Try again."

"Huh?" He looked at her blankly, but started to reread the letter. He frowned. "Are they trying to sell him something?"

She nodded. "It's one of these vacation home communities. They let you stay there for a weekend, but it's hard sell all the time."

"Tom would love that, wouldn't he?" Huck turned the letter over, reading the back. "But look, they have already reserved one of the following prizes for him: a thousand dollars in cash, a hot air popcorn machine—"

"Does he get to choose between the two of those?"

"—a set of luggage, a motocross bike—that would be okay—five hundred dollars in cash—"

"I think Tom has a lot of popcorn in his future."

"Oh, wait, Mom, this is a heartbreaker. Is Tom still married to Diana's mom?"

"I don't think the divorce is final until December, but what difference does that make?"

"He can't go. The fine print says married people have to go as a team."

"He'll be crushed."

Huck laughed and put the letter back in the envelope. "Should we send it to him? I told him you would."

"I would what?"

"Forward his mail."

"What are you talking about?"

"Mom! What's wrong with you? It's not such a big deal, is it? Forwarding some crummy mail. *I'll* do it if you're going to weird out over it."

"I'm not weirding out; I was . . . Wait a minute, Huck." Suddenly this seemed important. "Did you and Tom talk about this?"

"Sure, down in New Orleans. Somebody asked him for his address, and you could tell he felt strange about giving them Diana's mother's address so I said that he could use ours, that we'd forward it, that you'd always know where he was even if his dad didn't. There was nothing wrong with that, was there?"

"No, Huck," she said slowly. "No, there wasn't."

She took the envelope, this computerized letter addressed to Mr. Thomas J. Winchestee.

It was a good, solid piece of American junk mail. There was nothing more ordinary, more worthless.

Except that it told Curry how wrong she had been about so many things.

Subconsciously she always expected the worst to happen. When Huck had been in New Orleans, she had talked to him on the phone at least twice a week, she had gotten postcards from him, Tom had called to say he was safely on the plane for the first leg of his trip home, and still, when she was waiting at Watertown, she hadn't expected him to get off, she had assumed he would have vanished en route.

Again and again she did things like that. When

Tom had told her about Trish's miscarriage, right away she assumed he had been exposed to Agent Orange and he was dying.

She was crazy. She really was.

Yes, people die. Everybody got around to it sooner or later. But that didn't mean you lived your life as if they were all going to do it next week.

She was just as bad as Tom used to be. He had gone around setting up situations where he was guaranteed to fail so that he could have a nice, happy time feeling like a failure. And she sat around assuming that people were always going to leave her, that no one would ever come back.

Well, Huck had come back, and by God, Tom would too. He wouldn't stay, any more than Huck was going to stay, but he wasn't going to disappear as he had before. He had called her to let her know where to reach him in Illinois, and she was sure that if she called and asked him to come for Thanksgiving or something, that he'd come.

Janelle had been wrong. "Don't make yourself silly with hope." Curry's problem was that she didn't hope enough. Tom had asked her to call him back and she was so certain she'd never see him again that she hadn't bothered. Which was the way to ensure that she would never see him again.

Sure, there wasn't anything you could do about dry spells; you just had to wait for them to be over. But this wasn't the weather; she could do something.

Curry felt giddy. "Listen, Huck, let's call Tom

and tell him about all these sun-kissed popcorn poppers. I think he has a right to know."

Huck seemed to think it a fine idea. "I'll go upstairs."

"Don't pick up until I finish dialing," she called after him.

She rummaged around one of the kitchen drawers and pulled out the piece of paper with Tom's address.

She dialed and it started to ring. "Okay, Huck," she called. "You can pick it up."

"Hi, Mom," he said over the sound of the phone ringing.

"Hi, Huck." Parent-child communication at its finest.

Click. "Thank you for calling the Charlton Motel. Can I help you?"

"I'd like to speak to a guest if he's in. A Mr. Thomas J. Winches-tee."

Huck started to choke.

"I think he just stepped into the dining room. Shall I go see?"

"Please," Curry answered.

The line went blank as they were put on hold. "Waitresses always know who Tom is," Huck volunteered.

"I'm sure they do."

"Isn't this fun?"

"Paying long distance to talk to you? Yes, it's great fun."

Click. "Hello?"

It was Tom. Living, breathing, speaking—Tom.

"Hi, it's Curry."

"Cur—"

"And me too," Huck put in.

"What's the matter? Is something wrong?"

Nothing was the matter, not one little thing. "No," she said, "we just called to tell you that we think you ought to patch things up with Trish."

"What?" The line was silent for a moment and then—"This should be an interesting phone call."

Huck started to tell him about the Holiday Resorts' sun-kissed white beaches.

Curry could imagine what he looked like. He would be dressed as always in his well-worn jeans and a blue work shirt. As soon as he realized they were all joking, he would lean back against the wall, the phone tucked under his chin, his hands thrust in his pockets, a warm, lazy grin on his face.

"I sure wish I'd known this last week," he said at last. "I just called in every chit I had with that woman to get her to agree to take child support. But if I'd known that something important was going to be coming up..."

"Them's the breaks," Curry told him. "But we're going to have some sun-kissed turkey here on Thanksgiving. Shall we set a place for you?"

It took him a moment to answer, but when he spoke, his voice was as casual as if she'd asked him to cross the street. "Sure. I said I'd be in St. Louis right after Thanksgiving, and since your place is on the way and all, I might as well—"

"What do you mean, on the way?" Huck interrupted. "You're in Illinois, aren't you? Don't you know where St. Louis is?"

"Huck," his mother said sweetly, "shut up."

He didn't. "Well, isn't Bemidji on your way too? Why don't you stop and pick up Diana?"

It was, Curry later reflected, a fine moment in a woman's life when she realizes that she has given birth to a genius. She wondered if Mrs. Edison, Mrs. da Vinci, and Mrs. Shakespeare had been as pleased with their little boys as Mrs. James was with hers.

"I can't make any promises, Huck," Tom was saying. "That's up to Diana's mother. But I'll talk to her; I'll give it my best shot."

Tom was willing to try. Tom was trying.

"Don't let up on her because she's a girl," Huck advised.

Tom laughed. "Thanks, Coach."

Just as Curry had known it would be, Tom's best shot was very good, and a couple of days later Trish called her to say that it was fine if Diana came for Thanksgiving.

Of course, Curry suspected from the quiver in Trish's voice that it wasn't the least bit fine, that she wasn't looking forward to her first holiday without her child any more than Curry would. But Trish was willing to let her go and she was being as gracious as she could about it.

"I'm so pleased that you asked her," Trish said. "She's just thrilled."

"Excuse me, Trish, but isn't Diana always thrilled about everything?"

Trish laughed. "It does get tiring."

What a nice woman you are.

Curry was confident that Trish had not been a

good wife for Tom; she had expected the wrong things of him, she had wanted him to be a clean-shirt-at-supper-say-grace sort of husband.

And maybe she felt guilty about that, because she certainly seemed determined to be a very good *ex*-wife, and Curry thought she was making a fine start.

When Huck got home from his date, she told him that Diana was coming.

"Excellent!" He held out his hands, which she obligingly slapped. "That's just perfect. It will be like the summer all over again."

"Ah . . . Huck, it won't entirely be like the summer."

"What do you mean?"

Curry was dreading this conversation. It wasn't fair. In the movies, kids were always terribly sophisticated, about seven steps ahead of their parents on all counts. But in life, at least in her life, Huck was leaning against the kitchen counter, looking at her with an expression of the most innocent inquiry. You would have thought he didn't know where babies came from.

"You know how special Tom is to me."

"Yeah, I think he's great too."

Not quite in the same way. "And you know there's never really been a man I've cared about since your father died."

"So?" He was still looking a little blank.

Oh, for heaven's sake, why was she pussyfooting around? She wasn't asking his permission. "Look, Huck, I love Tom, and not just as a friend. I love him as a woman loves a man, and so at Thanksgiving, he'll be sleeping in my room."

Huck had seen all those movies too, and he knew exactly how he was supposed to react—bland, bored, faintly approving.

It took him a moment, but he made it. "That's nice, but I'm not surprised."

What a liar. "Of course you're not."

He turned and opened the refrigerator, looking for something to eat. "Were you sleeping together this summer?" he asked from its depths.

Curry sometimes thought that the refrigerator functioned as the family confessional booth; Huck could say things from inside it that he couldn't anywhere else. "Toward the end, yes."

"Why did you keep it a secret?"

She was not going to tell him that she was trying to shelter him. He would hate that. "Because of Diana. Tom was still married to her mother. We didn't know how she would react."

"That makes sense." Huck straightened, emerging from his chilly cocoon empty-handed. "But she does really like you, Mom, and remember, she's the one who always said that Tom was happier when he was here with us than he was any other place."

"I remember her saying that. It meant a lot to me."

"Hey—" Clearly Huck had been struck by a thought.

"What is it?"

"You know, Mom, once Tom and I were talking—" He stopped, flushing.

"Huck, if you can talk to Tom about sex, I think it's wonderful."

"Well, okay...we were talking about it, and

Tom was telling me that it isn't always great, especially if you don't love the gir—the woman. And then he went on, saying that he had only loved one person, and he talked about her, and it was really clear just how much she mattered to him. I've never heard him be so positive about anything except maybe reusing hundred-year-old nails. Anyway, I assumed he was talking about Diana's mother, since he married her and all ... but, well, do you think it's possible that he was talking about *you*?"

And Curry had no idea that she had the confidence, the certainty, with which she answered, "Yes, Huck. Yes, he would have been talking about me."

Chapter Fourteen

"Dad, I can't *breathe.*"

Tom let go of Diana and, stepping back, with his hands on her shoulders, took a look at her.

She was wearing a navy-blue down vest. Under the vest was a burgundy sweater with her initials monogrammed in pink. Under the sweater was a burgundy, navy, and pink plaid blouse. Under the blouse was a white turtleneck dotted with little pink and navy strawberries. What she might have on under the turtleneck, he did not know, but it did seem like an awful lot of clothes for one person to be wearing.

On the other hand, he thought she and all her clothes looked simply wonderful. Her blue eyes were sparkling, and she was blushing and laughing.

How different picking her up at the airport had been this time. Last June, he had approached her slowly, quietly kissing her cheek. As they had waited for her luggage he had lifted his arm to put it around her shoulders, but had let it fall, not knowing if she would mind.

But this time, as soon as she saw him, she had shrieked and, dropping her carry-on bag, had run to him. He had caught her in a hug so tight that she had to protest.

Tom retrieved her bag from where she had started her sprint, and in a few minutes they were in the truck on their way to Gleeson.

"Isn't this *great*?" she gushed. "To go have Thanksgiving in a white farmhouse. Doesn't that just sound unbelievably American?"

Tom had never thought about it. "I guess so. But tell me about your flight. Did you change planes all right? Did any weirdos follow you into the bathroom?"

"I didn't go. But, Dad, the *neatest* thing did happen. There was this lady—she was from Sweden, and do you know what? She didn't speak a word of English, not one word. Do you believe that? Isn't that terrific? I've never met anyone who didn't speak English. It sounds so neat to listen to them. Have you ever met anyone like that, Dad?"

"Sure."

"What do you mean 'sure'?" she demanded. "When? Where?"

"When you were little, when I was overseas."

"Overseas? Dad, when were you overseas?" Diana was clearly enchanted. "Overseas—that sounds so glamorous."

"It wasn't. I was in Vietnam, you knew that."

"Oh, that's right," she said. "My history teacher says we may study that this year—if we have time, that is. I guess they don't always make it through World War Two. You don't talk about it much, do you?"

"About Vietnam?" Tom sometimes had trouble keeping up with her. "Huck would say I don't talk about anything much. But, listen, Diana, if you want to know about it, just ask. It's not the sort of thing to chit chat about, but if you ever want to talk seriously about it, I'll do my best."

Tom felt like his saying that was a big step for him, but Diana wasn't impressed. Her attention had apparently darted elsewhere, and in a moment she gave herself away. "Ah . . . how is Huck, Dad?"

Tom managed not to smile. "As far as I know, he's fine. I haven't seen him since Labor Day."

"Did the two of you have a good time in New Orleans?"

She asked that every single time she spoke to him, and each time Tom felt guiltier and guiltier that he had not brought her down for part of the stay. "We had a very good time, and I hope that you can save a couple weeks next summer so you can do a project with me too."

"What?" Suddenly the world was bright again. "A project with you? Me? Oh, Dad, you're joking!"

"Not at all. Would you like to?"

"Like to? Are you kidding? I mean, Mom said you might ask me for a weekend next summer, but not for a whole *project* because I'm a girl and all."

Tom shook his head. "Huck's stronger than you, but you're much better at detail than he is.

There are projects that he wouldn't be much help on, but you'd be lots."

"Really? Me?"

Tom thought it amazing how Huck and Diana—who seemed, to him, like the most astonishing, extraordinary creatures who had ever drawn a breath—could have such uncertain opinions of themselves. Oh, well, it probably had a great deal to do with being fifteen and sixteen.

"Yes, you. But you'd have to work."

"Oh, I wouldn't mind. Where would we go?"

"Where do you want to go?"

"Hawaii," she replied instantly.

He laughed. "I'm sorry, but I don't have a single contact in Hawaii. Would Newark, New Jersey, do instead?"

"New Jersey..." Diana breathed, her eyes glowing. "Oh, Dad, you're kidding! That's on the East Coast. That would be *great.*"

Actually, Tom had been kidding. "The East Coast it is, then, but I can't promise New Jersey."

"That's okay," she said magnanimously.

But if it hadn't been okay, if she had her heart set on spending August in the center of industrial Jersey, Tom would have built a Burger King if that's what it took to get them there.

As they neared the turnoff to Curry's, Diana took a little pouch out of her purse and rolled down the window. "Is it okay if I move the mirror?"

"Sure."

Tom used his right driving mirror and it always took him forever to get it adjusted just as he liked.

That was one of the things that was hard about traveling alone, adjusting the driving mirror.

He glanced at his daughter, who was brushing something pink across her cheekbones.

Adjusting the driving mirror was just *one* of the things that was hard about traveling alone.

When Diana had finished doing whatever she was doing to her face—Tom couldn't see that she looked one bit different, and he suspected that Huck, who was probably the point of this primping, wouldn't either—she settled one of her many collars and then carefully readjusted the mirror, getting it surprisingly close to the way it had been before. "Is that right?"

"A little to the left...now up a bit...that's good."

At least one of the women in his life understood about having things exactly right. The other did not.

On the other hand, one thing a person could depend on was that Curry James would never twist a car mirror around so that she could check her makeup.

And in a minute he was turning into her drive.

Diana, who sometimes exhibited a startling amount of sense for someone who was related to him, reached over and blasted the truck's horn.

So before they had even pulled up to the barn, Curry and Huck were tumbling out of the house, laughing and calling, running toward the truck. Tom, usually so deft, fumbled with his seat belt and impatiently thrust open the door of the truck. Curry crashed into him, her hair whipping across his face, over his arms, as he pulled her close. He lifted her up, swinging her around, hugging her tight and hard.

At last he put her down.

"I should have done that when you turned up in June." She was a little breathless.

"Curry? Curry James?" He started to brush the hair off her face. "My word, it is you. I was afraid it was a rabid dog, out to bite me."

Curry was not one for missing an opportunity, and she promptly sunk her teeth into his shoulder. And for a moment Tom very much wished that their children weren't standing ten feet away.

But only for a moment.

"Hey, Tom—"

He turned at Huck's voice.

A sudden tightening. *Huck...oh, Huck...*

But then Curry's son grinned, and things were okay again. It was good to see him.

Everyone was chattering. Diana was telling Huck about the lady who spoke Swedish. Huck was telling Tom about a new house going up on the other side of town, trying not to be impressed by what Diana was saying. Curry was honestly impressed and kept asking Diana how she knew it was Swedish, at least, that's what she was doing when she wasn't interrupting Huck to say that the bank was robbing those poor suckers who were just trying to build themselves a decent American home.

"Can I have a beer?" Tom, who never thought of himself as a whimperer, whimpered.

Curry laughed, her wonderful, clear laugh, and

held up her hand, silencing the multitudes. "Huck, take Diana's stuff up to her room," she ordered. "Diana, get your pathetic father a beer. Tom, you—"

"I can carry my own stuff," Diana interrupted and raced off into the house, Huck following after her.

Tom went around to the back of the camper to get out the duffle bag he carried some clothes in. Just as he was stepping out Diana danced up and thrust a beer in his hand. "Here you go, P.F."

"P.F.?"

"Pathetic Father—I like it." And she was off again.

"I am never going to forgive you for that," he told Curry calmly.

"Yes, you are, because I told Huck about us. You can take your things up to my room."

"You're right; I forgive you." He had been wondering how they were going to manage that. "Did you feel weird about it?"

"I did indeed. I always thought the worst thing that could happen to a female was having to tell her parents that she was going to bear an infant out of wedlock. That can't be half as bad as telling your son that you are sleeping with one of your childhood sweethearts." She laughed. "Actually, once I got started, it wasn't a problem at all."

"Did he mind?"

"He didn't seem to, but who knows?"

"I guess I should say something to Diana."

"Do you want me to?"

"Of course I don't," he lied nobly. "It's my right as a parent to make a total hash of this all by myself." He slung his duffle bag over his shoulder and started to march off, whistling the "Colonel Bogey March."

"Remember," she called after him, "Huck has my old room. I sleep in what was my grandmother's room."

"It must be harder to climb out that window."

"I'm getting old; I use the stairs these days."

The farmhouse had three bedrooms: the large front room that apparently Curry slept in now, the little room that had once been hers and was now her son's, and the third one, which Tom had always thought of as the guest room.

He deposited his things on top of Curry's bed, which was made up with the nearly museum quality quilt that she used as casually as if it were a corded spread from the Sears catalog. Then he went across the hall.

Diana was unpacking. She smiled as he sat down on one of the twin beds, and she held up something green. "Do you like this, Dad? It's new."

"I'm not sure what it is, sweetheart. But the color's pretty."

She started to explain; Tom got lost at "dropped waist," but he stayed put, listening to her, thinking about this room.

Curry and Huck had moved in here when they got married. He remembered how Huck had complained that the room had twin beds; it took them three months to work up the nerve to buy them—

selves a double, and even then, they had drawn straws over who was going to tell Curry's grandmother.

How Huck had loved being married. Curry's grandmother had always regarded the two boys, Huck and Tom, as nuisances, as two very large horseflies. But once Curry married and Huck moved in, Gran kept telling him how lovely it was to have a "man" in the house again—a very sweet word to eighteen-year-old Huck.

Tom remembered one sunny afternoon. Curry and Huck had been back from their honeymoon for about a week, and he and Huck were building a new chicken coop at his father's place, trying to figure out what to do that evening.

"Oh, wait," Huck cried. "I almost forgot—the very best thing—"

"What is it?"

"You'll have to guess."

"The hell I do." Tom heaved a board at him.

Huck ducked and laughed. "Okay, but it's great—you aren't going to believe it: *Curry doesn't have a curfew anymore.*"

"What?" Curry's 11:00 P.M. curfew had been the fixed point around which all other plans were made. "We can stop off at Curry's at ten thirty," they would plan, "then she can be out of the window by quarter to eleven..."

"That's right," Huck announced proudly. "It was her idea. I mean, it would have never occurred to me. A couple nights ago we were going out and she just fixes her grandmother with this look and says that we might not be home by elev-

en. Me, I start to crawl under the kitchen table so I
wouldn't get buried when the roof caved in, but
no, the old lady says, 'You do what your *husband*
sees fit, girl. He'll take care of you.'"

"What? Curry has a husband who can take care
of her? Do we know him?"

Huck bowed and laughed.

Tom started back to work. "I don't see that you
are so much better equipped to 'take care' of her
now than you were a month ago."

"What do you mean? I was perfectly willing to
let her get in under the kitchen table with me.
And, anyway, it's beneath a fellow's dignity to
have to stand in the backyard waiting for his wife
to crawl out the window."

His wife! Tom drove a nail in sure and hard. She
had a name, for God's sake. Why didn't he call
her Curry? "His wife" indeed.

And all afternoon as they worked, as they
passed tools back and forth, positioned boards
together, Tom kept noticing Huck's left hand. He
still had his scar, but it had been joined by another
symbol, an unfamiliar gold wedding band.

But now, eighteen years later, there was no
trace of Huck in this room, no sign that he had
lived and slept here. The double bed was gone;
the room was neat, hardly ever used. In fact,
Curry had spoken as if the room were Diana's
own. "Take Diana's stuff up to her room."

He liked that—that there was a room in Curry's
home for his daughter.

Which brought him to the reason he was here.
"Diana?"

"What, Dad?"

"Listen, I know this will come as a surprise, and I don't want you to think it has anything to do with you—"

Why was he talking like this? Why was he apologizing?

Maybe because it's not Diana you're telling this to. Maybe you're talking to Huck.

He started over. "While we're here...ah—"

Diana had turned, now curious, and as he looked at her the memory of Huck's laughter, his freckles, his dancing brown eyes, faded and Tom worried only about how this would affect his daughter.

What was he supposed to say? Should he mention Trish, that they both had their own lives to lead? Should he— Oh, hell, he should just do it.

"While we're here," he repeated, bracing himself for whatever might follow—tears, anger, bewilderment, he had no idea what to expect—"I will be staying across the hall with Curry."

Diana calmly unfolded a blouse. "Oh, I know that. Huck told me."

"He did?"

Diana went over to the closet and hung up her blouse. "Sure."

Diana was pulling off the perfect nonreaction that is the goal of every teenager, and Tom was a little irritated with Huck for telling her. If she hadn't been prepared, he might have some indication of what she was feeling; now he didn't.

Wait a minute. Who was he to complain about this? Of course Huck had told Diana, and when

Hollywood made a movie of it, they could call it "Son of Stick-together-and-answer-straight."

"It doesn't bother you?" He hoped God did not allot each human so many words for his lifetime, because if so, he had just wasted four of his.

"Of course not." Diana came over and sat down next to him. She slipped an arm around his shoulders. "Dad, Mother went through the agonies of the *damned* before she let Phillip sleep over while I was there, and they are getting married as soon as the divorce—" She stopped, her eyes suddenly sparkling with what Tom considered a very dangerous light. "Oh, Dad, are you and Curry—"

"No."

"Why not? I thought you loved her."

"Yes, I do, but—"

"But what?"

How could he explain it to her, that there were still so many memories, so many— "I'm no good at being married, sweetheart."

Spending three weeks with Huck had taught Tom how to recognize a "grown-ups are weird" expression, and one certainly crossed Diana's face now.

Well, he had to agree with her. Maybe not about grown-ups in general, but certainly about himself. He was weird, but what could he do about it?

Any hopes that anyone might have had of a quiet family evening were instantly dashed when it turned out that Diana's one homework assignment for the vacation was, as luck would have it, to memorize the "quality of mercy" speech from *The Merchant of Venice*.

"You know," Tom reflected, "I pay the state of Minnesota a whole wad of money every year for the privilege of owning property there. I sure wish they'd manage to spend it in some way that didn't end up making me hear about thorned monarchs."

"*Thorned* monarchs?" Diana asked. "Is that like in Christ? A crown of thorns?"

Curry laughed. "Good try, Diana, but it's *throned* monarch. Don't listen to your father. He and Huck's father tried to pull that one on me."

"What's this 'tried to pull' crap?" Tom scoffed. "We succeeded. You fell for it."

"Dad!" Diana was disapproving. "Did you really do that? That was *mean*."

"It certainly was," Curry agreed.

Tom grinned at her and turned back to Diana and Huck. "Don't you want to know what she did to deserve it?"

"No, they don't," Curry said instantly. "They think they do, but they really don't."

"Listen, Diana," Huck was saying, "the thing to do is tape it and listen to it over and over."

Tom glanced at his watch, wondering if the stores were all closed. If there was ever a young woman who needed a Sony Walkman, it was Miss Diana James Winchester.

"Actually, I think the problem is that I don't

really know what it is about," Diana said. "I thought maybe it would be easier to memorize if, well...if I, like, *understood* it."

The other three stared at her. It had never occurred to them to try understanding the passage when they had been serving their turn at this hard labor.

But Curry, budding schoolmarm that she was, thought understanding the lines was a wonderful idea, and they spent the rest of the evening trying to figure the thing out. A regular family poetry reading. Tom decided if this was going to be a daily thing, he'd ask to do "My Sweetheart's a Mule in the Mines" next. They'd have a better shot at that one.

But at least this gave him an excuse for standing up at nine thirty and announcing that he could not tolerate this for one more instant, and that he was going to bed—something he had wanted to do from the moment Curry had rushed into his arms.

She managed to tear herself away from Shakespeare and come upstairs with him, leaving Huck and Diana alone with the verse. Tom guessed that the literary discussion would continue for at least another thirty-five or forty seconds.

And then, at last, he was alone with Curry.

She closed the door and turned to face him, her hands on her hips. "You took my child into a topless bar."

"Your child isn't a child anymore, madam."

"He was until he got into your clutches, you filthy varmint."

He laughed. "It's *vermin*, Curry, filthy vermin." God, how he loved her. "Did he tell you?"

"Goodness, no. But the rest of town did. Apparently, he told his friends, which had the same effect as printing it in the paper."

"He hated it, you know."

"I know. He actually told his friends that."

"He did? " Tom shook his head, impressed. "I wouldn't have at his age."

"And do you know what else? This is just between you and me, Tom, because he doesn't know that I know, but—"

This was just like the old days, when they had told each other everything.

He listened as Curry told him how Huck had refused his first girl.

No, maybe this was *better* than the old days; nothing Curry had ever told him then could have pleased him as much as this did now.

"What an amazing kid he is," he said. "I know of only one other person who would have—" He stopped.

"If you are talking about his father"—Curry assumed a lofty expression—"then you're wrong."

"Oh, Curry, *do* tell . . . no, wait, I already know. It was with, ah, what's-her-name . . . don't tell me, I've about got it . . ."

"Shut up, you idiot. Of course it was with me."

"That's not how *he* told it."

"Well, what about what you told Huck? Huck, my son, that is."

"What did I tell him?"

"He says that you told him that sex was really awful, that you hated it."

"I said no such thing."

"He says so—that both times you had been with a woman—"

"*Both* times?"

"—that you felt like it was an utterly wasted five minutes."

"Five— Well, that's right. I really hate it. I just do it to be polite."

"But your manners stink, they always have."

"Why do you think it only takes me five minutes? Now, come over here so we can get started. I want to get this done with so I can go to sleep." He looked at his watch pointedly.

"Are you going to keep time?"

"That was seven seconds. You've got four minutes and fifty-four seconds left."

"And you can't subtract."

"I can. I just thought I'd give you an extra second or so because I'm such a swell guy."

She made a face at him and sat down on his lap, facing him, her legs on either side of his. He kissed her. "Oh, Tom," she sighed. "I'm so glad to see you."

He pulled her closer and started to brush his cheek against the soft flannel of her shirt. "And I'm so glad you don't wear as many shirts as Diana does."

She laughed. "I couldn't believe it . . . and they all *matched*. I couldn't do that if my life depended on it."

"Then it's fortunate that your life doesn't depend on it."

She swung her legs up on the bed, curling them behind him, and she moved against him, familiar, confident. He rested his head against her breast, just giving up to the glorious feel of her body rubbing against his.

Everything he had said to Huck was true. Every word. When you love a woman, then it is different. This wasn't pleasant friction against sensitive nerve endings; this was Curry.

The world went warm, golden. He ran his hands along her legs; he could feel his body start to move with hers. This was Curry, this was love...

He grasped her hips, trying to stop her. "Look, Curry, I was joking about the five minutes."

She was kissing him, his neck, his ear, her breasts brushing against him. "I know that." Her jeans were still tight against his, moving, caressing, exciting.

"I just thought I'd better go on record with that, because if you don't stop what you are doing, I don't have a prayer of making it even to five minutes."

She laughed and, linking her arms around her neck, leaned back, pressing her thighs even closer to his. "Whatever are you talking about?"

"Come on, Curry, give me a break. At least let me get out of these jeans."

"Oh, all right." And Curry flung herself on her back, arms and legs outspread like a martyred virgin.

"That's more like it. But this works better if you take some of your clothes off before flopping down." Tom's were already half off.

She sat up, heaving a sigh. "You really ask a lot sometimes."

"I do not," he defended himself. "You just have to lie there and try to remember to breathe every so often."

"I think I can handle that."

"Great breathing, Curry," he said an embarrassingly few minutes later.

"Thank you." She propped herself up on her elbow. "You know, if I didn't know better, Tom Winchester, I'd say that it's been awhile since you've done that sort of thing."

"Is it so extraordinary that I might want to be faithful to a woman?"

"It certainly is." Then suddenly her eyes went soft. She shook her head. "No, Tom, no, it isn't."

He pulled her down to him, letting her hair spill across his chest. "And I suppose you're one of these women who expects a man to tell her that he loves her."

"I don't expect it, but it would be nice."

She sounded serious and he looked down at her in surprise.

"You never have, you know," she continued calmly. "I know you do, but it wouldn't hurt you to say it."

"Are you sure I haven't? Not even just before I—"

"Not even then."

"Oh, come on, Curry, everybody says I love you then. Even complete strangers do."

"You don't."

"Well, then, let's try again, and I'll do my best to work it in."

"Work what in?" she asked innocently.

"Me gritting my teeth and choking out the fact that I love you, you nitwit."

"Why, Tom, you do say the most romantic things."

"Yes," he agreed. "It's one of my specialties."

Tom had had Thanksgiving dinner in this house many times before. Curry's grandmother had always had them over—he and his father, Huck and his mother. It had been deadly. The only fun part had been how mad Curry got when he and Huck would tell her that "sticking together" did not include doing the dishes with her.

But doing dishes—and they had always helped her—was nothing compared to what she was planning for today. She had been to the grocery store and that was it.

When Tom came back from seeing the Jenkinses, the family who'd bought his father's house, Curry greeted him by thwacking him in the stomach with a bunch of celery. "Chop this."

"What?"

"I have a history paper due Monday. And it was either get that done and not stuff the turkey or stuff the turkey and spend the whole weekend writing."

"History? I knew that that Wheeler fellow had it in for me."

"Not just you. Everybody's working."

Indeed Diana was at the table making pie crust and Huck was opening cans of pumpkin.

They didn't seem to mind, but then Huck was used to such abuse from his mother, and, of course, Diana was crazy enough to think it was going to be fun. "No, Dad, you'll see, it will be great. Mother's kitchen isn't nearly big enough for four people to work in."

Tom thought that he really ought to take his daughter to Newark next August. Serve her right. "Why do you think I built it like that?" he asked her. "I wanted to be sure I never had to go in it."

"Shut up and start chopping," Curry ordered.

Naturally her knives were duller than his screwdrivers, and so he went out to his truck, got his whetstone, and started to sharpen them. Curry promptly cut herself and bled all over the turkey.

"I meant to do that," she told them. "It's a new way of basting."

"Hey, Mom," Huck asked her. "Now if the turkey asks you any questions, do you have to answer it straight?"

"Darling," she returned with a pointed look, "I talk to enough turkeys already."

God only knew why, but Diana thought that this was incredibly funny, and she stood there, laughing helplessly, the pastry blender dangling from her hand.

Tom took his whetstone back out to the truck. Sharp knives were important, but even having the blades exactly right was not as important as Curry's hand.

As he came back in he paused at the kitchen door, looking through. Diana and Huck were at the kitchen table. Huck was seated, a pile of pale green celery in front of him. Diana was standing, rolling out a pie crust into a nearly perfect circle. Huck was saying something to her, and she was blushing. Curry was at the counter, her back to the room, but she had craned her head over her shoulder, and she too was smiling at what Huck had said.

How precious the three of them were. Everything he held dear was in that warm, bright kitchen. For a moment Tom ached to be a part of their lives.

Well, you are. They love you; they need you.

Oh, sure they did. Diana was getting a stepfather, and Huck... well, yes, Huck had needed him some this summer, but that was only by default. As for Curry, she did love him, but Curry James didn't need anyone.

Sunday came painfully soon, and suddenly Diana, who knew only half of the "quality of mercy" speech, was saying good-bye.

"I had a marvelous time. We really should do this again," she told Curry.

"That's fine with me. Come whenever you want; I'm always here."

"What about Christmas?" Apparently Huck thought the arrangements should be definite.

"Oh, I'd love to," Diana sighed, "but Phillip was going to take Mother and me skiing."

"Well, we'll work something out," Curry said. "Now scoot along, you two; you've got a plane to catch."

In what Tom considered to be the noblest gesture of his entire life, he was letting Huck drive Diana into Watertown. He himself was off to St. Louis on Monday to do some work for a couple of antique dealers.

Huck and Diana took off, and Tom went into his truck to get his tool belt. The cord on the lamp in Curry's bedroom was fraying. He thought it dangerous, and she was willing to let him replace it.

"What are you doing for Christmas, Tom?" she asked as he came back out.

"Me? I haven't a clue. I used to go to Bemidji, but I guess I won't this year. Diana won't be there, and even if she were, Trish will have just gotten married. She's not going to want me around."

It was funny, he'd never really liked much about Bemidji, he didn't think of it as home, but it was...well, a center. Somewhere to go for holidays, an address to give people. He didn't have even that anymore.

"You know you are welcome to come here."

He didn't say anything for a moment. And then—"You know what I would really like...I mean, if you don't mind and all—"

"What?"

"Instead of coming for Christmas, I guess I'd like to come for Huck's opening game."

"Oh, Tom." For a moment Curry looked as if

she might cry. "That would mean the world to him, it really would. But you could still come back for Christmas too."

He shook his head. "That doesn't make any sense; they're too close together."

"Stay the whole time. You could make table legs or whatever it is you do for the St. Louis people."

"No, I couldn't do that."

Curry walked to the house as if she were going back inside. She opened the screen door, but then let it fall shut. She turned back to him. "Is this what it's going to be like for us, Tom, a few weekends a year?"

Slowly he strapped his tool belt on. *A few weekends a year.* She was right; it wasn't enough. But he didn't see any other way.

He was leaving tomorrow, and he'd be alone. He wouldn't have stopped minding being alone before he'd be back for Huck's first game. Then he'd leave, and it would start all over, the leaving, the minding, the coming back.

It was an odd way to live.

"It's too bad you can't come with me," he said at last.

"It's too bad *you* can't stay."

"My work—"

"Don't blame your work, Tom." And then— "Don't you think it's about time you said goodbye to Huck?"

"To Huck? I just—"

He stopped. Oh, that Huck.

"My son says that you told him you'd never

said good-bye to his father. Don't you think it's about time you did?"

It was a warm day for November, really almost Indian summer. The sunflower stalks still had a few fading blossoms and the—

"Sometimes I feel like you're so close to working things out. You're starting to feel good about yourself. You're not so withdrawn, so solitary. You're letting yourself love Diana . . . and me and my son too. But just when I think it's really going to work for you, I can see you waiting, watching, expecting Huck's father to come walking around the corner of the barn. He's not going to, Tom. He's dead."

The barn was brick red, the color barns always are in this part of the country. It wasn't a big barn, this barn wasn't. But still someone could be just around the corner, and you wouldn't see him.

"You made a joke about him." It was like she was pleading. "Wednesday night you made a joke about him. You've never done that before. It's a step, Tom, the first step. Aren't you ready to take a few more?"

He had to say something. "Like what? Put flowers on his grave? Go find his name on the memorial?"

"If that would mean something to you, then, yes. Or you could reread *Huck Finn*. You haven't, have you?"

"What good would that do? It's only a book."

"No, it isn't, not to us. And I know you've tried to read it. Maybe you made it through *Tom*

Sawyer, but not *Huck Finn.* On the top of the third page, you had to quit, didn't you?"

On the top of the third page ... She was exactly right.

"Oh, Tom, it killed me too. I thought I couldn't stand it, but I read it."

He had tried to read it once, this greatest of all American tales, of course he had, but after that passage, he had to close the book, never to open it again. He had read that paragraph just once, and still he remembered every word.

Miss Watson was telling Huck Finn about heaven:

Then she told me all about the bad place, and I said I wished I was there. She got mad then, but I didn't mean no harm. All I wanted was to go somewheres; all I wanted was a change, I warn't particular. She said it was wicked to say what I said; said she wouldn't say it for the whole world; *she* was going to live so as to go to the good place. ... I asked her if she reckoned Tom Sawyer would go there, and she said not by a considerable sight. I was glad about that, because I wanted him and me to be together.

... *him and me to be together* ... That's all he wanted, just for Huck and Tom to be together.

The barn was red, and it dropped a dark, heavy shadow. He could be there in the shadows, maybe he was down by the creek, but somewhere—Tom had to believe it—somewhere Huck was waiting.

"It would only have to be for a minute," he heard himself say. "I would only need him here for a minute."

"Why?" Curry sounded far away—almost as far as she had been when he was in Nam, remembering her. "Tom, why?"

"Because there's something I have to say to him, something I didn't know until it was too late."

"What is it? Is it something you can say to me?"

The chrome on her car was loose, it just needed a couple of rivets. A couple of rivets would hold it fast.

"No"—he wasn't sure if he was the one speaking—"it wouldn't matter to anyone else...just to him and me. And it's *him* I have to tell it to; I owe it to *him*."

"Oh, Tom, no, you don't." Curry had come to stand next to him. She was crying. "He knew that you loved him."

"No, you don't understand..."

"I know you never said it; you were only boys. How could you say that you loved each other? But, Tom, he knew. And anything you owe Huck, anything you've ever owed to Huck, you've more than paid by what you've done for his son. What matters about Huck now is his son. My boy needed his father this summer, and you were here because he couldn't be."

Tom looked away. He couldn't stand to see her cry, but, oh, God, didn't she understand? Why couldn't she understand how much he needed to talk to Huck, how badly he needed to say just one thing to him? It would only take a minute, even less than that.

No, of course she couldn't understand. That had been clear from the very beginning; he had seen it right away—that Curry didn't know.

So what was the point of trying to tell her why he couldn't let go? *Face it, Winchester, you're off the deep end, wanting to say something to a man who's been dead for fifteen years.* No wonder Curry had sounded horrified. Who wouldn't be? She was out in the middle of nowhere, with a certifiable lunatic on her hands.

"One more crazed vet ax-murders childhood sweetheart"—that's what the headline would read.

Except he would never, not ever, do anything to hurt her.

She had sunk down to the steps, and he sat down beside her. "Oh, Curry, don't cry. I didn't want to make you cry."

She sniffed and wiped her palms across her cheeks. "It's okay. I probably don't cry enough." She paused for a moment. "And you probably don't either."

"Cry enough?" Tom couldn't remember when he had last cried.

She stood up and put her hands on his shoulders, looking down at him. "I'll never love another man as long as I love you, but that's all right. I'd rather have a few weekends a year with you than all my days with anyone else. But we'll never have more than that until you can accept that Huck is gone."

He was shaking his head. He couldn't, he couldn't ever accept that.

"Tom, we've always heard about dry spells, that there's nothing you can do about them, that you just have to live through them. Well, that's true, but this is different. We're not powerless; we can make ourselves happy, but you've got to say good-bye to Huck first."

She was right. She always was. It was a long time before he spoke. "But I don't know how, Curry, I just don't know how."

Chapter Fifteen

There wasn't anything else to say. They went inside. Tom put a new cord on Curry's lamp, and she started to work some trig problems. He installed a pneumatic door closer on the screen door so that it wouldn't bang anymore.

Huck called. Diana's plane had taken off late; he was leaving for home now.

For lunch, they finished the last bits of turkey. Curry went back to her homework, and Tom looked for more things to repair.

It was a flat, empty Sunday afternoon, their last remaining hours together poisoned because he was leaving tomorrow.

The phone rang again.

Curry glanced at the clock but didn't get up.

"Do you want me to get that?"

She shook her head. "It's just Huck, calling to say he's stopped at somebody's house." She finished her problem before standing up. She pushed her hair over her shoulder as she reached for the receiver.

And then, astonishingly, Curry, strong, unshakable Curry, went white. Her hand flew to her throat and her shoulders hunched.

In a moment Tom was at her side. She seemed very small.

"Is he going to be all right?" she was asking, her voice shaking.

Huck! Something had happened to Huck.

"You don't know," she gasped. "How can you not know?"

Tom took the receiver from her loosening grip. "This is Tom Winchester. I'm a friend of Mrs. James's. Could you please tell me what happened?"

Curry had buried her face in her hands. He pulled her to him.

"Oh, Tom," the phone answered. "I'd heard you were back. This is Jody Vaughan, I mean, Jody Smith—"

Tom had dated Jody Smith once or twice.

"I'm a nurse in the emergency room, and they just brought Huck in. He's been in a car accident, and—"

A car accident! No. Our parents—that's what happened to them. Not another car accident.

Curry was now pulling at his arm. "Come on, Tom, let's go. We've got to get there."

He kept his arm around her, holding her still. "How bad is it?" he asked the nurse.

"I don't know. The doctor is with him now, but I knew Curry would want to get here as soon as possible."

"We'll be there in twenty minutes."

Curry didn't cry in the car. Tom almost wished

that she would. She just sat, numbly, blankly staring out the windshield at the flat road.

"If he was drinking, I'll..." Her voice trailed off, but Tom knew what she had been about to say.

If he was drinking, I'll kill him. Careless, automatic words—"I'll kill him"—made excruciating because he might already be dead.

She buried her face in her hands, and her voice was faint, sounding nothing like herself. "Oh, God, not him too. Please not him too."

The words tore at Tom. *Not him too.* So many people had already died: her parents, her husband, her grandmother. Had a part of her always been waiting for this, expecting this? That her child would die too?

How had she been able to stand it? How *would* she stand it?

Huck had been so happy all weekend, talking about the start of basketball season, teasing Diana about memorizing her speech. Was that it? Had he been thinking about free throws and rebounds instead of the road? Had some brief flash of inattention, some pleasant thought about Diana, diverted him, then becoming the last thought he would ever have?

What had his father's last thought been? Had it too been of some sunlit adventure, or had his mind been full of fear and the jungle's darkness, of the numbing struggle to survive?

Jody was waiting for them at the entrance to the small hospital, holding open the glass door. Tom recognized her immediately and took her arm, hoping to guide her away from Curry in case the news was bad, but Curry had to know. "Where is he? How is he?"

"He's going to be fine." Tom felt Curry slump against him. He put his arm around her, holding her, feeling her tremble. Jody went on. "He's been cut badly, but that's it. There's no telling what would have happened if he hadn't had his seat belt on, but he did and—"

"Where is he?" Curry spoke quickly now. "Can I see him?"

"Of course. But the doctor's still with him, and we need some information from you first, though." The nurse handed some forms to Curry.

"I need to see him." She turned to Tom. "Please, Tom, I need to see him now."

He looked down at her; why was she asking him? What could he do?

Anything she asked of him. Anything at all. At least, he would try. "Listen, Jody, let her go in. She's not going to get hysterical or faint at the blood, you know that. You can make an exception for her. I'll fill out this stuff." The nurse was shaking her head. "Now, Jody"—Tom touched her arm—"if that were your boy in there, you'd want to be with him."

Jody's eyes went soft and she turned to Curry. "Okay, Curry, just keep out of the doctor's way."

He was waiting for Jody when she came back out into the hall. "Is he really going to be all right?"

She nodded. "His face will be scarred, but if they care enough, Curry and Huck could go down to Sioux Falls and have a plastic surgeon take care of it."

"That's—" Tom stopped, suddenly unable to speak. They might have lied to Curry, but all this talk of Sioux Falls and plastic surgeons; Jody wasn't lying. Huck was going to be all right. He really was.

The world blurred, and Tom ducked his head. *You ass, you aren't going to cry, are you?*

Jody tactfully flipped through a chart, and when he looked back at her, his gaze clear again, she spoke gently. "Tom, there's something maybe you should know." She took a breath. "When they brought Huck in, he kept saying something about a child."

"A child?" Tom stared at her. "He didn't run over a child, did he?"

"I don't think so, nobody's brought a child in, and the people who called the ambulance didn't say anything about a child. The ambulance crew's gone back out to check, but Huck was awfully upset about it."

"Has he said anything else?"

Jody shook her head. "They are sewing his face; he can't talk until they are done. But I thought you'd better be prepared."

"Yes, yes, of course."

What if Huck had killed a child? Huck, straightforward, frank Huck, just now moving to the halfcourt line between being a child and an adult. What if a small child were now dead because of him? How would he be able to live with himself? Sixteen and a killer.

Oh, Curry, he's going to need you. Are you that strong?

"Now, Tom." Jody's voice broke into his thoughts. "You promised to fill out those forms."

The tiled corridor was lined with chairs that had little arm desks and Tom moved to one of those. He glanced back over his shoulder. "Jody, it was nice of you to let Curry go on in."

Jody shrugged, smiling a little. "Well, there's one condition."

Tom raised his eyebrows.

"If you're back here to stay, you've got to promise to keep away from me. You can still talk me into anything."

Tom smiled at her, hoping his smile was not as tired as it felt. He could not remember what it was that he had talked her into doing twenty years ago; it hardly seemed important.

Curry had dropped her shoulder bag onto one of the chairs; it was the purse Huck had gotten her in New Orleans. Tom pulled out her wallet, flipping through it to find her Social Security number, her Blue Cross number, and all the other numbers that the hospital wanted. For the most part, the form seemed straightforward; Huck was a minor; the responsible adult was his mother; she was a student, a widow, insured, etc., etc.

When Tom had nearly finished, the glass door swept open and a man hurried in. Without a glance at Tom, he went straight to the nurses' station. "Is the James boy going to be all right?"

"The doctor is still with him," Jody answered. "Until he is finished, we can only discuss the condition of a patient with the family." But in her kind way, she had stressed the "we" and then had gestured at Tom, silently suggesting that the man talk to him.

Tom hurriedly finished the form and stood up. "My name's Winchester. You were asking about Huck James?"

"Do you know anything? Is he going to be all right?"

"They told his mother that he would be, that he's cut badly, but he'll make it—"

"Thank God." The man slumped against the wall. "We were so sure—his car was such a—and there was so much blood, and the ambulance people wouldn't tell us a thing."

"You saw the accident?" The man nodded. "Then what's this about a child?"

"It was my son, our youngest."

And Tom knew, without asking, that the child must be all right; otherwise, the man would not be so concerned about Huck. "Tell me."

"It was such a warm day . . . our kids were playing in the drive"—the man sounded as if he were retelling a bad dream—"just the sort of thing they do all summer. And usually they're careful because we live right on Route Nine, but this time the ball went into the road and our four-year-old son didn't look. He just charged right out and the car was coming. It couldn't stop in time, there was no way."

Tom swallowed hard, he too seeing every parent's nightmare: a frozen image, Diana in front of a car and he powerless, unable to do anything to save her, and then her body, twisted and bloodied on the shoulder of the road.

"It just seemed so certain, so inevitable," the man was saying, "but that boy, I don't know how, he jerked the car right off the road; then she rolled and hit a tree."

"He didn't hit your son?"

The man shook his head. "No. That's what we couldn't believe. He must have thrown the car into reverse at the same time he turned. It was—I don't know if I could have done it, if I would have had my wits about me enough." The man cleared his throat. "We'll never be able to thank him for what he's done."

"Gentlemen."

It was the doctor, old Doc Reynolds. Tom said his name, and the man introduced himself as George Hauser and then continued quickly. "Is he going to be all right? My wife and I would never forgive ourselves if he isn't."

The doctor assured them that Huck would be fine. "He's on his way to a room now. You can go on in, Tom. They're both asking for you."

The room was down the hall, and Tom knocked softly before he went in. Huck was in bed; Curry was in a chair at his side, holding his hand.

At the sound of the door they both looked up. Huck looked pale against the white pillow, his freckles more prominent than usual. Black lines of stitching crossed his bruised cheek as if he were a scarecrow with a face sewn together out of blue-and-tan rags.

His voice was a little slurred; he couldn't open

his mouth all the way. "I wasn't speeding, Tom. Really I wasn't." It seemed important to him that Tom understand this.

He's confused, Tom thought. He can't understand why this happened when he hadn't been doing anything wrong. He still expects the world to make sense. If something bad happens, it has to be someone's fault. Adolescents thought that way—bad things were punishments, and punishments had to be earned.

Adolescents, hell. Grown men walk around for fifteen years wondering what they've done wrong, what they've done to make their best friends die.

"I know you weren't speeding," he assured Huck. "In fact, Hauser says that it was one of the alertest pieces of driving he's ever seen. They're mighty grateful to—"

"Hauser?" Huck said blankly.

"The little boy's parents." Then Tom asked him carefully, "You do remember the little boy, don't you?"

"Little boy?" Curry asked, suddenly frantic. "What are you talking about? A little boy? Was a child involved?"

"Yes." And at her gasp, Tom explained quickly. "It was a four-year-old. He ran out into the highway without looking. Huck rolled his car rather than hit him."

Curry again groped for her son's hand, and Huck, more teenager than hero, eyed her carefully to be sure that she wasn't mad at him. "And I threw it into reverse. I knew what it would do to the transmission, Mom, but I didn't know what

else to do. The kid, he looked so, well, so small.
And helpless. I just had to—''

Suddenly Huck turned to look at Tom, his eyes
questioning. "Did I do the right thing?''

"Absolutely," Tom replied instantly. "Absolutely. You had no other choice.''

For the first time in his life Huck had felt the
impulse that had lead men to save women and
children first; he had felt the code, and he must
have felt that only a man could understand.
Another man.

He was growing up.

"I don't know." Huck's voice was getting a
little dreamy. "When I saw that kid...he looked
so little, I've never felt that way before.''

"No. But you will again." Tom looked down at
Huck. "Often.''

If you are lucky, that is, Tom amended silently. *If
you are lucky, there will be a boy someday and you
will look down at him, feeling for him just what I do
for you now.*

Huck was blinking.

"Did they give him a sedative?" he asked
Curry.

She nodded.

"Does this...mean I'll...missing the opening...''

Huck was sound asleep when Doc Reynolds
came in. The doctor looked at him, felt his pulse,
and then spoke. "Curry, he'll be out all night.
There's no reason for you to stay.''

"I want to," she said immediately.

The doctor shook his head. "You mothers are

all alike," he said, but his tone wasn't severe. "At least, let Tom take you out and get something to eat."

She shook her head. "I couldn't eat a thing."

Doc shrugged and turned to Tom. "Go get her something and not the coffee shop food."

Tom was glad to have something he could do for her. "Do you need anything from home, Curry? A sweater? A book?"

"A sweater, yes, a sweater would be nice."

When he got back home, Tom found that they had left all the lights on and the back door wide open. He made some sandwiches and gathered up some fruit and cookies. Then he went up to her room and rummaged around, finding a sweater. There was a stack of books on her nightstand and he picked up a few.

And the last thing he did was track down the home number of the antique dealer in St. Louis. "Don't expect me until I get there," he told him. "Something's come up, and I can't leave."

Chapter Sixteen

Huck was kept in the hospital for three days, and by the evening of his last night there, he was feeling much better, and his room was filled with his friends.

Knowing that the boys would all prefer to be without adults, Tom and Curry went back home. It had been the first time they had been alone since they had heard of Huck's accident. Curry had been at the hospital most of the time; when she wasn't there, Tom was.

As he held open the screen door for her, she spoke. "Tom, thank you."

"Opening a door isn't that hard. You probably could have done it yourself if you'd tried."

"You know what I mean."

He shook his head. "Anyone would have helped you out in an emergency like this. There're a lot of people in this town who are on your side. Any one of them would have dropped everything for you." Curry's refrigerator was now packed with casseroles, scalloped potatoes, and molded salads; people had been calling, stopping by the hospital, willing to do anything for her.

"Oh, I know that. But all this bustling to and from the hospital—that's the easy part; I didn't need you for that."

Tom looked at her blankly. "Then I don't understand. That's all I did, things anyone could have done."

Curry sat down at the kitchen table and she stared at her hands for a moment. "You remember how on Sunday I was saying it seems like you'd almost gotten everything together for yourself?"

He nodded.

"Well, it was that way for me too."

"For you?" What did Curry need to get herself together about? No one had his head screwed on as straight as she did.

"This summer I realized that I have this thing about people leaving. I assume that every time anyone ever leaves that they'll never come back."

Oh. Yes, of course. Of course, she'd have problems with that. No wonder she seemed so independent and strong. She didn't dare let herself need people; they'd only leave her.

"In fact," she continued, "when you and Huck went off to New Orleans, subconsciously I was assuming that I'd never see either of you again."

"Curry—"

She held up her hand. "Obviously, I was wrong. Huck came back, and then you did. And I realized I could stop living my life like everyone I loved was going to die next week, and then..."

"And then you thought that Huck had died too."

"Yes," she said flatly. "And when we were driving to the hospital, I didn't know how I was going to make it. I used to think I'd been through the worst; I didn't think anything could be as hard as losing a husband at twenty-two, but I was wrong. Losing my son would be worse."

"They call it Nature's Joke, burying your child."

"It would be some joke, all right, but, you know, Tom, every other time bad things have happened to me, I've had to face them alone, and the one thing I knew, the only thing that got me to that hospital without falling apart, was that I knew I wasn't going to have to face this one alone."

She believed that. She honestly believed that.

"But you could have," he said slowly, "you could have done it on your own."

"I know I could have, but Tom, I've looked trouble in the eye so often: Huck's father dying, Gran going batty on me, Myra being sick for so long. When a woman has to face that much heart-ache alone, it changes her, it does strange things to her. You talk to women whose lives have been that hard, and they just aren't like other women. But I still am; I'm tough, I'm real tough, but I'm not hard yet. And facing this alone, that would have made me go hard."

Tom knew what she meant, and he could see it, Curry's strength becoming granite, her grit becoming flint, her warmth and laughter buried under the stony struggle to survive.

She went on. "It happened to the pioneer women; the women who had first settled here. This prairie was so desperately isolated, their lives were so blankly comfortless, that they had to go hard, harder than a woman ought to be. They survived all the trouble, through all those lonely winds, but the cost must have been higher than any one of them could have dreamed. And I would have survived my son's dying, but I would have paid a terrible price."

Tom listened to her, her words so lovely, her sentences so graceful and flowing, so unlike her usual speech. This was what she must mean, that there was a poetry in her, a poetry that the demands of her hard life had choked just like buffalo grass on a short-grass prairie choked out the violets.

"You would have kept that from happening to me, Tom," she continued, her voice low. "I don't know if you believe it of yourself, but I believe it. You wouldn't have let me down; I know that as well as I know anything."

And with deep certainty, Tom knew it too. If Huck had died, or if Huck had killed that child, Tom would have never left her. He would have stayed for that. He didn't know what good he would have done, but he would have stayed.

"Yes, Curry, I would have been here with you." And he picked up her left hand, touching his forefinger to hers, the two white scars meeting. "It would have been a first for me, but I would have stayed."

And Curry smiled, the diamond-bright smile

that had lit up his memory for years. "Now, surely there's food around here," she said lightly. "I've carted enough stuff to other people that they owe me."

Her voice was like it had been before, the brisk, practical Curry, but Tom knew, even if no one else ever would, that this was only the side of Curry she chose to show. There was more, a sweetness and beauty that needed a little shade against the hot prairie sun if it were to survive.

Curry needed him.

"There's enough Jell-O salad in the icebox to feed even Huck," he told her. "What do you want for supper?"

"Not Jell-O. But something solid would be nice."

"I think there's chicken and ham."

It was the most routine talk, but wasn't this what days are made of, what life is made of, the routine, the ordinary, occasionally punctuated by poetry and tragedy? Why had the routine once frightened him so, made him feel so trapped?

As they ate, Curry flipped through the mail that had been accumulating. "What's this?"

He glanced at the blue sheet of paper she had in her hand. "The form I filled out when we first got to the hospital."

"I thought you didn't fill out forms." She clearly didn't remember how he had taken the form from her.

"I don't make a habit of it, but in a pinch I can do it."

She skimmed through it. Suddenly she looked

up and smiled. "This is sweet, Tom. You listed yourself as the 'next of kin outside the home.'"

He shrugged. "I guess that was stupid, since I'm using your address these days. I should have put your friend Bonnie." It had never occurred to him to list anyone but himself.

"Well, the little box is hardly big enough to describe your relationship to Huck." She was teasing.

"That's why I left it blank."

Curry looked up at him, surprised. "No, you didn't. You put in 'uncle.'"

Tom froze. He did not remember doing that. He simply did not.

George Hauser had been asking about Huck— he had been hurrying to finish the form and talk to him. He must have done it absolutely unthinkingly. Oh, God, after all these years...

"Well, I'm proud of you," Curry was saying. "At last you're doing things my way, telling the closest approximate lie. 'Uncle' is five spaces and a reasonable—"

"It's not a lie, Curry," he heard himself say. Why was he saying this? *Why?*

Because, at long last, he was going to answer straight the question that had never been asked. He was going to say it.

"Huck's father and I were brothers."

"Well, of course you and Huck were like brothers." Her voice was easy, her smile pleasant. "Goodness, most of the time, Huck and *I* were like brothers."

"No, Curry. Huck and I weren't *like* brothers. We were brothers, half-brothers."

Her fork clattered to the plate. "What on earth are you talking about?"

"Huck's father, Howard James—he was my father too."

Curry stared at him. "You don't mean that."

"Didn't you ever wonder why my father, my legal father, and Huck's mother weren't in the car that night?"

She shook her head, her mouth open. "Not really. Weren't they baby-sitting? Like my grandmother was with me?"

"No. My mother and Huck's father—my parents—had finally decided to run off together, and your folks were in the car, trying to persuade them not to."

"My God, Tom—" she faltered. "Your mother and Huck's father...your parents...I don't understand."

"I don't know all the details. But apparently, my father, I mean, my stepfather—" Tom gave up and started using names. "Apparently, Cal Winchester came back from the war, his war, in pretty bad shape. Not physical problems, but mental. He was a man ahead of his times, I guess. It sounds like clinical depression, but, of course, in those days, they just thought of him as having a lot of bad days. And Howard James was everything the opposite. He'd done great in the Marines, but he was still glad to be home, all full of plans and enthusiasm, just like Huck would have been...and you know what Myra James was like."

Curry nodded, remembering her mother-in-law, a faded, complaining woman. "But, Tom, you and Huck were born within a *week* of one another."

"I know," he said bitterly. "Howard was still sleeping with Myra, although my mother wasn't sleeping with Cal, which was the mistake, because it meant that he knew. I guess that they all did." He gestured at his eyes, so surprisingly blue. "Apparently, Howard James had these eyes. We didn't know that because all the pictures we ever saw were black and white."

"But what about those pictures? They all seemed so happy in them."

"I think they were just trying real hard. You know those stories we heard about what fun the six of them always had together? It was always your grandmother that told them, not Cal or Myra James. The two of them never told those stories because they weren't true. Sure, they did all those things together, things that were supposed to be fun; they were all trying to convince themselves that this would work. That they could go on being friends, three happy families, but the whole time, they all knew that Cal Winchester wasn't my father."

"But why did your mother and Huck's father wait so long to do something? I mean, we were all two at the time of the accident."

"Times were different then. Remember, they'd all grown up in the Depression, they'd just been through a war, they were probably all desperate for some sort of stability. There was a lot of talk in those days about how families had to stay together.

So they tried and apparently managed for a few years. It's really sad when you think about it, what they all must have gone through. But Cal probably made my mother's life impossible, and it must have reached a point where Howard just couldn't stand by and watch her misery any more. He must have felt responsible for both women, both my mother and Huck's. But my mother probably seemed more miserable than Huck's, and you know, if he was anything at all like Huck was, he would have felt like he had to do something."

"Tom, where did you find all this out? I've been here my whole life, and I never had a clue."

"When I came home that one time after the service. Dad was talking about kids, telling me that I would regret it forever if I didn't have a son, that a man needs a son. But things were so awful with Trish then; I couldn't imagine how I was ever going to spend the rest of my life with her. Of course, I couldn't tell him that, so instead I was snide, and randomly asserted that the Winchester name and bloodline were not so superb that they needed to be preserved through the ages. And then he told me that it was a generation too late to be worrying about that."

Suddenly Tom's voice changed, and he told her what it had been like, coming home, how hard it had been. Even turning into the drive had been hard, knowing that Huck no longer lived down the road.

It had been in late January, bitterly cold but without any softening snow. The mud had frozen into ridges, the tire tracks preserved until the spring thaw. The landscape was harsh, the choke-cherry trees were bare and gray, and the wind was strong enough to break the limbs of the elms. It was a world without Huck.

His father's house had been cold; even Tom, who cared little about physical comfort, noticed. He had offered to insulate or caulk, put in better windows, a new furnace. But his father railed at him about Trish and Diana, about how unhappy he'd be if he didn't have a son.

"I don't know that having a son has made you so all fired happy."

And then his father, the man he called Dad, had said that he had never had a son.

In shock, Tom had insisted on details, the steady, miserable accumulation at last convincing him that he had a brother. Or rather that he had had a brother.

Only after Huck was dead, had Tom learned that they'd been brothers.

"Do you understand, Curry? That's why I left without seeing you. I came over here; I was across the creek and in the orchard, and I just couldn't. I was too blank, too numb."

"I still wish you had come."

"I couldn't. I would have told you, I couldn't have helped it, and I knew Dad wanted to shoot himself for telling me. He and Myra had kept it secret during all those years when we were little. I guess it was horribly important to her that no one ever know, and he didn't want her to find out that he'd let on. And I figured I owed him that much. I know I owed you, but I owed him too. I wasn't his, but he raised me. And so I let you down."

"Yes, yes, you did," Curry acknowledged, "but I forgave you a long time ago even without understanding why you did it, and it's time you forgave yourself too."

She twisted her napkin. This explained so much. Why Cal Winchester hadn't loved Tom; the man was raising a boy who wasn't his own. It explained why Mrs. James hadn't treated Tom better; his bright blue eyes always reminded her of what her husband had done.

The stories that that woman had told Huck—about how wonderful his father had been. How those stories had oppressed him. He joined the Marines to prove that he was the man his father had been. And the stories had been lies.

But all that was in the past. What Curry cared about now was Tom. What did this explain about him? Yes, it explained why he hadn't come that day. And it explained why he was so uneasy with the notion of stepfathers—he'd been raised by one who resented him. But what else did this explain about Tom?

She knew this was going to sound terribly unsympathetic, but she had to say it. "Tom, just what difference does knowing this make?"

"What difference?" He stared at her. "All the difference in the world."

"Do you think that would have changed things? That there would have been something better between you and Huck had you known?"

"Well, for starters, we didn't both have to be over there."

She had no idea what he was talking about.

"In Vietnam," he said impatiently, "brothers don't have to serve in the same war zone. Don't you see the joke? If we'd known, if we could have gotten it declared legal somehow, then once I got there, he could have come home. And I could have gotten there before he...before he—"

"Before he died." Curry could say it. Then she shook her head. "It wouldn't have worked that way. Even if you had gotten your birth certificate changed or whatever, Huck wouldn't have come home, not at your expense, not ever. And you know it."

Of course he knew it. If he honestly believed that this secret had caused Huck's death, he would have been unspeakably bitter.

"I guess I do," he said slowly. "But after he died, I felt so guilty, like I was responsible, like I should have been able to prevent it. And then when I found out about this, it seemed like this would have been the way. I held on to that for a long time—maybe to punish myself—but, of course, you're right. If we'd known, it just would have meant that I wouldn't have gone. It wouldn't have changed what happened to him."

"And you didn't know."

"Isn't that ironic? All that time we were pretending to share the same blood"—Tom flicked his thumb across his scarred finger—"we really were."

"You said the other day you wanted to tell him something." She remembered how horrified she had been by the blank, helpless misery that had been in his voice. "Was it this?"

He nodded. "I felt like I'd give anything, even my own life, just to have him alive for another minute so I could look at him and call him 'brother.'"

Call him "brother." Suddenly it all made perfect sense to Curry—why Tom so longed to have known. It was the same mistake he made again and again. Words had too much power for him.

This time she was going to say it aloud. "Oh, Tom, you did know your brother; you acted like brothers, you loved each other like brothers; you were brothers—you just had the wrong word for it, *friends* instead of *brothers. Brother* is just a word, a label. What counts is the love, not the word that describes it, and you and Huck had that love. You didn't need the label, and you shouldn't mourn it—it wouldn't have changed anything. If words mattered as much as you believe they do, then it would have been enough for Cal just to call himself your father, but it wasn't. The word didn't make him love you."

She took his hand. "Tell me the truth, Tom. All these years when you've been saying that you were a lousy father and a worse husband, haven't you been thinking that your greatest failure of all was as a brother, because you'd been a brother without knowing it?"

He nodded reluctantly.

"But that's so wrong. You were a wonderful

brother to Huck, just as he was to you, and the remarkable part is that you did it all on your own. You didn't have parents or society telling you that you should love one another because you were brothers, you just did it by yourselves. There is no way, no earthly way, that that can ever be called a failure. You succeeded with Huck more than most people ever succeed with anyone."

"Curry, I don't know, I still feel like I want to tell him."

"Of course you *want* to tell him, but you don't *have* to, and anyway, you can't. When you can't have something, you've got to figure out what you do have and go with that. Huck's not here. What you've got is me and the fact that I know. When you left in August and I thought I'd never see you again, I told Bonnie about us, and it helped, knowing that she knew we'd been lovers. And it may help you, knowing that I know you and Huck were brothers."

Tom didn't say anything for a while, and then slowly he began to talk. It was extraordinary. Over the years he'd been through every one of his memories, searching for signs proving that he and Huck were brothers. Of course, they looked nothing alike, and their most basic mental abilities were different—Huck could imagine while Tom could execute—but Tom had found resemblances.

"It was nothing we'd noticed at the time, after all, we were kids and we probably thought the whole world was this way, but—"

Their reaction times had been identical; in sports, they had both been quick, rather than fast.

They could remember concrete phenomena easily; they both had trouble remembering abstract concepts. Neither one had ever broken a bone, although they had often deserved to; they almost never got cavities. Their military physicals had measured their vision as considerably better than twenty-twenty.

Tom remembered things about Huck that Curry had forgotten, and he had treasured every detail. Each resemblance, no matter how slight, mattered to him, because these resemblances made it seem real, made it seem like Huck had been his brother.

So Curry listened, late into the night, hoping, praying that as he spoke, it was becoming less important that Huck would never walk around the barn and hear these things for himself.

At last he had said all that he could. He tried to thank her for listening, but she just pressed her fingers to his lips. "Tom, I understand. You don't need to say anything more."

"I guess we should try to get some sleep, then."

But Tom didn't sleep that night. Curry woke to see him standing at the window, staring out. She didn't say anything, and then in a moment, he silently pulled on his jeans and a sweater and left the room. She heard the stairs creak and then the screen door open and close.

She went across the hall, looking out the window of Diana's room. The winter moonlight was pale, but she could see Tom, standing in the backyard. His hands were in his pockets, his shoulders hunched a little. And in a moment he bent his head, pressing his thumb and forefinger to the bridge of his nose. Curry wondered if he were crying.

Then slowly he started to walk, not through the orchard on the way to the house he'd grown up in, but across the field. Curry knew where he was going—to the empty lot where the little renter's house had stood.

He was going to start saying good-bye to his brother.

Tom was sitting at the kitchen table when Curry came down in the morning. She leaned over him, linking her arms around his neck, and kissed him.

"Did you lie awake all night thinking?" he asked.

"Not all night." She poured herself some coffee and leaned against the counter. "But I do need to know one thing. Am I anybody's sister?"

"Not that I know of."

"Well, let's not inquire too closely, okay?"

He laughed. "I hadn't thought about it, but I guess if any of us are related, it's a good thing it's him and me."

"That's for sure. Any other pairing would have gotten me arrested."

"Well, if you had been, I would have broken down and hired a lawyer for you."

"Thanks. Now what kind of Jell-O can I offer you for breakfast?"

"Scrambled or fried over-easy."

Curry made a face at him and started to pull things out of her crammed refrigerator, hoping that one of them would prove to be an egg carton.

As she rummaged she heard him speak. "If I ever decide I need a workshop, you'd let me have your barn, wouldn't you?"

Curry closed her eyes, leaning against the refrigerator door. He was thinking about staying. He really was.

Of course he could have her barn. He had her heart and her son's heart; what was a barn or two?

"No, you can't *have* it," she said. "But you can *rent* it."

"Then you'd have to pay to fix it up."

"The hell I do. 'Unimproved space,' that's what the lease would say."

"A lease? You wouldn't trust me?"

She'd trust him to the end of the earth.

And she'd had enough jokes. "Are you really thinking about staying, Tom?"

"It largely depends on whether or not you'll marry me."

She almost dropped the eggs she had found. "Marry you?" She shook her head slowly. "I don't need that, Tom, not if it grates with you. You tell me that you plan to stay, or at least come back when you go, and that's good enough for me; I don't need the legal things, I don't need the words, I don't need to be a wife."

He stood up, took the carton from her, and put his arms around her. "Curry, I love you, and I'm determined to make things work for us. Not getting married somehow suggests that we aren't sure that they will, and I'm not going to start on this expecting to fail. I've done enough of that."

Curry didn't even try not to cry. "Oh, Tom,

you can't know how wonderful that is to hear."

"Does this mean you'll marry me? Right away?"

She sniffed and laughed. "I'd really rather wait until your divorce is final, but if it's now or never, let's do it. You're the one who minds lying on forms, not me."

"I forgot about that," Tom said simply.

"That's why you need me, Tom Winchester, to keep these things straight. From now on, whether or not you're married is going to be a very simple question; even you will be able to figure out how to fill out that part of the forms."

As they drove into town to pick up Huck, they made plans.

"Were you serious about putting a workshop in the barn?" she asked. "Because I'm still planning to go through with this business of turning myself into a schoolteacher."

He nodded. "I don't want to give up working on houses altogether. But there are a lot of projects, especially helping people get started, that only take a couple of days. I thought maybe I could go on doing one or two of those a month. But I did promise I'd take Diana to the East Coast for a couple of weeks next summer, and I don't feel like I can renege on that."

"I hope you don't want to. But Tom, there's no reason in the world why we can't all be gypsies in the summer, you and me, Huck and Diana, if they want. I'll always be free in the summers; I can go anywhere with you."

"What? Curry James leave her house?"

She stuck her tongue out at him. "Only for three months every year, but we can do root canals on houses all summer long, if that's what you want."

"Root canals? Curry, that's dentistry."

"Whatever. I can't imagine you're going to let *me* near any of your tools."

"That's certainly true . . . but listen, don't you have to go to a university for a year or so?"

She nodded. "I can only get an associate's degree at the community college, but once Huck goes to college, I'll drive over to Brookings."

"Will you do a favor for me?"

"Name it . . . as long as it isn't your laundry."

"Take some sort of course in historical research. I do fine in the field, but when it comes to libraries and court houses and all that paper stuff, I'm not as good as I should be; it takes me a long time to find things. But if you have good research skills, we could be quite a team in the summers."

That sounded just wonderful to her. "Oh, Tom, that's *great*. We'd both be working historians together, we could go to all sorts of places, and I certainly don't mind filling out the forms to get grants. That would be a change, getting money back from the government. And then we could—" She stopped. "Am I sounding like Diana?"

Tom laughed. "Do I have to spend the rest of my life listening to my daughter ridiculed because she has a slight tendency to enthusiasm?"

"A slight tendency? She's a—wait a minute,

Tom." Curry glared at him. "I'm not such a nit-wit. Do you remember when I said she reminded me of Huck's father? Of course she does. She's his niece."

"Yes, she is."

"When I said it, you looked at me like I had been dropped on my head once too often."

"It was because I was trying hard not to kiss your feet. Of course she's like him. And that's been terribly important to me. That's what I almost said to you that day."

"What day? What are you talking about?"

"Don't you remember the day she left this summer? First she was telling you how proud she was because her middle name was James. Imagine how I felt. I didn't know it when we named her, but she and her blue eyes are part James. And then remember how you came over to my dad's house after supper, and we were talking about what Bonnie had said, that I hadn't been a total washout as a father?"

Curry nodded.

"Well, I think in some ways I do owe that to Huck. When I got back to Bemidji after seeing my dad, I felt so terrible about everything—I hated myself, I was close to hating Trish, but I couldn't hate Diana because she was related to Huck. And even as things got better, I was still fascinated by that part of her, the way she resembled him. I love her for her own sake now, and I probably always have, but for a while there, all that I could admit that mattered was that she was like Huck."

Curry watched him, this man, unspeakably pre-

cious to her, once so shattered that the only bond
he could admit to feeling for his daughter was her
resemblance to some other man.

"So that's what you'd been about to say that
day? That you owed it to Huck's fa—" She shook
her head; it was so easy to get tangled up—did
"Huck" mean her son or her husband? Did
"Huck's father" mean her husband or her father-
in-law? Did "Tom's father" mean Howard James
or Cal Winchester?

Oh, well, in this case it was easy. "Were you
about to say that you owe your success to your
brother?"

"My—" Tom broke off, his lips tightening,
clearly moved by the word she had used. "Yes,
and that's why I went a little strange when we almost walked in on the two of them—Diana and
Huck, this Huck, that is—they are cousins, after
all."

Curry shook her head. "I don't think that matters. They're so young. Huck likes Diana a lot,
and he respects her, but when she's not around,
he doesn't have any trouble getting involved with
other girls. He's not carrying a torch for her."

"I think it's the same for her too. Trish lets her
go out on only one date a week—the rest of the
time she has to be with groups—and apparently
that is a problem."

Curry laughed. "Did she hint that maybe you
should talk to Trish, try to get her to change the
rule?"

"My daughter is a living, breathing teenager,

with a great deal of common sense. Of course, she's trying to play her parents against each other."

"Then you're lucky you agree with what Trish is doing."

"Yes. I chose a woman of wisdom for my first wife. That's why I am entitled to such a fruitcake for my second."

"Don't complain, Tom Winchester; you don't know what trouble is. I'm marrying somebody who shoots rubber bands at me."

But as he threatened to crack an egg on her head, she went on thinking about Huck and Diana being cousins. No, it didn't matter.

What truly mattered, she suddenly realized, was that Diana was related to the other Huck, that she had inherited the same sunny temper, the relish for adventure, the unquestioning enthusiasm for the future.

Curry remembered what she had thought in the restaurant that night with Colin Wheeler—how something was missing from American life, that the bright promise of boys like the first Huck James had been lost forever.

But that wasn't so. True, the line wasn't direct; it hadn't gone from father to son, but from uncle to niece. But that didn't matter; rigged out in a pair of size seven designer jeans and a Lady Di hair cut, the determined sparkle, the bright-eyed grit, was still there. With young women like Diana Winchester around, no one had to worry about America losing its spirit.

On the way home from the hospital they told Huck about their plans. "Hey, that's neat," he exclaimed.

Tom looked at him suspiciously. "Are you sure?"

"Sure, I'm sure. Why wouldn't I be? I like you fine."

"Thank you," Tom said humbly.

"But what are you going to do about your work?" Huck asked. "Are you just going to visit us between projects like you did with Diana and her mom?"

Tom explained about his workshop in the barn and then about their summer plans. "Your mother will be our red-tape person, filling out forms, talking to the lawyers, and doing the more scholarly research, being the genuine historic preservationist, and you—"

"I get to be the unskilled, underpaid, exploited physical laborer."

"Exactly."

But when their eyes met, Huck's were shining. Then he turned back to Curry. "Are you going to change your name?"

"Goodness, I hadn't given it a bit of thought. I don't suppose it matters. It will take everyone in town five or six years to stop calling me Curry James."

"Which is," Tom put in, "about half as long as it would take you to get it right."

Huck didn't laugh. "If you change your name, Mom, do I have to change mine?"

"No, not at all," Curry said immediately. "Do whatever you want."

He looked at Tom. "Is it okay with you if I don't?"

"Absolutely. There's not a better name in the world than the one you have."

"Still ashamed to have me as a son?"

"Yes. I was lying to you when I said I wasn't."

Then Huck thought of something else. "This means that we'll be seeing a lot more of Diana, doesn't it?"

"I hope so," Tom answered.

"She'll be your stepsister," Curry pointed out. She was teasing Tom; she knew that this would not bother Huck in the least.

Indeed it did not. "Well, I guess I better go out and get a new rubber duck, then," he said.

Tom stared at him, but Curry spoke calmly. "I haven't the faintest idea what you're talking about, Huck, but I'm very glad that you added *duck* to that sentence."

"What *are* you talking about?" Tom asked.

"About baths," Huck replied. "Taking baths. Lots of guys I know, when they were real little kids, had to take baths with their sisters. They say they hated it, but in the interests of improved family harmony, I'm perfectly willing to take a bath with my new sister."

"That's good of you," Tom returned. The minute that he had asked Huck to explain, he had known that he was falling into a trap, but he couldn't resist this Huck any more than he could the other one. "But why don't we leave it up to Diana?"

"No, sir. You're Diana's father and you'll be my stepfather. You should order us to do it."

Tom was instantly serious. "Listen, Huck, I don't want you to think that things are going to change for you. I won't come in and play the stepfather, telling you what to do and all."

"What do you mean? You already tell me what to do."

Tom was horrified. "No, I don't."

"You don't order me around or anything, but you're always saying that if I do such-and-such, then such-and-such else will happen; you know, spelling out the consequences of stuff. And it sure seems like I always end up doing it your way."

Curry laughed, and Tom took his eyes off the road to glare at her for a moment. "Don't say one word," he threatened. "Not one word."

"What's so funny?" Huck asked.

"Tom has this thing about stepfathers," Curry explained, "and he will do just fine so long as we don't remind him that he is one."

"I think I can manage not to call him 'Papa,'" Huck said graciously. "But I don't imagine it would change anything if I did."

At home, they ate lunch, then Huck lay down and ignored all the homework he'd missed while Curry resolutely got to work on all that she'd missed. Tom went out to the barn and thought lovely thoughts about pegboards, bench vises, power saw tables, and wives and sons.

At three thirty a Dodge Dart and a Chevy van

drove up. Within moments, the kitchen was full of Coke bottles, red-and-black letter jackets, a couple of footballs, and a platoon of Huck's friends.

"Is this what I have to look forward to for the rest of my life?" Tom demanded as he pulled Curry out to the safety of the autumn afternoon.

"Just for two years; then he goes to college."

"That's terrific. I'll have gotten used to it by then, and I'm crazy enough that I'll miss it."

"Life's tough, Tom."

He put an arm around her shoulders and they started to walk. They didn't go through the orchard to the house where he'd grown up—that house had new people living in it, a bright, noisy family whose children would, in the years to come, fill its kitchen with their own laughter, letter jackets and Coke bottles.

The Jenkinses were the right people for that house. It really was a good house and it deserved a family. It hadn't had one for many years.

Curry and Tom, although they were glad of their new neighbors, took the other path, across the road to the swimming hole.

Fall had come late and warm to South Dakota. The fallen cottonwood leaves were still fresh, rustling underfoot in deep, yellow piles. Tom went to the creek's edge to look at the tree limb that stretched along the bank.

"What are you thinking about?" Curry asked.

"Swings. I was wondering if this limb will still be good for one in fifteen years."

She went up to him and put her arm in his.

"That's a nice thought—Huck bringing his kids back here to play, or Diana bringing hers—their kids playing where we played."

"This is an adventure we hadn't planned on, Curry, having grandchildren together." He put his arm around her shoulders. "I vote we spoil them."

"Sounds good to me, but let's not get too gung-ho about it just yet. I don't mind pushing Huck, but not on this."

"As the father of a fifteen-year-old girl, I have to agree with you there...but speaking of planning adventures..."

Curry leaned her cheek against him, knowing that he was about to speak of him who had planned so many of their other adventures.

And he did. "You know this long-awaited meeting with Huck's father that it seems like I'm not going to have?"

"What about it?"

"Well, all these years, what I've thought about is what I would say to him. I never thought about what he might say to me."

Curry looked up at him inquiringly.

"I think he would be real disappointed with me. He'd groan and shake his head. 'What's this with Curry?' he'd say. 'You've had *years*. What took you so long?'"

Curry laughed. "Forget him. I want to know what took *us* so long."

"Well, you know me. *I* like to get things right, and getting things right takes a long time. Sometimes it does take years."

"Do you think you've got it right now?"

"It doesn't get any righter than this."

The wind swirled about them, and as they walked back to the house the leaves tossed up, stirring around their feet. The grass beneath the leaves was still green, growing in tufts dense and thick from the summer rains. It had been a good year for South Dakota.

The dry spell was over.

ABOUT THE AUTHOR

Kathleen Gilles Seidel was born in Lawrence, Kansas, and received her B.A. from the University of Chicago. She attended The Johns Hopkins University and was awarded both an M.A. and a Ph.D. in English Language and Literature.

Kathy's first published work was in the Harlequin American Romance line in April, 1982. Her titles include: *The Same Last Name*, #2; *A Risk Worth Taking*, #17; and *Mirrors and Mistakes*, #57.

Kathy currently resides with her husband, Larry, in Virginia.